To: Barbara.

Anthology
2014

Ink Splinters

Best wishes from: Breda x.

DEDICATION

This collection is dedicated to all our relatives, friends and colleagues who have been supportive of us in our various writing endeavours.

You guys know who you are and we are grateful

CONTENTS

Page No	Title	Author
5	The Cambrian Invasion	Brian Carroll
13	My Yellow Jumper	Anniekate Gillroon
15	Total Footballer	Kenneth Nolan
25	The Red City	Volker Gebhart
26	My Side	Alda Gomez
27	Stolen Voices	Brian Carroll
30	The Silent Sound of Winter	Breda McAteer
31	Free Nelson Mandela	Camillus John
33	The Radio	Brian Browne
35	Help	Alda Gomez
36	Good Sons Are Relative	Pat Nolan
44	Letters	Bláithín Ní Liatháin
45	The King is Dead	Harry Browne
66	Above and Below the Earth	Breda McAteer
68	Kicking My Mother In The Head Trilogy	Camillus John
83	Master Mariner	Frank George C. Moore
85	Memories	E.M. Olivander
87	Beast	Susan Cooney
88	Laura's Trek	Cathy Power

98	Santry Park 26 March 2013	Bláithín Ní Liatháin
99	Heat	Katie Dwyer
102	Earth Tree	Anniekate Gillroon
104	Paddy and the Bog Body	Brian Carroll
107	Chronos	Susan Cooney
108	The First Time I Fell In Love with A Junkie	Camillus John
111	Saturday Lunch	Kay Dunne
112	Louisbourg	Mimi Goodman
120	Season's Haiku	Bláithín Ní Liatháin
121	The Top Hat	Brian Carroll
133	Grave Digger	Frank George C. Moore
135	Santa in Africa	Geralyn Rownan
153	Peter's Painting	Breda McAteer
154	The Story of a Boy	Brian Browne
164	In A Second	Susan Cooney
165	Dublin Clocks	Pronsias O Mordha
166	Sarah's Tale	Brian Carroll
169	Leaving Town	Katie Dwyer
170	Life is Not a Bowl of Cherries. It's a Pie	Geralyn Rownan
224	Literary Assassin	Frank George C. Moore
229	To A Prompt	Bláithín Ní Liatháin

230	Stories From 'The Village'	Martina Carroll
268	Never Spare a Tear	Alda Gomez
269	Sunny Side Up	Brian Carroll
271	Classroom Windows	Bláithín Ní Liatháin
272	Creative Writing Workshop	Frank George C. Moore
275	Story from the City, Dark.	Anniekate Gillroon
278	The Saponification of Henri de Franoux	Brian Carroll
280	Rose Garden	John O'Farrell
290	Bon Chance	Frank George C. Moore
306	Biographies	All
317	Praise From The Critics	Camillus John

THE CAMBRIAN INVASION

Brian Carroll

Fothergill picked himself up and gingerly felt his ribs for cracks. The three thugs clad in white had given him a good going over. There was no motive for the attack, they were simply looking for some sport and he had the misfortune to cross their path that evening on the way home from the library. He got to his knees and picked up the books that lay scattered around him. 'The Orthorhombic System' was undamaged and just a bit dirty. He gathered the books together and cleaned them off as best he could with the sleeve of his overcoat. He struggled to his feet and groaned as he felt the pain course through his bruised kidneys. He walked out from under the overpass, he was wary because he could still hear shouts from the direction in which the young louts had departed.

Thankfully, he was going in the opposite direction. He made it to the nearest bus stop and it wasn't long before his bus arrived. It took him longer than usual to mount the steep steps and he could see the bus driver raise his eyes to heaven as he flashed him his travel pass. The driver pulled away without pausing and Fothergill was sent spinning down the aisle of the bus by the sudden acceleration. He grabbed the handrail on the back of a seat and managed to flop into the seat behind without falling. He winced at the pain in his back and clutched the bundle of books under his arm more closely to him. He told himself it would be all worth it, that his experiments in crystallography would revolutionise the world and that his name would be remembered.

The events of this particular evening however, he just wanted to forget. He had just made it home inside his front door when he looked at his wristwatch to check the time. Then he remembered that the young ruffians had relieved him of it, along with his wallet and his wedding ring. But it was the loss of the watch that pained him more than anything else. It was the first prototype that employed nano-crystals. Even though the artificial intelligence he had programmed into it was rudimentary, it was irreplaceable. He hung up his muddy overcoat on the hat stand in his dimly lit hall and glanced in the mirror at his shocked reflection. His thin white wispy hair stood up in disarray. He limped into his study and went over to the huge table which occupied most of the room. Its surface was covered in apparatus of obscure and arcane function. He spoke to no-one in particular,

'Well, my little amphibolites, how are we this evening?'

To his great surprise he thought he heard a response, but that was impossible surely, he thought.

'Crystals can't talk now, can they?'

He sat in his favourite armchair and lit his pipe. He puffed away and began to relax a bit from the day's ordeal.

He hummed a little tune to himself and an idea began to form in his mind.

Fothergill was not a vindictive or vengeful man but his beating at the hands of the drugged-up thugs did not dispose him well towards his fellow man. He had thought originally that if he could develop his artificially intelligent silicates to the stage of rudimentary consciousness that they could be trained to perform onerous or dangerous tasks. Perhaps they would even be good companions for old loners like himself. But his current frame of mind lead him to conjecture that his work would more likely be used to construct weapons of war. He put these dark thoughts aside and went back to his experiments. Presently he was intrigued by the possibilities a course-grained piece of granite was showing. It had well-developed dark Muscovite flakes along with good coarse K-feldspar phenocrysts. Using piezo-electricity and sub-sonic frequencies he had succeeded in getting it play back a very simple tune. In deep bass notes it had mastered do-ray-me when struck at just the right angle with a heavy wooden mallet

This was as far as Fothergill had progressed in his work and he felt at an impasse. He sat heavily in his armchair and puffed away on his briarwood pipe. He was idly toying with a piece of Tourmaline when he noticed something strange. The hefty lump of granite had changed its tune. Not only that but it sounded like it was improvising, more like a jazz singer of the twenties than a seven kilo cube of igneous rock. He stood up from his armchair and approached. Instinctively he began to wave the piece of Tourmaline in the direction of the granite and bizarrely enough it seemed to be responding. As he brought the crystal closer its tune would raise in pitch and tempo. If he withdrew it, it returned to its deep bass notes. Fothergill was in equal parts amazed and perplexed. Was he losing his marbles? Had he just taught an inanimate chunk of rock to sing?

He pondered the title of the paper he would publish in Nature. 'Improvised micro-tonal arpeggios in Caledonian Adamellites.' He rubbed his chin with satisfaction. It was cause a sensation for sure. He would be welcomed back into the Geological Society with open arms. Even the unpleasantness that had previously lead to his expulsion would all be forgotten. He would have the last laugh. He would show them what a true genius he was. The scientific world would bow at his feet and pay homage to his greatness. But then he snapped out of his reverie and remembered that he was an outcast. No one would listen to him. He must conceive of a way to publish his discoveries without anyone knowing that it was he who was behind it all. He had a vision of a great granite statue – a statue that sang. But whom should the statue portray?

'Why not the great Professor Fothergill?' he said.

He grinned broadly at the mirror and his crazed reflection grinned back at him.

Some hours later in the local infirmary the orderlies wheeled the gurney at a leisurely pace down the dimly-lit corridor. Fothergill lay upon it, stone cold and beyond all knowing. He had achieved his goal, at least in part. His experiments with igneous rocks, tuning them to emit musical notes had yielded unexpected results. He had carelessly left a piece of Cambrian limestone, crammed with trilobites, close to his piezo-electric/sub-sonic vibrational field apparatus. The six hundred million year-old arthropods had become animated somehow. They could hardly be called sentient, being composed entirely of calcium carbonate. But something of the original organic intelligence must have remained. They sought out food and they found it.

Fothergill must have been blissfully unaware that his beloved trilobites had devoured his brain while he slept. It must have been something to do with the energy field generated by the human brain that attracted them. What no-one knew however was that hundreds of tiny re-animated trilobites were now let loose on the world. Having fed on the old man's brain-tissue, who knew what they would be capable of next? Fothergill's experiments had succeeded beyond his wildest imaginings but not even he could have foreseen the plague of flesh-eating brain parasites that he had unleashed on the world. He would have been proud of his achievement if he had not been their first victim. Now he lay in the morgue and the trilobites continued their search, silently seeking out fresh grey-matter. Invisible and inconceivable, the pre-historic creatures set about re-establishing their pre-Cambrian dominion over the Earth.

The post-mortem examination of Fothergill's remains was inconclusive. One strange detail did emerge however and this was the entire and complete absence of his brain. Small traces of finely crystalline calcite were found in his brain case but no trace of grey matter whatsoever was found. The Chief State Pathologist was puzzled by this abnormality and brought the matter to the attention of the police who promised to put their best man on the case.

So it was that Detective Myles 'Snowy' Nugent found himself lumbered with the case of the mad scientist with the missing brain. Nugent was not all that amused by it but was compelled to investigate nonetheless. He took Murphy with him to the dead scientist's lab just in case it was a set up and someone was yanking his chain. The deceased had been found in his armchair. There were no signs of violence except that the poor fellow's brain had gone AWOL. When Nugent saw the Professor's lab however, he was convinced that something was amiss. It was Murphy that spotted the musical rocks first. Or rather he had dropped one of the specimens and to their great surprise it had played three descending musical notes quite clearly.

'Did that feckin' rock just play a tune or am I hallucinatin'?' said Murphy pointing at the offending piece of granite on the floor.

'Sure sounded like it to me,' said Nugent, 'here let's try some of the others.'

So they tried out all the other rock samples they could see in the lab. Nugent found a huge wooden mallet and went about bashing each in turn. Each of them had its own particular tune, some more musical than others. The dark heavy basalts were low key and sombre while the lighter pale granites were more tuneful and melodious. A piece of dark grey limestone labelled 'Cambrian Trilobites' yielded no music at all. But there was something about this particular specimen that caught Nugent's attention. It looked porous and on giving it a good thump with the mallet it shattered into a thousand tiny pieces that flew in every direction. Nugent thought he saw some shape to one of these shards and bent down to pick it up. As he reached out his hand however the small piece of limestone uncoiled itself and scuttled away under the couch.

10

'Jaysus, Mary and Joseph,' he said, 'the bloody rock just ran away. Look,' he said, dragging Murphy over by the shoulder.

'What're ya talkin' about boss? Rocks don't move,' said Murphy.

'This one bloody-well did,' said Nugent, 'here, give us a hand with the couch.'

The two of them tilted the couch back, something scuttled away and this time Murphy saw it. He saw it run over his shoe and up his trouser-leg. He started squealing.

'Jaysus, get it off, get it off!'

He was hopping about on one leg and batting at his trousers with his hands. Nugent grabbed him by the arm and made shushing noises at him.

'Don't feckin' move,' he said, 'keep very still. It's on yer neck.'

He picked up a phone book from the nearby desk and carefully approached Murphy who was looking very pale. The little grey creature made a dart for Murphy's left ear. Nugent swung the telephone directory.

Nugent took the piece of limestone home with him since nobody seemed to care about how the old science geek had died anyway. He put it in an old Tupperware lunchbox which he placed carefully in the back of the fridge and promptly forgot all about it.

Several weeks later however, he was on his way home when he saw two squad cars parked out the front of his house. When he got to the hall door he asked the uniformed officer there what all the commotion was about. He just stared at him with vacant eyes and drooled. Then Nugent saw the trail of blood trickle from his left ear. He sidestepped him and ventured down the hall toward the kitchen.

He stuck his index fingers in his ears on instinct but he could still hear the shouts and bangs from inside. The shouts were followed by squeaks, then gurgles. It didn't sound good. He peeked around the corner of the door and saw three uniformed bodies spread out on the lino. One of them was face-down at the back door. He'd gotten the door open but hadn't made it out. His left foot was still twitching and Nugent saw one of the little grey beasties crawl out of his right nostril. It flew out the back door like it was electrified or something and Nugent groaned.

'Oh hell, now they've escaped,' he said, 'How am I gonna explain this to the Super?'

What on earth could he say to them? That the fossilised remains of tiny sea-creatures that have been extinct for the last five hundred million years have been re-animated somehow and are now vicious predators with a taste for human brains. He didn't think so. They would have locked him up in a padded cell without further ado. No, he must come up with a plan and come up with one fast before a plague of flesh-hungry trilobites took over the world.

MY YELLOW JUMPER

Anniekate Gillroon

She was an easy person to be with
My oldest sister
Used to say to me
On her summers back to us
'Take a step back, and think,
Then tell me what you want me to do'
When my frightened frail face
Looked for her
Looked up to her
Her long silky black hair
Falling across my arms
As she hugged me

At Christmas
Taking my yellow jumper
From the soft cream paper
And her note
And her promise
To be back to climb Knocknarea
and warm our toes in the sand
Watching the dangerous waters at Strandhill

The last yellow jumper she sent
Was too big for me
It wrapped around me
As if to keep out
A treacherous cold happening

It all started with her ache
In the top of her head
The ending was all over for her
At the end of October

13

That Christmas I folded my year old
Yellow jumper and slept on it
To stop the ache in my head
As I closed my eyes
And whispered to her
That this was the thing
That frightened me most.

TOTAL FOOTBALLER

Kenneth Nolan

There I was at the training ground of the great Ajax of Amsterdam, ready, willing and able to take my place in that great midfield beside other young starlets like Clarence Seedorf and Edgar Davids. It's August 1995 and the team had just been crowned Champions of Europe for the fourth time in the clubs history. I had thought it was getting a little ridiculous how I had not been picked up by a professional team in England yet and at 19 years old in four months' time I had better get my skates on and do something about it. The reason a scout hadn't picked me up was obvious to me, style of football of course! "Get rid of it", "push up", "out, out, out" … These were the type of shouts I'd hear from the touchline while playing for my local team in Blanchardstown. 'They know nothing about football' I thought. They don't know what to do with a player with my technique and passing ability.

I had my so called big chance, or chances, trials with Shelbourne F.C. and Shamrock Rovers but they couldn't see my talent. All they wanted was big physical lads who could play 'set piece' football and run like the clappers all day. And an English team wasn't gonna see it? Not with the type of players they produce. No 'Total Football' was the only way for me. A proper footballer should be playing for a proper football club in a proper footballing country. So when the guy at the reception said "We only choose from our academy, we have scouts throughout Europe who choose, you cannot just come here and join Ajax, I'm sorry" "but Bert! I have come all the way from Ireland, if Mr. Van Gael could just see me play for ten minutes. Please!" I'm sorry, he said, and insisted that I leave.

All those years ago standing there in the reception at the Ajax training ground where which I had thought would be the start of a glittering career and a wonderful life for me, denied by Bert but little did I know it would actually be the beginning of a life of crushing disappointments, similarly failed audacious attempts of achievement, gut-wrenching embarrassments and misery that that 18 year old (averagely talented footballer) couldn't even imagine was humanly possible.

I spent three weeks of that August in Amsterdam, discovering Ecstasy pills for the first time and for some reason being arrested by the Dutch police, who in a very short time alerted my family to my behaviour and whereabouts, the first knowledge they received of such. Apparently I was a bit of a celebrity back in Dublin my face adorning many a lamppost and takeaway window.

My brother came to Amsterdam to collect me, he is eleven years older but seemed like fifty years older than me at the time. The following month or two hidden away in my bedroom at the family home I found uncontrollable grief set upon me, rivers of tears followed by anger, concluding with periods of staring at the wall in silence. It was around about this era that I first remember phrases like 'Lunatic' and 'Headcase' from the mouths of my friends and being the first to be nominated for any risky endeavours. Sometimes I would revel in it and other times I felt a terrible shame were upon I disgusted myself beyond comprehension.

Seven years later I made the first attempt on my life. In a short space of time I was let go from my third job in as many years and more importantly dumped by who you might call in that old fashioned soppy way 'The love of my life'. Linda and I were together for two and half years before she finally had enough of me. She had the brightest red hair of a traditional Irish Cailin, a beautiful smile and an exceptionally kind nature. The funny thing was, I spent most of my time trying to tell her and trying to show her how much she meant to me only for her regular complaints to be that she could never get through to me and that sometimes I treated her like a complete stranger. We were classmates at school and I always valued the fact that she never laughed when other kids were teasing me. She'd help me at most subjects I was weak at which was in fact 'most subjects'. I never had the nerve to ask her out at that time as she was/is way too beautiful for me. Then at Stephen Conway's sisters 21st a few years later we ended up in company together and thanks to my old friend alcohol I managed to blurt out how I had always fancied her. It took a while after that to become a couple but eventually it happened and I had by my side the type of girl or in fact 'D' girl' I always wanted.

In a short space of time she had forgiven me a lot more than many women would forgive in a lifetime. One infidelity that she found out about, countless disappearing acts, failure to have rent money for the apartment and short periods were I just simply couldn't talk to her. At certain periods my sex drive would be through the roof, she would say it's overboard and unnatural, I didn't see it as anything out of the ordinary. One particular occasion sticks in my mind when after a massive argument she said "John, there's something wrong with you, you really need to get help babe".

The final straw for her came when she miss-carried our baby in the tenth week of term. I was down in Kilkenny trying to buy cheap tractor engines at the time, another get rich quick scheme. I unfortunately couldn't be reached for a couple of days. I don't know much about farming equipment but I have always known a lot about getting pissed and Kilkenny is a great place to do so. The drive back to Dublin was dreadful! I tried to put the twenty two missed calls to the back of my mind by convincing myself that 'nothing could be that important' but indeed it was.

When I got home and found out what had happened the fright nearly caused me to vomit. She wouldn't speak to me for days. I went over to her mother's and insisted she speak to me, I began to beg forgiveness to anyone who would listen before her father and brother took to beating me severely. I think I accepted every blow received without retaliation and I didn't feel much physical pain until the following day. She eventually spoke to me again and against the will of both families we gave it another go which lasted about a month before she casually told me "It's over. I don't want to be with you".

I had been getting casual depressions since my teen years, out of the blue with no explainable reasons. People would just say 'Ah he's a cranky fecker' or 'John's in his flowers again' however, now it seemed I had a legitimate reason for misery and I committed to it wholeheartedly. After a couple of long weeks of being unapproachable and uninterested in anything around me I swallowed twenty odd pills and drank half a bottle of Southern Comfort.

I was found in time fortunately or unfortunately depending on how I look back on it at certain times. My stomach was pumped out and I have no recollection of this.

I woke four days later with my whole family at my bedside, my poor mother as white as snow. Two more long weeks in hospital, followed by a couple of months of mindlessly boring therapy sessions at the psychiatric unit outpatients department. Every session started with the question "How do you feel this week?" and included the question "How are you adjusting to your medication?" and usually ended with the phrase "We'll take it up from there next week". They might as well have giving me a gun there and then so I could do the job with a little more panache next time.

Eventually it was the beautiful game that brought me back to some semblance of happiness. My interest was revived by watching matches on television. Then I began to play again when some friends organised a weekly five a side game in the local sports hall and asked me along. The guys began to notice the skills I had and I was always first or second pick each game. Once there was great laughter in the shower rooms when my friend Paul told the story of me showing up to play for Ajax. "You didn't really do that did you?" I was asked. I answered no, "of course not, don't mind him".

I got to a stage where I was playing three times a week and would even join in a kids game whilst passing if I was allowed to. After no time at all I was playing eleven aside on Saturdays at Leinster Senior level and I was head over heels in love with life again. I spent hours on the computer entering fantasy league teams into various competitions online. I was spending at least half of my weekly money gambling on televised matches and had totally rekindled my passion for football if not regained an obsession. That summer Ireland had qualified for the World Cup in Japan and Korea and a certain Cork native refused to play. 'Could I have done a job in midfield in his stead?'

I have to admit the thought did cross my mind. The country was on a high as we progressed to the second round, so was I, in fact I didn't sleep more than three hours a night for a fortnight. Spain knocked us out as you may know and I took to catching up on my lost sleep.

The following year, 2003, I made an unwise decision to go on a three week holiday with the guys to Thailand. I had been feeling good in myself. I hadn't drunk alcohol in nearly a year and I was confident that a dark period of my life was over. I lasted four days into the holiday before I began drinking. Six lads in a beach paradise, on the holiday of a lifetime, it was inevitable I suppose. I spent a week and a half getting smashed, sleeping two hours a night and eating very little. I was hearing phrases from some of the lads like "You mad bastard" which were unsettling flashbacks to the past. However, I was also frequently told that I was the best craic ever so I ignored the signs.

Then I made an impulsive decision to head back to Bangkok alone five days before we were due to fly home from there. Whilst there I sought out every cheap prostitute I could find to have unprotected sex with, an average of maybe two or three a day thinking I could catch AIDS. Yes believe it or not that was the plan. 'Screw as many girls as possible in a skewed attempt at a sneaky suicide'. This way, I rationalised, I could spare my family that sudden sharp shock of grief. No it wasn't exactly a masterplan, however, fanciful thinking and reckless disregard of my body and person was nothing new to me and I did enjoy the sordid adventure of booze, sex and drugs amongst the other dangers on those chaotic, busy streets. I made the flight home, seated with Derek, unfortunately. "You've got to get a grip of yourself for fuck's sake. You'll get yourself into serious trouble". With enough miniature bottles of whiskey I managed to fall asleep for most of the flight home and avoid the taunts both inside and outside my head.

What I did bring home from Bangkok was easily cured with a course of antibiotics and three months later there were no lasting effects to be found. At this stage in my life my football talents began to disappear again, just like the Ajax side of that particular period and my love for football was soon stone dead replaced by alcohol and cheap drugs. Back living with my parents but soon asked to leave, my father said "You're an alcoholic John", I could only laugh at his ridiculousness. There were so many things wrong with that assessment, I never drank in the morning and I didn't drink every day, plus I was only 26 for God's sake! I could do denial, it came naturally to me.

I continued to use alcohol and managed to just about get by. When necessary I could make people believe that I was a perfectly functional human being. I could play in all the positions on the field 'so to speak' just like a Total Footballer. I had a gut feeling that alcoholism wasn't the root of my problems, its main necessity for me was in helping me sleep.

In the latter part of 2004 I was on an even keel again. I moved into a flat on Dublin's North Circular Road. I was also back on good terms with my family. The flat was shabby enough and so small that 'A cat couldn't swing a mouse in it'. However, it was sanctuary until it occurred to me that the constant traffic outside was quite noisy. I couldn't sleep a wink for four days straight and alcohol had lost its sedative power, even when I did nod off I dreamt I couldn't sleep so perhaps I was actually asleep all along. Anyway, I was a nervous wreck and paradoxically only loud Rock Music settled me down. In an attempt to release the pressure valve I slashed at my left arm twice with a Stanley knife, blood spurted everywhere then poured out of the wound very readily. First came panic then a genuine feeling of restfulness came over me. I felt ten times better but I knew I'd have to put off a slumber for a little longer until I got to the A&E department. I wrapped my arm as tightly as possible in a towel and went down to the street to seek help. Officially this incident counts as a suicide attempt but as I look at the wounds on my arm it's noticeable that they are closer to my elbow than my wrist. To tell you the truth I don't think I've ever really tried to kill myself.

My arm was stitched up and in a couple of days I was sent to a different part of the hospital to see if they could stitch up the wound in my head. A few weeks into my stay sitting in front of Dr. Casey, a man I was vaguely familiar with, I heard the term Bipolar Disorder. He had said a lot leading up to it that didn't register due to the drowsiness, I was actually wondering would I ever be alert again. Indeed those words sharpened me up a little. He continued, "Looking at your history you seem to have been showing severe symptoms since your teens and perhaps this diagnosis is a little overdue".

2005, was a year of adjustment back at the family home in Blanchardstown. A complete change of lifestyle, no booze or bad food but plenty of drugs! Anti-depressants and the mood stabilizer Lithium. Lithium is there to keep a manic depressive in neutral, it dampens down emotions and moods high or low and maintains the thought flow at a comfortable steady pace, eliminating manic episodes. At first all it done was bring on constant nausea and thirst, I must have put the founder of Riverrock's kids through college with the amount of mineral water I drank. It became easier after a while and achieved its desired affect I guess. I developed a strict exercise regime but resisted the impulse of playing football again, much like avoiding an old lover.

Month after month passed and I settled in to the life of a very boring person. A friend told a joke one day and the other people present fell about laughing. I attempted an uncomfortable chuckle but I was acutely aware the gag deserved better. I couldn't laugh from the heart anymore! And I feared I would never truly experience any real positive emotion again. The medication had done exactly what it was supposed to do and that was to nullify the extremities of the mood swings I was prone to, to keep me level, or in the middle you might say, not going much above or beneath that middle line, which basically makes a person incapable of feeling any real degree of grief or joy. That's the funny thing about an illness that causes people to lose touch with reality, its state of recovery becomes perversely the very thing that seems unrealistic. Well I guess it's a fair price to pay for no more times of being so low I could rip my own heart out or so agitated that a raised voice could cause me to tremble with anxiety.

I knew Linda was still living in the area and I was surprised we hadn't crossed paths. I had heard that she was fairly settled with another guy and her life was going well. Then one day in June 2006 we met at the local pharmacy. I don't know why but I said I was collecting hay fever medication, "I didn't think you suffered from that" she said. We hugged and I felt easy warmth from her. I should have known that would be the case, there was never any malice in her. Her belly was huge, and she spoke about the excitement of having her first child, which was to be born very soon.

I felt genuine happiness as I congratulated her and as we parted she looked back knowingly and said "John, I'm glad you're doing better with your health". When I got home, I turned on the TV. I had the house to myself for the first time in a while. There was a World Cup match on between Argentina and Serbia-Montenegro which I forced myself to watch. I was uncomfortable at the start but I settled down and started to enjoy it as the game wore on. Argentina were playing some really good football, swift passing and good movement throughout the team.

Rodriquez wins the ball in his own half and lays it off, he, Mascherano, Cambiasso and Riquelme begin popping it about between themselves. Riquelme conducting the orchestra with his touch and vision. There must have been 20 passes before the ball finds its way out to the left hand side, then Riquelme and Saviola play a one/two, Riquelme plays a sublime ball with the outside of his right foot back to Saviola, Saviola clips it into the box where Cambiasso plays it for Crespo, Crespo takes a touch and back heels it into the path of the onrushing Cambiasso who rifles a left foot shot into the roof of the net! I was on my feet with joy at this stage clapping as though I were at the stadium, a fearless joy! The type of natural joy one gets from the simple things in life like total football.

THE RED CITY

Volker Gebhart

The city changed the very second Karen put her red glasses on. At first she didn't recognise her own street. Then she didn't recognise herself in the shop window. Karen walked slower ahead. Somewhat cautiously, she moved one foot in front of the other. As if that would change anything. The collision, still – it was unavoidable. It happened in slow motion. When Karen hit the Volkswagen on the pavement her glasses didn't get a scratch. She looked up at the sky as if to check something. Then she felt the burning pain in her right knee. But Karen knew what mattered was that she kept walking. It was in passing that she left a handwritten note on the windscreen. – The sky looked amazing. Karen knew that it could explode any second. She started running.

MY SIDE
Alda Gomez
I stayed on my side of the bed,
out of habit or complacency,
oblivious of any side, but there.

I stayed on my side for ages.
Yes, stayed there,
cherishing it like a sacred land,
on my side, warm but fearful,
alone in tears at times.

A side can be as important as an angel,
a side, my side, your side, whose side?
As important as an angel, to be cherished,
so I did. I cherished it, my side of the bed,
with your empty space touching my elbows,
your absence creeping into my dreams,
your voice quieter and quieter inside.

Unaware of where I was, there I stayed,
fearful and warm, scared and joyful,
but frozen until one day.

I woke up during the night and felt alive,
but uneasy and uncomfortable,
I moved to the other side of the bed,
stretched out, arms wide open,

and I felt the expansion of possibility,
and I felt the ridicule of my frozenness,
and I felt the freedom of infinity,
and I awoke fully open and excited,
ready to leave no space for you,
ready to cherish all my sides.

STOLEN VOICES

Brian Carroll

Hans Wilber von Groppeninck was positioned at the back of the auditorium nursing some kind of arcane apparatus in his lap. As the famous tenor took to the stage he opened the lid and folded out what looked like the earpiece from an old ear trumpet. He attached a black winding handle to the side of the mysterious black box and began cranking the machine into life. Onstage the singer had just launched into 'Vesti La Giubba' with great gusto and the audience sat upright in their seats in rapt attention.

Slowly but surely something began to happen to the tenor's rich deep voice. As Groppeninck wound his contraption and chuckled to himself, the great tenor's voice decreased in volume and increased in pitch until in a few moments he was left squeaking like a mouse. He clasped his hands to his throat as he tried to summon his voice into action but all he could manage were a few hoarse croaks. His face burned bright crimson as he tried to apologize to the audience for his sudden incapacitation but they had already begun to talk amongst themselves. Some had risen to their feet muttering, 'shocking, disgraceful' and other oaths. The stage curtain came down abruptly as the tenor held out his arms in mute helplessness.

Meanwhile at the back of the theatre, Groppeninck was poring over his device and writing a label on a jar which he placed in a small wooden case along with several others of its kind. The inscription read 'Caruso, Enrico – 1907'. Groppeninck was still chuckling to himself as he left the auditorium with his stolen treasure. The headlines in the newspapers the next day read, 'Another famous tenor robbed of his voice'. The articles went on to speculate that some nefarious forces were at work and blamed variously Bolsheviks, Anarchists and Serbian Nationalists. Groppeninck read these reports with something like amusement as he tinkered with a contraption in the basement of his aged mother's dilapidated mansion

'Wilber! What are you doing down there? Come up here at once and eat your dinner before it gets cold and I have to give it to the cat again,' said Madame von Groppeninck.

'Stupid bloody cat,' said Groppeninck as he set about strapping the poor bedraggled creature into a chair, complete with all sorts of tubes, wires and electrodes. He loaded one of the labelled jars into the machine to which the cat's head was now attached and began to wind the cranking handle on the side of the machine. The unfortunate feline tried to struggle free of his restraints but he was held firmly. The tortured creature began to meow pitifully as sparks flew and low humming vibrations shook the chair violently.

Gradually the cat's meowing deepened in tone and became a rich and melodious tenor voice. It was unmistakeably that of the great tenor Enrico Caruso and no-one was more surprised by this than the cat himself. He'd never heard himself sing before, much less in such beautiful tones.

Madame von Groppeninck barged into the basement room at this moment and berated her son,

'Stop torturing the cat will you? You're making a god-awful racket. And put my blasted ear-trumpet back together will you? Your dinner's on the table, now come and get it before it gets cold.'

She twisted his left ear and led him with her up the stairs. Hans Wilber von Groppeninck winced as he was led on his tip-toes with a meek, 'Yes, mother.'

The cat meanwhile amused himself by singing 'Una Furtiva Lagrima' and was well pleased with the results.

THE SILENT SOUND OF WINTER.

Breda McAteer

Snowflakes are falling,
Icicles melt against my skin.
While I shelter from the cold winter chill;
The trees welcome the white dew
That kisses their naked branches
With gifts of shining crystal.

I shiver as I shield myself against
The cold crisp air,
As my body has no defence
To frost that bites!

I wish I was like a tree
That stands tall with every season.
And in the winter, let the snow decorate me
With white stars that falls from the sky.
If I were to embrace the serenity hidden
In the harsh winter chill,
I would share this gift of magic
With gratitude while it lasts.

FREE NELSON MANDELA

Camillus John

I'm blue in the face telling people why I'm blue in the face. A Specials song was slapped onto the turntables by a mod D.J. in a wooden youth club when I was thirteen. Unlucky for some. Free Nelson Mandela. Free. Free. Free. Free. Free. Nelson Mandela. Every man Jack and Jackie were up on the dance-floor. Compelled by a known force within and without. Everybody dancing to ska. Mile a minute. Sweaty. Jump around the place. And not only that. Frogs.

Everybody had green skin. Hoppy legs too. And their insides went electronic. Their lips were huge, pouting and pink and they danced with wild expectations. Couldn't stop. Expecting everything now. The entire youth club were giant electronic frogs with pink lips. Music had turned them into. And the message was highly political yet they danced, then pondered hard on the significance - understanding by osmosis who this person was, ransacking their parents' minds when their got home for more information later - of this black man of cardinal import.

I looked down and my thighs were green too, my voice croaky and insides eeeeelectronic, my pen having gone astray in the sheer rush, my lips large and pink, leaping now from note to note like a class-conscious flying superhero, the off-the-beat snare drum skanking my body in glorious skank, skank, skanks.

And Eric -

"I'm Eric Earwig and I'm brave.

I sing songs so you won't be afraid.

I hear my Earwig chums.

Eric and the Earwigs.

HAIL!   Eric and the Earwigs."

- Earwig was brought to life in the mind and scribbled pages of this particular giant electronic frog with pink lips in a 1984 Ballyfermot youth club. When I was thirteen. I am a writer. No? I'm blue in the face telling people why I'm blue in the face.

THE RADIO

Brian Browne

A radio sits on its purpose built shelf beside the window: this shelf is quite high up and the radio bears the brand name of Philips, which I am told means that it came from an exotic place far away called Holland. On this particular day the news is on and it's that time of year when the Pope gives his blessing called "Urbi Et Orbi" which means "To The City and The World" Now we live in a home steeped in a strange brand of Catholicism which is unique to Ireland and consequently when the announcer says "And now we have the Popes blessing" Mother instructs us to get down on our knees and be ready to receive this precious gift from the pope himself. We dutifully do so and are filled with a sense of wonder at the solemnity of this strange sonorous voice reciting the familiar phrase of the benediction "in nomine patris et filii et spiritui sancti".

The announcer then informs us that the Taoiseach Mr Eamon De Valera has said something to the effect that we must accept our responsibilities as good citizens and put up with some further misery or other (the more things change the more they remain the same) The radio receives its power from a fitting which was actually designed to take a light bulb. This fitting was pressed into service to supply power to any and every electrical apparatus which found its way into the living room, whether the socket was suitable or not. In most cases the appliance should not ever be plugged into an unearthed two pin light socket, none the less it was the only source of electricity and therefore the clothes iron was duly plugged in there when the washing had dried sufficiently. This iron was already an ancient contraption and prone to break down, when it gave trouble father would take it apart with relish and play with the elements, which resembled sheets of stiff silver paper in the exact shape of the iron.

Father's universal fix for anything electrical was the silver paper from the Sweet Afton packet. He would carefully re-make broken connections between the elements and then reassemble the offending item. The result of these repairs was that if and when a hand came in contact with any of the metal parts of the apparatus there followed an electrical shock. Nor was the iron the only appliance in the house which was quite literally shocking. He also went so far as to wire the house in similar fashion to the wiring of the universal source in the living room. The result of this endeavour was that the electric cooker was a stimulating experience for anyone who used it, especially if a metal spoon was employed in the stirring of the contents of a pot or a pan. The radio was perhaps the one thing which was not amenable to the "fix" of silver paper, its interior glow of strange lights were responsible for its magical ability to be more of a portal to the outside world than that of the window it sat beside. The window after all only showed us the yard while the radio showed us the world only limited by our own imagination.

HELP

Alda Gomez

I need to help you because
I cannot bear to look inside.
My pain is too strong, too alive,
too stale, too rancid, too painful a pain.

I need to help you save yourself,
small one, because I'm lost.
I need to find a way to wave
my self-hatred good bye,
to turn it into love, into wings
of change for me, for you, for us.
And you are so fragile,
so fresh, so naïve, so delicate,
it seems.

So why are you so angry at me?
Why do you not accept my help?
Why do you nail those fierce eyes
of yours into my neck?
Why do you tell me to stop it?
Why do you not understand that
it all comes from a deep deep love?

A need to help you because
I cannot bear to look inside,
into a pain that is too strong, too alive,
too stale, too rancid, too painful a pain.

GOOD SONS ARE RELATIVE

Pat Nolan

Golden Oldie to rescue Royaume-Uni from nul points curse, Veteran Crooner Rides Again, and similar headlines, broke the news that Engelbert Humperdinck was to represent the UK in the Eurovision Song Contest 2012. I hadn't registered the name for years but willy-nilly I was back in 1966.

It was Christmas Eve, and sleeting. I was sodden but I knew my mother would have the fire blazing and my dinner ready. And the school holidays stretched ahead.

But when I got home Mr. Colgan, from next door, was ensconced on the couch, sucking in every drag of his cigarette and looking miserable. I recognised the signs. At thirteen, I was inured to those bearing witness to life's rich tapestry. Having the living room, and my mother, commandeered by the self-absorbed needy was a nuisance you hated but got used to, like static on the radio. My mother beckoned me into the kitchen. 'What's he doing here?' I hissed.

'I had to ask Mr. Colgan in. He spent his Christmas bonus on drink and Cora threw him out. I couldn't leave him crying on the doorstep.' my mother replied, somewhere between defiance and defence.

'But he'll be here till Stephen's Day' I said, the horror dawning.

'He'll be gone in a while,' said my mother. 'What he did is awful irresponsible. I don't know how she's going to

36

put food on the table, but its Christmas and she'll have to take him back in.'

The Colgans, like ourselves, were a family of ten, but given to realising their potential for woe more often. Peter, Mr. Colgan, was a skilled tradesman with a fine tenor voice and a fondness for drink, the former activated by the latter. Mrs. Colgan, Cora, enjoyed high blood pressure alongside a portfolio of womanly complaints.

The Colgans had a different texture to their lives than us. In their house I first tasted bread with sugar instead of butter, a culinary delight my mother forbade point blank. When we only had radio, for years the Colgans enjoyed a rented, and frequently repossessed, television on which we had been invited to watch Pope John's and President Kennedy's funerals.

The creative side of the Colgans found expression in the eldest son, Dan, who burned a hole in several layers of blankets so he could smoke comfortably in a wintry bedroom. In consequence, he was fussy about his bedclothes and arranged these to the highest standard of military precision.

After Dan, there was Peter Jr., the success of the family, who had gotten a start as a messenger boy in the Brewery and had just graduated to labourer. There was then a run of daughters who worked variously in the jam and sweet factories, followed by a number of minor children.

Dan's career was peripatetic. A charmer, he was respectful to my mother and the other neighbours. He was considered resourceful. When Dan was home from England he took charge of feeding the dog, Elvis Colgan.

We all knew that was because he would feed Elvis a daily tin of cat rather than dog food at a saving of 1d per day, parlaying his entrepreneurship into 3.5 cigarettes a week. These days, he would fancy himself for *The Apprentice*.

On the whole I liked Mr. Colgan. He was genial and generous, the more so when drunk. My father, on the other hand, didn't get drunk but no one would accuse him of either trait. Still, I was used to Da and I couldn't see what a doleful Mr. Colgan, with no half-crowns for deserving boys, brought to the Christmas party.

In the meantime he was there to be put up with.

How many strong cups of tea can one man drink on a raw Christmas Eve afternoon, while Santa Claus on Raidió Eireann tells of his imminent journey (Santa's, not Mr. Colgan's)? An awful lot, it turned out, but in maturity I appreciate there was a need for both occupation and rehydration.

The time crawled. My mother was trying to make small talk: difficult when avoiding the obvious seasonal topics. So she bustled around with the Christmas preparations, and prattled on about the murder in Rathmines. All that week the evening papers had shocked with their tale of an elderly spinster, aged 59, bludgeoned to death. For the sake of £37 in the till. At work in a drapery shop. In the middle of the afternoon.

I sat by the fire wishing my father home, a novel emotion. I took comfort in his ultimate weapon. He could glare for Ireland. He would loathe Mr. Colgan's presence. He didn't like Mr. Colgan all that much in the first place, on account of the drink, Peter being a better singer, and the

Colgans being a large family. My father strongly disapproved of men other than himself having large families.

Then, as Santa left the North Pole, there was a knock at the door. I answered it, to be met by Mrs. Colgan, red-eyed and agitated. The distracted look of a woman with ten people to feed and no turkey, I thought.

But all she said was 'Oh, Annie' to my mother and 'Oh, Peter' to Mr. Colgan. And then, 'It's Dan. He's in trouble.'

Peter added concern to his expression even as he grasped his transgression had been trumped. My mother hugged Cora, asking 'That's terrible. Has he been caught out by the Army?'

My mother's reaction was entirely reasonable. What Dan did at irregular intervals was go to England and enlist in one or other branches of the British forces. He would stick it for a few months, then desert and arrive home. Always with presents.

With hindsight I realise Dan serially joined up from lack of options rather than as an actual career choice. He would join the Navy, say, after a short stint in the Army. Or enlist in the Army in another town. A character who wrote his own character references he was limited only by the forces' configuration.

Cora, distraught, responded, 'It's not the Army, Annie, it's the Guards. He's been arrested. They say' and her voice shook, 'he did the Rathmines murder and they're going to charge him'.

My mother was stunned. Peter yelped as his cigarette burned his already deep orange fingers. I was pretty shocked myself, glad I did not have £37 to have incited such an attack nearer home.

My mother, combining reconciliation with action, said, 'It must be a mistake, Cora. Sure, was he not in England? Let me get my coat. Come on, Peter. We're going over to the Barracks to get this sorted.'

To me, she said, 'Tell your father where I am when he comes home, and do a couple of boiled eggs for his tea. There's a banana for yours.'

Mrs. Colgan beseeched me 'Tell Philomena where I am when she gets home.' Philomena was her eldest daughter. This I did when she got home from seasonal cheer at the jam factory, although I only said Dan was in trouble with the Guards. I didn't feel it was my place to tell her brother was a killer, or that there was no turkey for her dinner tomorrow. I saved those details for Da and my own sisters and brother.

My mother got home about eleven o'clock that night, bone-weary. 'Paddy, you should go to bed' she started on me. But I wanted to know what was happening. We all did. I waxed indignant, 'I've had a terrible day. I had a banana for my tea on Christmas Eve and I've missed Midnight Mass'.

She gave in and told us what she had gleaned. 'Cora was expecting Dan home for Christmas but the Guards say he came a week early. According to them he spent his last few bob on presents. He was staying at his girlfriend's house, whoever she is, and on the day of the murder he stole

40

a bike, then robbed the shop and killed that poor woman. He made his getaway on the bike, but there are witnesses to his comings and goings and they've fingerprints as well. They're going to charge him and he'll be up before the judge on Stephen's Day.'

'They won't be able to see him till after he's charged,' she continued, drawing breath. 'Peter himself is sober as a judge and Cora's in a state of shock. I'll get up early tomorrow and go and tell Fr. Neville so he can visit them.'

She looked at my father. 'I believe the Guards, Billy. I think he did it. There was always something a bit off there. And, now I think about it, a lot of times he skipped off to England all of a sudden. Maybe it's not the first time he's done something, here or there.'

'Will he get Christmas Dinner in the barracks?' I asked.

'He will', she replied. 'But I wouldn't say that's what's on his mind now. Their minds won't be on their dinner either but we've a big turkey. I'll give them half of ours after I cook it.'

Even my father didn't object to this profligacy. So we all went to bed, in a roundabout, sheepish way as surprise Christmas presents had to be set out.

Next morning my present was there, my very own record player. Complete with three singles to launch my collection. No longer would I have to depend on the wayward needle and muffled sound of our radiogram, worn out by Mario Lanza.

True to her word, my mother divided up the turkey, and even the stuffing, so the Colgans had a corporal work of mercy for their dinner. She had also collared Fr. Neville at early mass. Instead of passing the afternoon with a bottle of Redbreast and a nice snooze poor old Fr. Neville had to spend it delivering a spiritual work of mercy to the Colgans. I envisage him assuring them that, whatever his failings, Dan was a good son. Well, everything's relative, including sons. I suppose he hadn't beaten any family or neighbours to death.

My mother had asked Cora and Peter in for tea that evening. As she said to Da, 'It's the worst thing that could happen to anyone' (apart from being bludgeoned to death, I thought) and 'It's not their fault. It'll help them to talk about him.' 'The papers will do enough talking about him' was Da's retort.

And so they joined us. The shock had affected them with a kind of role reversal. While Cora knocked back the cream sherry, Peter took prim little sips of his brandy.

My mother asked Cora 'who is the girlfriend?'

Sobbing, Cora replied, 'Philomena says she's from the flats.' As if they hadn't suffered enough.

For diversion, my mother turned to me 'Paddy, show Mr. and Mrs. Colgan your Christmas present and play them something'. And so I loaded the three singles, the music a rest from talking and thinking.

The plaintive strains of the third single rang out as Engelbert pleaded *Please release me, let me go'*. As import dawned, my mother pucked me and motioned

42

fiercely to turn the record off. But as I reached out to reject it I heard a humming from Mr. Colgan and then he began to sing along with Engelbert, as he clasped Cora's free hand, and sang to her and for her and for Dan and for the poor woman from the drapery. We all joined in, because what else would you do?

 And then I played it a few more times before Cora and Peter went home to face their own family, tomorrow's ordeal, and the literal and figurative trials ahead of them.

What goes around, comes around, I'm thinking. In a few months' time Engelbert will undergo his own trial, by the Eurovision jurors. If he does badly he will only face the prospect of oblivion not a theoretical death penalty.

LETTERS
Bláithín Ní Liatháin

Tied together with a brown velvet ribbon,
The letters, once so precious so private,
Keep the past present.

Declarations of feelings of longings
In poetic words, stirred the heart of youth,
Love is not letters; love is presence.

I should shred these letters
But there are none else.

THE KING IS DEAD....

Harry Browne

Edward pulled his charger to a halt. "What can this dolt want" he demanded "Doesn't he realize that I'm busy here. If this is not important I'll have the dog flogged"

The trembling messenger approached diffidently, offering the sealed parchment to Prince Edmund, Edward's younger brother, who, in his turn passed it to the Prince.

The Prince, weary from his journey from the Holy Land to Sicily impatiently broke the seal on the imposing missive. Reading the message his face blanched and he swayed in the saddle.

Edmund, seeing the prince obviously upset, rushed to his side and grasping his arm to steady him he cried "What is wrong, brother, it must be bad news. Has anything happened to the Princess Eleanor?"

"Nay, brother, our father has died in Westminster. I am now King of England" His head bowed with deep sorrow he went on "We did not always see eye to eye but I deeply loved him and I will grievously miss him in the future"

Edmund immediately jumped from his horse and falling to his knees cried "Let me be the first to pledge myself to your Majesty".

Edward climbed from his horse and standing bareheaded in the hunting field received the homage of all the assembled, English and Norman nobles who had accompanied him to the Holy Land.

"My Lord" Roger Clifford, one of Edward's knights spoke up "We should make all haste back to England and have you crowned. There is, after all no King in the realm until the coronation has confirmed him"

"Nay Clifford, in this you are mistaken. Before we left on the crusade to the Holy Land my father and I arranged for this eventuality. As we speak there is a great assembly in Westminster for my Father's funeral. All the great Magnates assembled there are swearing fealty to me and a new tradition has been started with the cry 'The King is Dead, Long live the King'. From this moment forward England shall never again be without a King, even for an instant" Edward could not have foretold that this tradition would continue for more than seven hundred and fifty years, but he had, perhaps unwittingly, placed a very early foundation stone in the English constitution.

His mind was not concerned with such thoughts, however. "Before we return to England, Clifford, we have business here in Europe. I have sworn a holy oath to wreak vengeance on the De Montfort brothers for their foul murder of my boyhood friend and cousin Henry of Almain. Simon has escaped my wrath by dying some two years agone, cursed by God and condemned to the seventh circle of hell, steeped to the neck in a river of boiling blood, for killing his cousin, and mine, on the steps of the altar of St Sylvester in Viterbo. Guy remains at large, hiding behind his wealthy wife's skirts, but he has been excommunicated by Pope Gregory the tenth and he is, therefore vulnerable to my justice. We go to Rome to ask the Pope to negotiate his delivery to me"

"Scribe" Edward called "Send this message to England 'Edward by the grace of God King of England'" the message continued with detailed instructions to the three remaining regents of the five who had been appointed by Edward and his father Henry III before he set off on the crusades. In his message he informed the regents that, urgent as was the need for his presence in England, there were a number of matters which also needed him in Europe, not least the requirement to deal with the de Montforts and the necessity to satisfactorily sort out his position in his Dukedom of Aquitaine, a long standing area of dispute between himself and his relative Philip III of France.

Travelling through Italy on his way to meet the new Pope Gregory X, Edward's friend and sometime companion in the crusades they were greeted everywhere with rapturous welcomes. Edward was young and well set up and had a beautiful young wife, both of whom had returned from the crusades and they were very well received on their journey to Rome. Unfortunately for Edward's plans however, he found no appetite amongst the

Italian nobility for providing aid in his vengeful quest to bring Guy De Montfort to justice.

Finding no help in his main task Edward and Eleanor continued on to Rome where they found that Gregory X had gone on to Orvieto, some sixty miles further north. Nothing daunted they travelled on and were met with great pomp and ceremony by Gregory.

Here they delayed for a number of months endeavouring to bring de Montfort to justice. Appealing to Gregory Edward complained "Has nobody in Italy any regard for the laws of God or man? This miscreant has grievously offended the sanctuary of the church, murdered a defenceless man whose only offence was that he was related to me and compounded his crime by mutilating his corpse. Where can I go to seek justice against this man?"

"I am deeply sorry my friend" Gregory replied "My hands are tied in this matter. de Montfort has a rich wife and her family is very high in society both here and in France. He has, therefore, powerful protectors and it would be unwise for others to try to bring him to heel. As Supreme Pontiff I can excommunicate him a throw him in prison for a time but under no circumstances can I deliver him to your justice!"

With this Edward had to be satisfied for the moment and he decided to proceed to the next order of business, his estates in Gascony and his duties and entitlements as Duke of Aquitaine, a title which he had inherited from his father Henry III.

Arriving in France after a gruelling trip through the Alps Edward and his party was met by a delegation of Bishops and Nobles from England.

"My Lord and Liege" The spokesman for the group addressed Edward after they had all sworn their allegiance to him "Matters in England require your urgent attention. We have been awaiting your arrival in Paris this three months and more. There is trouble in the Marches and the Magnates there are continuing their feuds with each other, there have been several uprisings against your rule in parts of the country and lawlessness is rife throughout your domain. Your country is in dire need of your Majesty and we entreat you to return with all haste"

Assuring them of his concerns for his realm Edward said "I will return to England as soon as possible but whilst I am in France there is the matter of my lands in Gascony to be dealt with. During my late father's reign matters there have given rise to grave concerns. I am now Duke of Aquitaine as well as King of England. The actual extent of my holdings there and the fealty of my subjects are both in dispute. This matter is more critical than England at this moment and must be dealt with first" He sent the delegation home with his assurance that, as soon as matters in Gascony were settled he would immediately travel back to England.

"Edward" Since becoming King only Eleanor was entitled to address him by his given name and then only in private "I think it best that I should go to Gascony whilst you go on to Paris to see King Philip there. I am expecting your child again and I am certain that this will be a son. Whilst we are in Gascony I would like to see my brother King Alfonso of Castile, if I am right we can ask him to be Godfather to the baby"

Edward was in a peculiar relationship with King Philip III of France. Both he and Philip had very recently ascended their respective thrones and they were related to each other also. Philip, however was the undisputed overlord of all France and Edward was subservient to him as Duke of Aquitaine, a province of the French domain. This relationship demanded that, at some point Edward should submit, on bended knee to Philip as his liege lord. On the other hand Philip had a responsibility to acknowledge Edward's rights as lord of that province.

So it was that these two brother kings, equal on all levels, except in the case of Gascony, met in Paris in late July 1273. Edward was in a tricky position, he needed the legitimacy of his Dukedom to be established and acknowledged by Philip, but on the other hand his personal honour would not permit him to bow down too low to one whom he considered his equal.

Fourteen years earlier, on the 4th December 1259, their respective fathers, Henry and Louis had dealt with the same issue with a typical political fudge. Henry had knelt before Louis and pledged that, as far as Gascony was concerned, he was Louis' man. When Henry tried to clarify exactly what he meant by this declaration words seem to have failed him "We will do appropriate services" He declared "until it be found what services are due for these things, just as they have been found"

When Edward's turn came he was hardly any more definite in his choice of words "Lord King" he said, kneeling at Philip's feet "I do homage to you for all the lands I ought to hold from you" and with this unsatisfactory and ambiguous pledge both of their Royal highnesses had to satisfied.

Edward left Paris for Gascony in August with the intention of beginning the process of clarification of his rights and privileges in his Duchy of Aquitaine.

He declared to Clifford "Just as I have done homage to Philip as my king, I require my subjects within the duchy to do the same to me as their duke. Let it be known throughout my province 'By voice of herald and by sound of trumpet' that I want to create a written record of the services they owe, my tenants shall be advised to assemble at my coming and furnish me with the requisite information"

Having passed through Bordeaux, where, as well as accepting the homages of the citizenry, he was received with suitable pomp and ceremony, Edward proceeded further south to the town of St Sever, where he received the same acknowledgement from the leading lords of the duchy, and where the laborious process of registering their obligations to him began.

Just as Edward was basking in the adulation of his faithful retainers, however, his plans were rudely interrupted by the rebellion of the greatest lord in Gascony (after Edward himself that is).

At a tournament arranged in his honour in the town Clifford whispered in his ear. "Gaston de Bearn, whose lands lie in the hills along your realm's southern border, has rejected your overlordship and declared that he will not bow down to you, or any foreign King. He has a history of causing trouble. During the rule of Simon de Montfort as your father's seneschal he had been the chief ringleader of local resistance"

"He can hardly be blamed for hating de Montfort" Declared Edward "A viler creature than him can hardly have been put on this earth. My sympathies lie with this de Bearn already. de Montfort, however is far away and in an Italian prison. Wherein lies the de Bearn's objection to me as his liege lord now?"

"It seems to have stemmed from a disagreement with the duchy's new seneschal, Luke de Tany. de Tany has a somewhat arrogant way with him and it appears that he has ruffled de Bearn's feathers somewhat. He refuses to appear before your Majesty, claiming his independence under King Philip III of France"

"It is a great pity that Roger Leybourne died a couple of years ago. He was an excellent seneschal, defending my father's rights and privileges but also having due regard to the rights of his subjects" Edward mused "Unfortunately this business will force me to break off my administrative agenda and embark on a military expedition to put him in his place. It is very vexatious, I have more important issues which need my attention"

de Bearn's chastisement took a long time. Within a three weeks Clifford had good news for Edward "Your highness we have captured the dog de Bearn. He was hiding in a pigsty on one of his farms and his soldiers had all deserted him"

"Be very careful how you refer to members of the nobility Clifford" Edward admonished his second in command "Particularly in front of the troops. Remember that de Bearn, scoundrel that he is, is a distant cousin of mine and as such is to be treated with respect" he struggled to conceal a smile as he spoke for, truth to tell, the image of de Bearn cowering in a malodorous pigsty appealed to his sense of justice.

de Bearn refused to go quietly however. Having agreed surrender terms he immediately broke them and fled to his castle in the foothills of the Pyrenees. Recapturing him called for a new campaign which demanded Edward's presence for the remainder of the autumn and into the winter. Finally at the beginning of 1274 the pestilential Vicomte was finally brought before Edward in chains.

Gaston de Bearn was brought before Edward and apparently suitably chastened and promising fealty to his rightful Duke said "My Lord Duke, I am sorry for any transgressions which I may have committed against you. I would submit that I was driven to them by the actions of your late father's seneschal, Luke de Tany who was a cruel and unjust steward of your realm"

With typical magnanimity, Edward allowed him to go free, having first sequestered a large part of his lands in forfeit for his offences.

de Bearn however immediately appealed to Philip III, and the French king on receiving his appeal and seeing it as a heaven sent opportunity to put Edward in his rightful place in relation to himself, revoked the dispute to his court in Paris

This was a devastating blow to Edward's authority in Gascony. If he was subject to the King's authority in Gascony, then it followed that any decision by him in Gascon affairs was subject to the authority of the French King by virtue of his superior rights as lord of the realm.

If the duke of Gascony was properly subordinate to the king of France, it followed that any Gascon who was disgruntled by a ducal decision could appeal to the higher judgement of the French king's court.

"This is intolerable" raged Edward "I cannot bring my legitimate subjects under my own control in Gascony but that they may apply to the distant king in Paris for redress from my judgments. Philip is undoubtedly enjoying my discomfiture over this affair and revelling in his superiority over me as a consequence. God's curse upon both him and de Bearn, I shall have to abandon my campaign against the traitorous rat and leave him to Philip's justice and the good offices of my lawyers at court"

Dispirited by his frustrating lack of closure regarding de Bearn Edward decided it was time to move on. Winter had been wasted chasing Gaston, and Edward had had to abandon his intention of returning to England by Easter.

"We will spend the spring finishing the survey of my ducal rights and then go back to England, we shall hold a parliament in Bordeaux in March and receive the submission of my people" Edward announced, plainly dissatisfied with the onerous position with regard to Philip's overlordship, but unable to do anything about it.

As Edward and Eleanor left Gascony in April bound for England they were met on the road by another messenger. "My Lord" said Edmund, once more in company with the royal party "It is a message from the burghers of Limoges where the oppressed citizens are keen to acknowledge you as their lord, unfortunately the local Viscountess will have none of it. She too is determined to resist your authority"

Edward and his party hastened to Limoges to deal with this new upset but the Viscountess had shrewdly forestalled him. She, in her turn appealed to Philip III, who was only too pleased at the frequency with which opportunities arose to display his superiority were accumulating.

Finally, at the end of July Edward reached the French coast and set out for England. He had not entirely wasted his year in France. During his stay in Gascony, he had cultivated good relations with his neighbours, the kings of Navarre and Aragon, and had concluded alliances with both.

Eleanor, meanwhile, had been delighted to meet up with her half-brother, Alfonso X of Castile, for the first time in twenty years. The Spanish king had travelled to meet her at Bayonne, where he had become the godfather to her newly delivered third son: Alfonso junior had been sent back to England ahead of his parents in June.

"Looking back on my visit to Gascony" Edward lamented "It has, overall, been most frustrating. I have made a start on firmly establishing my authority within the duchy, but there are pockets of resistance still festering there. My situation with regard to my brother King, Philip remains most unsatisfactory. He is undoubtedly enjoying my discomfiture but for my part it is insufferable that I cannot exert unfettered authority over my Gascon subjects, both lowly and high born. However my presence in England is also crucial so the Gascon question must remain open for the present time"

Edward and Eleanor were met at Dover on 2 August 1274 by Robert Burnell, Bishop of Bath and Wells and sometime Archbishop of Canterbury, although he was rejected for this office by the Pope. He was a long-time friend and confidante of Edward's and had been the senior member of the council which had ruled England since Henry III had died. In fact, popular legend has it that, following Henry's death, Burnell had moved into his royal palace.

Edward's arrival in England was greeted by a tremendous sense of popular excitement. Partly it was the fact that Englishmen now had not one, but two crusading heroes to boast about; partly the fact that, after almost four years of absence, Edward had kept his public in England waiting for such a very long time. There was also a sense of relief at his safe return, and the prospect of better royal rule that only a resident king could provide. Over and above all these considerations, the populace were, undoubtedly, buoyed up by the knowledge that the country was about to witness a coronation.

Effusively greeting the King, Burnell said "Welcome home my lord King. Your presence here is sorely needed. There are many matters which need your personal attention and the sooner they can be addressed, the better. However before bothering you with affairs of state, there is the matter of the coronation to be dealt with. It is, as you well know more than four decades since your revered mother's coronation and even longer since your sainted father was crowned as a boy of nine years"

"You are King already due to your fathers' and your foresight in arranging matters before you travelled to the Holy Land" he continued "However although the royal title has passed from him to you and that you are indisputably recognised as King by all and sundry, it still remains that we must call upon the Almighty to bless your rule and for that we must have a coronation"

"Fortunately also, the fact that there was no longer the need to rush matters means that organisers of the ceremony have had months rather than days to make their preparations, and this in turn means that we can produce a programme of celebrations which will be suitably majestic. This will be a coronation which will be remembered whilst England exists" Burnell allowed his enthusiasm to show.

On Saturday, 18 August Edward and his entourage rode into London. The mayor and citizens had adorned their city 'without consideration of cost' with silks and cloth of gold. Not just the citizens themselves, we are told, but all the magnates of the kingdom, both clerks and laymen, had gathered in the capital to cheer the arrival of their new king.

Edward's entry into London on a Saturday was highly significant. Very likely what the citizens and visitors were witnessing was the birth of the custom whereby a new king would ride from the Tower of London to Westminster on the day before his coronation. Here again Edward was establishing a custom which would endure for centuries.

The Tower had been redecorated and cleaned up in advance of the King's arrival, and, at his personal request, the mayor had cleared the clutter from Cheapside, London's main market, and the route along which later 'vigil processions' would travel.

Edward then another started what was to become new tradition in 1274, one that would continue until the seventeenth century. Ceremoniously processing through London, Edward followed a fashion laid down by his father, who had loved to indulge in such showy excesses. Large public showpieces were one Henry III's most successful endeavours and he could usually be relied upon to get them right, unlike his political initiatives which often went spectacularly wrong. In fact, much of the detailed long-term planning for Edward's coronation can be traced back to his father's initiative.

Edward announced to his assembled courtiers "I will spend the eve of my coronation in prayer and contemplation much as I did in Burgos when I was about to be knighted twenty years agone. I am about to assume an enormous responsibility and I must seek the comfort and solace of some time spent with my God"

"I shall stay the night in the Painted Chamber. It was here that my late father died, and in 1274 his spirit still remains about the walls. This was his favourite room in the Tower and he, himself had it prepared for my use this hallowed eve. It is seemly that I should lie here before this momentous occasion"

On the wall directly behind the royal bed, the king's painters had created a coronation scene. The subject, naturally, was Edward the Confessor, being crowned by a crowd of bishops. On either side, outside of the curtains that closed around the bed, King Solomon's guards stood watch. Henry's aim, we must assume, was to provide his son with appropriate images on which to reflect during his vigil. Edward was to ponder the example of the Confessor, and the Wisdom of Solomon.

On Sunday, 19 August, the day itself dawned. Edward, accompanied by Eleanor, led by the clergy and the magnates, in procession the short distance from the palace to the abbey. The new abbey, of course, was Henry Ill's greatest legacy, and Edward was the first king to be crowned in it.

Henry and his architect had been acutely conscious of Westminster's long-standing role as the coronation church, and had tailored the new building accordingly. Its ornate north portal was sufficiently huge to admit with ease those processing from the palace; the galleries around its transepts allowed spectators to view the proceedings from on high. The crossing of the church, where much of the ceremony would be acted out, seems to have been rendered deliberately massive for this reason.

On the day of the coronation, it was filled with a giant wooden stage. This was elevated so that those standing in the nave could observe the king, and, as an added touch of pageantry, of sufficient height that those earls, barons and knights among the congregation could ride underneath it. For Edward's coronation the north and south transepts of the abbey were filled with aristocrats who were not merely elaborately dressed, but mounted on their gaily caparisoned horses too

The coronation itself was a magnificent piece of religious drama. Solemn prayers were intoned, censers were swung, and candles and torches burned, glorious anthems rang out. It was many years since the last king's inauguration and many of the old practices had been forgotten and new ones introduced in their stead.

In the case of Edward's coronation, Henry III, as

well as designing the theatre, also contributed many details to the script. Later medieval kings, for example, would begin by making an offering at the altar of two gold figurines, one of Edward the Confessor, the other of St John the Evangelist, a 'tradition' introduced in 1274 on the posthumous instructions of the Confessor's most avid devotee

The English coronation service had changed (and has changed) very little across the centuries. The coronation oath, for example, Edward's next significant act after making his offering at the altar, had been a central part of the service since it was first devised in the tenth century.

By this long-established convention, the new king made three basic promises. Standing at his full six foot two inch height Edward spoke in a loud and firm voice "I vow before almighty God that I will protect the Church, do good justice, and suppress evil laws and customs. Furthermore I also vow before almighty God that I will protect the rights of the Crown"

This was, of course, a much more self-interested pledge as far the king was concerned, and one to which Edward would attach much importance later in his reign.

Edward then descended from the stage towards the altar and disrobed down to his undershirt, in order that the archbishop of Canterbury could anoint various bits of his body with holy oil. The most mystical part of the whole ceremony, it took place on a suitably mystical pavement of multicoloured marble mosaic, the work of Italian craftsmen, and another finishing touch supplied by Henry III.

The unction was the point where medieval practice drew on biblical precedent: the Old Testament kings, David and Solomon, had been anointed in this way, and, for this reason, the choir in Westminster Abbey sang the anthem *Unxerunt Salomonem* (They Anointed Solomon) while the act was performed. Traditionally this had been the critical part of the service, the religious ritual that transformed a mere man into a king and Edward, although king in name already, regarded it as the supreme spiritual moment. At this moment his rule became blessed, and the gifts of the Holy Spirit were bestowed upon him. In more practical terms, it meant that, in addition to the holy oil that had been applied to his breast, shoulders and elbows, Edward also had chrism an even holier oil, poured over his head, where custom decreed that it must remain for a full seven days.

Lastly came the investiture: the part of the ceremony where the king was re-dressed in the most elaborate royal fashion and adorned with all manner of symbolic baubles (collectively known as the regalia). These had tended to multiply over the years, with the result that by the thirteenth century the new king was weighed down with glittering ornament.

Edward was vested in a golden tunic, girded with a sword, and robed with a mantle woven with gold. A gold ring was placed on his finger, and golden spurs were attached to his heels. Once he was wearing his special coronation gloves, a golden rod and a golden sceptre were placed in his hands.

These items had for the most part been wrought in the early thirteenth century but, thanks to the enthusiasm and credulity of Henry III, by 1274 each was believed to have been an original first used by Edward the Confessor himself. When, therefore, Edward was invested with the greatest item of all, described in a later account as 'a great crown of gold, with precious jewellery of great stones, rubies and emeralds', he understood this to be the same object once worn by his sainted namesake.

Edward's coronation, therefore, for all that it took place in a magnificent new church, and despite the manifold small details of staging introduced by Henry III, was essentially traditional in format and stuck to a time honoured script.

Once the great gold crown had been placed on his head, Edward immediately removed it and set it aside, saying "I now lay aside this crown, symbol of my reign and solemnly declare here in the presence of God and this loyal assembly of my lords, barons and nobles that I will never take it up again until I have recovered the lands given away by his father to the earls, barons and knights of England, and to aliens"

This was a clear declaration if intent on Edward's part and clearly revealed the policy that would preoccupy him during his first years of government, and to some extent for the rest of his reign. He was determined to recover for the crown all that his predecessor, Henry Ill, had been forced to give away. The greatest beneficiaries of Henry's conciliatory attitude had been those closest to him, such as Richard of Cornwall, William de Valence and Simon de Montfort.

It would have been politically unthinkable, however, for Edward to have taken back these lands and rights and privileges from such men or their descendants, the right to hold a court, for example, or to take a toll, even the right to do justice on red-handed thieves with their own private gallows.

Rights could also be expressed negatively, as the right not to have to do something. Some landowners would claim that they and their tenants did not have to attend the king's court, or to answer the summons of his officials. Either way, in asserting and maintaining such rights or liberties, there was financial advantage to be had. Holding your own court, for example, meant you received the profits it raised in fines; not attending a royal court meant you avoided paying similar fines to the king.

Such rights and privileges could be very ancient and legitimate; they might also be officially sanctioned by the king. Henry III, when he found it difficult to obtain the support of his greatest subjects, was wont to appease them by granting just such exemptions. Often as not, however, rights and privileges were simply assumed by landowners who sensed that they could get away with it, and this had been the case during much of Henry's lax rule. Great men in particular had taken excessive liberties, shutting out the king's agents, his sheriffs, justices and bailiffs and creating what amounted to their own private fiefdoms.

Edward, speaking quietly to Robert Burnell, the leader of the regents appointed by Henry while Edward was in Palestine said "I am determined not only to halt this tendency, but also to throw it into reverse. I am, I believe well-qualified for the task. I am a more masterful man than my father and in the course of my struggle with Simon de Montfort I fought hard to earn the personal authority that my father had so visibly lacked" There was, as a result, little chance of anyone scaring or dominating Edward in the way that Montfort had scared and dominated Henry.

Similarly, Edward's crusade had further enhanced his standing, cementing his relationships with a powerful circle of friends of the kind his father had never known. The crusaders returned from the East as brothers-in-arms, their loyalties to each other, and above all to their new king, heightened by a sense of having been tested together in a great adventure.

With such men to support him, Edward would have no need to resort to his father's policy of appeasement in order to get his own way.

Edward spent much of his thirty five year reign reforming royal administration and common law. Through an extensive legal inquiry, Edward investigated the tenure of various feudal liberties, while the law was reformed through a series of statutes regulating criminal and property law.

Increasingly, however, Edward's attention was drawn towards military affairs. After suppressing a minor rebellion in Wales in 1276–77, Edward responded to a second rebellion in 1282–83 with a full-scale war of conquest. After a successful campaign, Edward subjected Wales to English rule, built a series of castles and towns in the countryside and settled them with Englishmen.

Next, his efforts were directed towards Scotland. Initially invited to arbitrate a succession dispute, Edward claimed feudal suzerainty over the kingdom. In the war that followed, the Scots persevered, even though the English seemed victorious at several points. In later years he obtained the sobriquet of 'Hammer of the Scots'

At the same time there were problems at home. In the mid-1290s, extensive military campaigns required high levels of taxation, and Edward met with both lay and ecclesiastical opposition. These crises were initially averted, but issues remained unsettled. When the king died in 1307, he left to his son, Edward II, an ongoing war with Scotland and many financial and political problems.

At the present day, Edward I is credited with many accomplishments during his reign, including restoring royal authority after the reign of Henry III, establishing Parliament as a permanent institution and thereby also a functional system for raising taxes, and reforming the law through statutes. At the same time, he is also often criticised for other actions, such as his brutal conduct towards the Scots, and issuing the Edict of Expulsion in 1290, by which the Jews were expelled from England. The Edict remained in effect for the rest of the Middle Ages, and it would be over 350 years until it was formally overturned under Oliver Cromwell in 1656.

He had sixteen children by his childhood sweetheart and wife Eleanor of Castile, eleven daughters and five sons. Only five daughters and one son, Edward II survived into adulthood. With his second wife he had two sons, who lived into adulthood and a daughter who died young.

He was justly termed a great and terrible King.

ABOVE AND BELOW THE EARTH

Breda McAteer

What's underneath the ground if left unturned?
Earthworms that multiply and thrive,
In the darkness of the soil, we tread upon each day.
Digging the earth beneath ground,
Disturbs the earthworm's living space;
But provides a welcoming home
For new seed, to bloom and grow.
What will the new growth bring?
A Flourishing array of flowers,

To welcome in the season.
If the new growth is forgotten,
An abundance of weeds to greet us.
But the weeds must die if we want our flowers to exist.
Yet the worms still multiply and thrive without our aid.

What about the trees that were cut down!
Did the Elderflower cry in pain
When the axe dug into the bark?
No one stopped to save the tree
That was blooming and flourishing in the shade.
The sweet scent was only missed when it was gone.

If all that can be seen is stone
When we look down upon the ground,
Yet the sky is always visible up above.

If the rich soil cannot be reached,
And the stony ground is left unturned;
The worms can live undisturbed in the safety of the soil.
Their home of darkness beneath the earth
That we tread upon each day.

The earth will always provide for us
New soil to meet the seeds we plant.
When the sky looks down upon the seed,
Our shrubs will bloom and grow, to welcome in the
season.
Visitors to our home, in the ground above the earth.

KICKING MY MOTHER IN THE HEAD TRILOGY

By Camillus John

BARKING

Interior: A room in a Pigeon Club on a Wednesday evening at approximately 7.30 p.m. It's a Creative Writing class. Twelve people or so sit around a few tables. They are close enough to chat.

Tom and Dick to be spoken deadpan and Henrietta hammed-up.

The Author stands up to speak.

The Author:	This first piece is called Capitalism.
Tom:	Woof
Dick:	Woof
Henrietta:	Shut up!
Tom:	Woof
Dick:	Woof
Henrietta:	Shut up!

68

Tom:	Woof
Dick:	Woof
Henrietta:	Shut up!
Tom:	Woof
Dick:	Woof
Henrietta:	Shut up!
The Author:	And the next piece is called Communism.
Tom:	Miaow
Dick:	Miaow
Henrietta:	Shut up!
Tom:	Miaow
Dick:	Miaow

Henrietta:	Shut up!
Tom:	Miaow
Dick:	Miaow
Henrietta:	Shut up!
Tom:	Miaow
Dick:	Miaow
Henrietta:	Shut up!
The Author:	I'm working on the Nordic economic model for next week.
By the way	- does anyone know how to spell moo?

Author sits back down.

THE PYJAMA GIRL

Interior: When the above author sits down, Dee Du enters the Pigeon Club and walks towards a back room where there is a poetry recital due to commence. She has to pass the group of creative writers and assorted others sitting around tables.

Martina & Bernard Barrister stand up and block her path.

Martina Barrister:	You're a scumbag! Get off the streets and change. You offend me.
Dee Du:	I just need to get by madam, please.
Bernard Barrister:	You're a lazy dole-sponging scrounger. Take those pyjamas off or we'll do it for you over there in that park!
Dee Du:	I can't, I'm late for a poetry recital in The Shack. Please!
Martina Barrister:	Who gave you permission for that?
Dee Du:	I didn't know I needed permission from barristers to recite poetry. I'll get it next time madam, I swear. Please! I'm reading Ginsberg's Howl today.

Martina Barrister:	Ginsberg! You're nothing but a whore. Your type have caused this whole recession. You make me sick. Hold her Bernard.
Dee Du:	Please let me go. I'm begging you.
Martina Barrister:	We own most of the houses in Ballyfermot now, little Miss Pyjamas, so we run things now. Do you hear?
Bernard Barrister:	Look at that crease on my trouser there Miss Scum. You could slice turnips on it. Those smiling sun pyjamas should never had seen the light of day.

(Martina pours a can of Dutch Gold lager down the front of Dee Du's pyjamas and punches her in the gut).

Dee Du:	Please! I'll ask next time. I swear!
Martina Barrister:	Punks. Good for nothing punks ye are!
Dee Du:	Punks? *(Stands up straight)* Yes, we're punks. I am punk. More punk than punk itself.
Martina Barrister:	Junky!

Dee Du:	You're middle class, you'll never understand. The most avant-garde statement of the past two hundred years and you see nothing.
Martina Barrister:	Lazy bastard.
Dee Du:	I'm bigger than Duchamp's urinal I am.
Bernard Barrister:	Pyjamas? You're fucking joking.
Dee Du:	Yes, pyjamas outdoors. I'm getting a bigger and better reaction than the first punks got on the Kings Road in London. Junkies. Scumbags. Lazy scroungers. Like Duchamp. Like Stockhausen. Like Dada. Like Punk!
Martina Barrister:	You've slept in those pyjamas like an animal.
Dee Du:	All jaws to the floor when I wear my pyjamas outdoors. It's that immense. Up there with punk. I am urinal.
	(A bell sounds)
Bernard Barrister:	Martina, quick! To the

tribunal!

Martina Barrister: You're lucky Missy. If there wasn't money to be robbed, you'd be dead now and lying naked in the park.

Dee Du: No. I think I'll read my own poem today and scrap Ginsberg's. Actually.

Martina Barrister: Stop talking about poetry - you're not allowed poetry - that's for us. Bitch! *(She punches her gut).*

Bernard Barrister: It's probably not poetry at all. It's probably rap.

Dee Du: Chocolate Charlie is playing today in The Shack. He's the chocolate poet of Landon Road. He writes all his words down with a chocolate pencil. Recites them. And then licks his notebook clean afterwards. Thus, eating his own words every time. He has no ego. And this makes sure that that doesn't change.

Martina Barrister: You bitch!

Dee Du: My name is Dee Du, not bitch.

(A bell sounds even louder)

Bernard Barrister: Martina come on! Time is money.

Martina Barrister: We'll be back with switchblades later - and accountants.

Dee Du: Chocolate Charlie has no ego but he teaches people how to swagger. Like Noel and Liam Gallagher.

Martina Barrister: Bernard, she wants to swagger now. I'm getting sick. Bernard just one kick please, I'm begging you? In the balls!

Bernard Barrister: No. We're going. Into the fucking car outside - come on! *(They run outside the pigeon club and get into a car and drive away).*

Dee Du: Ladies and gentlemen, my poem.

(Bows and walks into the room labelled, The Shack, for the poetry workshop).

KICKING MY MOTHER IN THE HEAD

Toni Thursday, with two tough looking female security guards behind her, enters the Pigeon Club. They walk up to München Minnie, a man in the creative writing group.

Toni Thursday: München Minnie, I know it was you who violently kicked my mother in the head yesterday morning with your big size twelve, cherry-red, steel-capped Doctor Marten boots.

München Minnie: And you are?

Toni Thursday: Toni Thursday.

München Minnie: But it's a Tuesday.

Toni Thursday: Even on a Tuesday, my name's still Toni Thursday. Did you kick my mother in the head?

München Minnie: Yes, I did.

Toni Thursday: So you admit it.

München Minnie: Of course.

Toni Thursday: Why?

München Minnie:	Plankton.
Toni Thursday:	What?
München Minnie:	I said plankton.
Toni Thursday:	What?
München Minnie:	The Fulmar is a bird of the open sea, and it eats plankton. As a result, it can spit for over a metre in length at its predators. I figure, if I eat enough plankton, I'll be able to kick your mother in the head for longer, harder and faster. For next month's competition like. The only downside is that my breath will become very oily and pungent.
Toni Thursday:	Arrest him now women. He's admitted to kicking my mother in the head. You all heard him.
München Minnie:	Hold your horses Toni. It's all perfectly legal. In fact, it might be compulsory. Read this letter first before doing anything Tone. Right? It might just save your life.
Toni Thursday:	*(Reading letter).* Dear

München Minnie, all under-utilised resources in the country must be used to their fullest capacity from now on in, and in particular, unemployed Irish mothers.

Toni Thursday's mother has now been officially interned to the 2014, *"Kicking Toni Thursday's Mother In The Head Competition,"* where she'll have to wear a safety helmet with yellow elbow-pads, keep a leg-speed measuring device at all times in her handbag, and be kicked in the head for fifty hours a week as per the new memorandum of understanding commencing January 2014. Please see attached for further information. Signed the government.

Toni Thursday: Hold it women. This letter looks official. It's got a rubber stamp.

München Minnie: Did she not tell you Toni?

Toni Thursday: No, she never said a word.

78

München Minnie:	Probably ashamed of the work that's all. She'll come round in a week or so. I know how she feels Tone. When I started at the Donut Factory I was too ashamed to tell people where I worked for weeks, months even. It was as if I'd failed miserably in life. I came around though, eventually. In the end like. Your mother will too Tone. Don't worry about it.
Toni Thursday:	We can't arrest you München, that's boxed off. We know that now. But it's a morally repugnant act. How can you kick my mother in the head and sleep soundly?
München Minnie:	I told you München. It's in the agreement. It's allowed. I sleep like a baby. Look at this print-out from her handbag, I'm not even in the first half of the league table. I'm not doing great at the moment *(Passes print-out over to Toni).*
Toni Thursday:	You're right there.
München Minnie:	My leg speed was a paltry sixty kph.

Your Ma's advice to me afterwards was to get my Docs resoled. And adjust my stance a little more to the right. The leader's was one hundred and eighty kph. Treble top.

Toni Thursday: I can see that. What if your kick misses her helmet completely and hits her face?

München Minnie: It won't. Anyway, it will only stun her for a minute, blood and mucus, a little headache perchance. That's all. There's no other way Tone. The country needs the pain. A little teeth loss, that's all. Look at the league table.

Toni Thursday: *(Perusing the print-out).* That's Black Eyed Susan from down the road. She's in third place. She's a kick-speed of 150! There isn't much in it now. At the top like.

München Minnie: You'd be faster Toni. Why not have a go yourself? I've application forms in the bag.

Toni Thursday: My own mother?

München Minnie:	You lose yourself in the technique and the physical preparation. It's the perfect meditation. You won't even be able to make out her face after your first kick, you'll be so in the moment. Go on Toni, kick your mother in the head and compete for the league championship. It's your duty. You know it makes sense. *(He hands Toni a kick measuring device).*
Toni Thursday:	Mind you, I was always fast at school. And it is for her own good, you say -
München Minnie:	Here's some polish for your Docs.
Toni Thursday:	Look, it's just measured my neck-chop speed at 80! And I wasn't even trying. Are we allowed to neck-chop her as well?
München Minnie:	Don't think so, but I'll ask the question. She can wear a neck-brace for protection - and a groin-guard too, if you want to go down that route like. No problems Tone.
Toni Thursday:	No. No. No. The kick is

obviously the superior art-form München. It tests your skill better. I can see that now.

München Minnie: Come on then, and we'll discuss the bones of this large over there in the lounge. They do a very nice plate of plankton.

They walk off towards the lounge with München Minnie's arm around Toni Thursday's shoulder, the beginning of a beautiful friendship.

MASTER MARINER

Frank George C. Moore

On some stormy night if your passin that way
and the winds comin' up from the sea

Boumme, boumme, boumee

The foghorn in old Dublin bay
sounded last night, for the last time,
or so the port men say.
I thought I heard the voice of Capt. Bligh
Dublin's master mariner, sigh out at sea.
He who tamed our Viking place
Between blue Howth head and Sandymount.
I heard him speak while guiding
night ships into port.
While I listened in my youth
Dreaming of voyages I might take
With goods away to France,
or to the Dutch man's Skagerrak
or the ports of the Afrikaans
or golden Venezuela, in the Americas
trading wine & tea or saviour Christ;
I a young sea missionary.

In the mist that touched
the window sash in my room,
in the bay of youth
as jazz played on long-wave radio
and the voices of the oceans called in mist,
"Acquire a master cert in life"
For no sound ceases, that guides ships.
As sea- captains sung jazz with Eartha Kitt

and old Sachmo played ship's bass
on the air ways of the world
guiding voyages into port.
Listen, if you pass down that way
you'll hear the sound although
the port men say its ceased
listen yet, for it echoes in eternal fog.
Boumme, boumme, boumee

E.M. Olivander

"God gave us memory so that we might have roses in December."
— J.M. Barrie

Memories, the good ones, nourish the spirit. They weave a tapestry of goodness and freedom and love through our lives. They are that bank of savings we can dip into when emotional cash flow runs low. They are our most precious keepsakes, something to keep forever, an inner time capsule. Like all keepsakes it is good to take them out once in a while. Remembering great moments like they had happened yesterday is like taking that dose of vitamin C to fortify against winter colds. These are a few of the special ones that sustain me to this day.

I remember my first day at school. First came the excitement; a sense of a new beginning and of growing up overnight. I was collected from my house by my next door neighbour, Nora from sixth class. To my five year old eyes she seemed more like an adult. The mile and a half walk to school seemed like the adventure of a lifetime. Then came the shock of seeing so many eager smiling faces at once. I had never been in a room with so many people at one time before. There were perhaps thirty pupils from low infants - as we used to call them back then – to first class. A sudden shyness kicked in. I was no longer the grown up girl that left the house that morning. I was a five year old again. . Nora left to go to her classroom next door. I ran after her, but to my consternation she kept walking. The teacher, also called Nora, gently took me by the hand led me back into the classroom. She looked at me with that déjà vu smile. She had seen it all before, and I would too, each September after that, with each new batch of 'low' infants.

I remember the smell of fresh mown hay and the sight of fluorescent green frogs, slithering away into hiding like naughty children caught raiding the larder. It was summer time on the farm and the call of the corncrake heralded the hay saving season. It was an exciting time of sunshine and freedom from school. There were hide and seek games among the hay cocks – or wynds as we used to call them. There was the novelty of dining outdoors in an era before picnics and barbeques became fashionable as people to busy to go back to the house had their meals in the fields.. Later there was the thrill of rides on the back of the hay float – a horse drawn low flat platform cart with a mounted winding winch which lifted the hay cocks on to the float and transport them from the fields to the barn. It seemed like a magical process to my child's eyes.

I remember seeing the joy on my father's face as he read that letter. I'll never forget the words he uttered: "We're very proud of you" His words rolled around in my ears like delicious chocolate. The source of his pride was the scholarship to attend secondary school that I had won – a valuable prize at a time when second level education was not free. I remember it so well because it was the first time he had ever said anything so special to me.

BEAST

Susan Cooney

He captivates pedestrians on pavements,
Perambulators in public parks,
Late night revellers on Aungier Street,
Surly security guards, and tots are transfixed
By his button eyes, cute furriness.

And yet, beware badger, wounded bird and rat,
Prowling mastiff, mouse, hissing cat,
And any soul against his master:
His bloodline impels him to the jugular.

He waits, tied outside a shop,
And barking, he anticipates.
Later, by his best friend's table sits
Stone still and craving.
At starlight, at his feet he lies
When, jolted from his strange dog dreams
He tries to lick away
What lies behind the nightmare cries

LAURA'S TREK

Cathy Power

Laura had got used to not having a man in her life and had stopped looking. Her last broken heart had come about when, she arrived into Dublin airport after a week in Paris with the man she thought would be the father of her children.

His wife was waiting at arrivals with two little girls by the hand. Laura had never suspected he was married. As they walked out the sliding arrivals doors to the waiting crowd, he caught her by the elbow and whispered urgently:

"That's my wife and daughters. Just go."

She glanced at the woman who was staring at Dan, looking angry and sad at the same time. Laura turned and walked away with her heart thumping and vomit rising in her throat.

She never saw Dan again. She sat in the women's toilet for a long time, waiting for her legs to work and for the wife to be gone, before she could go home.

Not only had Dan lied about being married and a father, but he never even spoke to her again, not even to get his things from her flat. He disappeared from her life, wouldn't answer her calls and, she presumed, didn't read the letters she sent him asking, at least, for an explanation.

He left her feeling, not only distraught, but like a fool that didn't realise what was staring in her face. His excuses for not turning up had to do with his shifts at work. She was left marvelling at her gullibility.

That was eight years ago and she had not been with a man since. Dan had destroyed her trust and she weighed up the odds and decided that lonely was better than deceived, heartbroken and devastated.

She was lonely to the point of insanity at times and spent many Sundays near to tears, even when she was making an effort. That meant getting out of bed and not resorting to spending the day in pyjamas with the laptop open, tweeting, Facebooking and watching miniseries on Netflix.

When she was up to it, she would get up, dress with care and go out, not always, but usually, alone. She would walk the dogs somewhere nice, go to a film or to some worthy cultural event and come home to eat, drink wine, watch evening television and go to bed to sleep soundly.

She had got used to it and had stopped staring at couples and trying to work out if they were happy or just tolerant of each other.

She wondered if they knew how lucky they were to have someone, seven days a week for company, to share food and drink, for him to take her elbow when they crossed the road, for the heat and bulk of a body in the bed and, of course, for sex.

All that had to be balanced against the rest: someone who might, again, deceive her, someone to judge her, someone who might, having wooed and loved her, reject her and leave her bereft.

She had always kept a rule about not consorting with the men at work, even before the Dan fiasco. She had never even considered the newly separated Joe as being available, at least not to her.

One February night, though, speculation about the threat of the company going into receivership led to fraternal drinks in great quantity at the nearest pub and after closing time, to her house. They were drunk and sufficiently afraid of unemployment to fall into bed together.

Laura was surprised by how much she enjoyed him. She was even more surprised about how much he enjoyed her. She had thought that the next man to touch her intimately would be the undertaker at the rate she was growing used to being alone.

He turned out to be not just a good lover, but easy in her company and undemanding of her. The joy it brought her was shocking. She was mortified by how happy he made her. She hated that it was that easy to make her lighthearted and good humoured, quelling her smiles so that people would not notice and suspect that they had a thing going.

There was no doubt that she found him irritating at times, but would tolerate him while asking herself if that was normal leeway between people in a relationship, or just her putting up with him long enough to get him back into bed. She never had managed to have sex without emotion though and although she tried her very best to be nonchalant and undemanding, she knew she was getting used to Joe.

The stress and mortification of it, sometimes made her want to end it all, but after getting used to being alone for years, she very quickly plunged again into a situation which she feared would end in tears and that the tears would be hers.

They didn't speak about their relationship, nor try to label it in anyway. It was an unspoken, usually two nights a week arrangement: Wednesdays and Saturdays and occasional Fridays depending on what was happening after work. None of the workmates knew for sure and no one asked straight out.

They never left the office together or arrived together or left the pub in the same taxi. They didn't talk about it and arrange it like that. They just didn't.

Laura knew that he didn't want anyone to know and decided not to push it. She didn't want anyone to know either to avoid the mortification that might come if told her he didn't want to be with her again. They didn't discuss previous loves in their lives, which relieved her of the shame of telling him it had been so long since she had sex before him. His exwife was never mentioned. She knew they had no children. He sometimes referred to "before", meaning when he was married.

It was in an effort, in this newfound good mood, to get out and meet other people that she joined the hillwalking club. She went out and bought the gear: boots, socks, waterproof stuff, things that hadn't been invented when she last went hillwalking.

Things were lighter and more expensive now. She tried everything on at home and saw that she looked uncomfortable and ridiculous. She got hot and redfaced just putting it all on in the heat of the flat. She became breathless bending over to unlace the big boots until she realised she should take off the jacket and woollen hat first.

She fretted about not being able to keep up, about needing to pee when they were on the hill, about just not being able to continue when the rest of the group was still going strong.

She had three weeks before a planned trek in Wicklow, so she set about training a little by walking faster and harder with the dogs in the park and even hauled out the exercise bike she had abandoned in the shed. When her thigh muscles screamed she convinced herself that walking would be different.

On the Saturday morning, she gritted her teeth and decided to make the best of it, knowing that this was good for her. She was making an effort, after all and trying not to be alone every weekend.

A look at the map showed that the walk would be about 20 kilometres and that the first half of it would be uphill.

She began with determination and almost immediately found that she could not talk and walk at the same time. Attempts by the others to be friendly ended badly when she had to excuse herself and pause to explain that she was out of breath or else plod along bravely nodding and smiling but not attempting speech.

The boots seemed very heavy and her left heel was already sore after a couple of kilometres. Worse, the skin on the inside of her thighs was starting to chafe despite the €29.99 spent on the super dooper hiking trousers which were supposed to be ideal for all circumstances.

She was desperate by the seven kilometre mark and tried to work out the logistics of turning back or getting off the track to somewhere she could rest, but without disrupting everyone else's fun.

So, in these unfortunate circumstances, it was almost a relief, when Laura broke her ankle by landing badly on a hardened hoof print of some wandering beast.

She was third in the group to make the leap across a narrow but fast flowing stream on the side of the hill, bordered by rock and heather. She thought she could make it and so, pushed a bit forward to get it over with, rather than stand back and let others go first.

She made a good fist of the jump, but as soon as her foot hit the ground she felt herself jolted violently to the right. She heard the bone snap. She was winded by the fall then and gasped as the others rushed to help her up. Laura saw how her foot was wobbling at the end of her leg, looking like it had been severed from the limb, with just the sock and boot holding it on.

She heard gasps around her as the others saw the damage and gently laid her down again from the one legged standing position into which they had hoisted her after the fall.

"I'm sorry," she said, over and over, while they told her she was alright and not to worry. She lay there on the heather, with something hard digging into her hip, looking

93

up at the sky with her tears streaming into her hair from the pain and mortification. Laura could hear when the lads stepped away from her to urgently discuss the options.

"We have to call out the rescue. We can't carry her for fuck's sake."

They decided quickly and Laura sobbed while Eoin rang 999 and asked for mountain rescue. The pain was excruciating by the time they arrived and despite the others taking off their jackets and pillowing her head with a rucksack, she was shivering and quiet.

The rescue people did their business efficiently and kindly, stretchering her down the track to a waiting ambulance. Eoin, who she did not know, came with her to the hospital but left her soon after, explaining that he had to take the lift back to his car, or he would be stuck there. "Is there someone I can phone?" he said.

"No, thanks. Just go," Laura said. "Sure, there's nothing you can do here for me now." But she would have liked him to stay, to be on her side in this strange hospital in shock and in pain. She was mortified by not really having anyone to phone.

Her mother was hardly able to walk herself with arthritis and would be more of a hindrance. Her one female friend, the one who even knew about Joe, was on holidays. Her brother was very wrapped up in his band and his work and they hardly saw each other. It was a hard lesson in solitude to think that really there was no one who sprang to mind instantly.

The window, to her left, became her only view of the world. The blinds were almost permanently open and she sweated in the unshaded bed when the sun shone.

She had never been to Tullamore before and had no bearings. She could see a green patch of grass and behind it a rusting fence of corrugated iron.

No one ever passed by, no animals appeared and even birds seemed disinterested in the space. She had been brought in by ambulance, so even if the pain hadn't blinded her, she couldn't have seen the entrance to the hospital or the streets that led to it.

The pink walls of the ward, the five pale women in it, the glass panel to the corridor and the view out the window were all she knew for sure.

Lying in her bed, plastered leg aloft in exquisite pain, she tried to imagine the layout of the hospital and even the town.

The pain was so constant and overpowering that she was never bored. The sleepless night was spent concentrating on the throbbing agony, rubbing a small piece of green marble between her index finger and thumb. Joe had given it to her one lunchtime before she was to see her dentist. It would help, he said, seeing her so nervous.

The medication trolley came at six, when it was on time. She could hear it approach for 17 minutes before that. First, a faint rumble, the sound of its metal lid being lifted and an almost inaudible squeak from its wheels.

Laura could hear the voices speaking around it and bit down hard on her lower lip not to screamingly implore the stupid women to stop chattering and come on, please, give me rest. Stop the pain. Let me sleep.

But no, she would turn her head, her body could not turn and watch the sun rise over the rusty fence and wait for sweet relief to come after last night's Fair City had been reviewed, the weather noted and tonight's plans announced. It was only when she had taken her meds, had her sleep and woken again that she could touch the part of her mind which was screaming at her that Joe was a thing of the past in her life.

She had not seen him since the Sunday morning as she set out on her hillwalking expedition.

He had kissed her long and hard.

"Mind yourself and I'll ring you tonight," he said

She wasn't at home to get that call, but by now, surely, he had heard at work what had happened. Laura couldn't get out of the bed so it was impossible to get to the phone on the corridor to ring him.

She couldn't bring herself to send a note with one of the crowd from work who made the 70 mile journey to see her. They would wonder why she was writing to him and even worse, someone might read it before giving it to him.

After a week of no contact from him she plucked up her courage and asked Belinda from advertising about him one evening when a few workmates came down to see her.

She tried to make it sound casual, although she knew that Belinda of all people, would have suspected there was more than a casual enquiry behind it. The minute she mentioned his name, she felt the atmosphere around the bed change. People looked at their feet and started muttering about having to make a move. Belinda seemed to blush slightly, before she cleared her throat and said:

"We haven't seen much of Joe, these days. I believe his wife isn't well."

"Really?" said Laura as she felt her face redden and frantically tried to absorb this information, while finding a subject onto which to change the conversation. She began to talk about a woman who had been in the bed opposite but had gone home that day.

When they were all gone, she cried. She hoped he would be man enough to contact her, just once at least, before she went back to work. It might be less mortifying that way. The pain would be private and no meds trolley would come to give her relief. Just as she knew she would never go hillwalking again, she knew there would never be another Joe in her life.

When Belinda came to see her the next time, she gave her the wording of the ad to put in the paper:

For sale: One pair of hiking boots, size 5, full waterproof suit, lightweight rucksack, with water bottle, travellite sleeping bag. Perfect condition, used only once. £250 o.n.o, Dublin area.

SANTRY PARK 26 MARCH 2013

Bláithín Ní Liatháin

Is this a day of Summer?
Summer warmth comes from the sky
A sky of cloudless blue.

Daffodils adore the trees
Trees unleaved hazed with green
Green of Spring not Summer faded.

Park is full of children's play

Play of others is milking warmth.

Warm sitting outside day.

Is this a day of Summer?
Summer without April and May?
June in March?

HEAT

Katie Dwyer

In Honduras, heat and sadness were the dominant aspects of my days. The sadness I invited—I had come to seek out stories of family separation and hardship, and lived daily with the reasons people would leave their country in pursuit of mine. But the heat was a surprise in its aggression as it seeped into every motion, every interaction, until I could not disassociate the sensation of damp, desperate sweat from the slow process of recording narratives.

In the busses we pressed up against one another, one solid, sweating mass of humanity in a creaking American school bus. The young men hung from the open door in the baking dust or hot tropical rain, on the edge and in the elements. Again and again a seatmate, or someone standing face to the shoulder of my foreign height, would ask what I was doing in their country and then, skin against skin, sharing sweat, would ask if I knew how she could find her brother/cousin/sister/son, who had been heard from last at the border of Tejas, some time ago. And, in a heat more intimate than that between lovers, I would take down a phone number and anticipate my search through prison databases and immigration detention rosters, searching for the carefully-spelled-out name scribbled on a crumpled piece of paper. Then I would make the phone call in the scant relief of the evening: "I'm sorry, I didn't find anything. God be with you." Or, both better and worse, "your son/nephew/sister/neighbour is alive and you can contact them. But they are incarcerated and you have to follow these directions to call…"

I was an anomaly, a sweating foreign entity speaking oddly inflected Spanish. I'm sure I was the topic of many conversations, and that my reputation for 'finding' the disappeared proceeded me. I had come seeking migration stories and they swarmed me—I never encountered a person without family living somewhere in my country of origin, or somehow lost along the way. Even successful migration stories were shot through with loss, as success meant that the money arrived but the relative was far away and often living precariously at the fringe of my society.

"He washes dishes but sometimes they do not pay him," I was told, and "sometimes he is thrown out of his house even though he paid in advance." "They are too scared to say anything to an authority." And I could understand why: all around me was evidence of the precarious prosperity of a loved one's successful departure, as well as the grim and silent desperation of those whose migrants had failed.

The stories overwhelmed me. The sadness was as constant as the heat.

Any relief was incomplete, lifted sometimes by watching American movies dubbed in Spanish with my host family, and being teased that the sun and mosquitos both favoured me. We sat on a concrete slab out of doors and images of my homeland played on an expensive TV, bought on credit, as the half-starved chickens scratched at the dinner scraps and the neighbourhood kids laughed or were silent. Children's shows from the Disney Channel played on repeat, the simplicity and polished colours on the screen dissonant with my surroundings: verdant desert lines of palm oil plantations in what used to be farmland.

The only break from the heat came for a brief breath time in the night. I'm sure my body was reacting to a change in temperature in the moderate cool of evening, but each night I would go to sleep sweating only to jerk awake sometime in the night shaking with cold. There were no blankets—why would there be?—so I would curl under a bath towel and shake until I could sleep again. I never mentioned this discomfort to my hosts—they were witness to the public nature of my struggle through the heat, so I suffered the cold in private.

I don't know whether my sadness could be described as known or hidden, but such emotion was common and appropriate there. Like the heat, it surrounded me. It was all around me, and was not mine anyway—it found me because I invited it: travelled the long distance and accepted the heat and weight of stories. For those whose narratives I recorded, loss and sadness were simply fact, noted but not remarkable until a sheltered, sweating foreigner was there to be surprised.

It is difficult, now, to say how each has remained with me. Heat is forgotten—the sunburn flakes away and what is left is skin that is damaged but appears beautiful, deliberately bronzed, refreshed.

Perhaps it is the same with sadness. The storytellers now distant but the memories remain, burning just under my skin.

EARTH TREE

Anniekate Gillroon

The day we cut down that tree, I wept,
The surgeon said it was dangerous,
And I said to him,
'How?,'
And he said, 'look it has shared bark,
It is too strong, leaning to the right, to the left,'
Oh!, it was just before the leaves opened,
That tree on your granddaughter's earth space, my mother's
earth space,
As the blade hit, the wounds shed sweet tears of sap,
The awful sounds as it hit the soft grass of early spring,
Sounds you must have heard, my great- grandfather over
there,
Where trees and earth and bloodied water all lay, beneath
soft faced young men,
Oh!, we never meant to cut it down, never,
They never meant to go over there and slice flesh with
metal, they didn't,
They were not even born on the earth they now had to slice
flesh for,
We kept rings of my mother's tree,
They lie peacefully in our garden,
I let rain and moss and fox touch them,
Now and then I touch them,
Some, we burned in a fire that warmed our house,
We have the piece that has all the wound marks of the
hatchet,
I even took a photo of it,
Oh!, how I wish I had a photo of you,
You, young man who had to see wound marks on flesh.
Over there where tears had no sweet flow,
Oh!, how I wish I could take you and show you,

Your granddaughter's child,
That she could say to you, you had to do what you did,
To have you rest on earth song by those fallen logs in our
garden.

PADDY AND THE BOG BODY

Brian Carroll

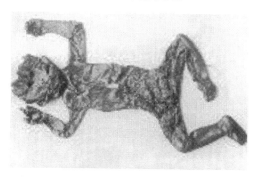

Paddy Mulligan was a man of few words, but he was made even more speechless when he saw what fell from the back of the truck as he walked home from the pub. It was a dark and bitterly cold November evening on Gardiner Street. The world was suddenly silent and still as Paddy stared at the bundle lying in the middle of the road. His first impulse was to keep walking but his curiosity got the better of him and against his better judgement he went to investigate.

At first glance it appeared to be the remains of some kind of arcane animal, charred and blackened by some ancient burial rites. But a closer inspection revealed it to be the mummified corpse of a child. Paddy gasped and stood pondering, scratching his chin. He glanced around to see whether he was being observed, he thought perhaps he might be the butt of some cruel practical joke. But he saw no-one and Paddy knew then what he had to do.

Bending down on one knee he scooped up the little bundle from the road as delicately as if it were a living

104

child. He was shocked by how heavy it was and he had momentary second thoughts about what on earth he would do with the thing. But he caught sight of the creature's face with its eyeless sockets and its skeletal toothy grin and he felt sorry for whoever this had been. He hefted the bundle over his shoulder and carried on his way back to the small terraced house not far away which he shared with his wife.

His biggest fear now was not what the bundle might turn out to be but what his wife would say to him. Paddy was a soft-hearted kind of fellow who was forever bringing home stray mangy dogs and birds with broken wings. His wife had become less and less tolerant of his altruistic tendencies over the years and would often not let him in the door of his own home until she was sure he didn't have some sorry-looking mutt or half-dead bedraggled cat hidden beneath his overcoat. But tonight he was in luck, he found himself unimpeded as he brought his bundle into the spare bedroom where he dropped it onto an old rocking chair.

As the thing rocked back and forth on the chair Paddy swore he heard it say,

'Thank you Sir, you have done me a great kindness. I will not forget your good deed today Paddy.'

Paddy was a little perturbed by this but he put it down to the whisky he'd imbibed that evening and he immediately retired to bed. He dreamt strangely of ancient Celtic rites, he saw a man taken out onto the bog and his throat was cut as a warning to the neighbouring tribe. He awoke with a start to the sound of a scream that sounded very much like it came straight out of an old black and white horror movie.

He struggled out of bed in the pre-dawn gloom and went to the spare room where he found his wife's body slumped on the floor, the expression on her face was one of abject terror. He felt her wrist for a pulse but there was none, she was stone cold dead. He looked at the figure in the rocking chair where it appeared now to be smiling at him. He thought he heard it say,

'Now we are free at last Paddy, together we shall avenge those who have wronged us.'

CHRONOS

Susan Cooney

Christmas trees on the New York
pavements, in the melting snow;
Festive baubles now tired, garish
In the weak millennial sun.

And the teenage crush we see
Now with a paunch,
Paterfamilias . . .
Dances on faded film, and –
Did we really wear those clothes?

The nineteen-eighties recede
Just as the War fled
round the corner from them.
Soon enough we'll be the links
Ourselves.

Second by millisecond . . .
Can anyone pinpoint
when the soil becomes seedling?
Like a landslide of change it grows
Increasing exponentially
Making us emigrants
Once our backs are turned.

THE FIRST TIME I FELL IN LOVE WITH A JUNKIE

Camillus John

The first time I fell in love with a junkie was a confirmation. I couldn't quite believe. Or more to the point, I could.

I recognised his face for I had seen it around the place on streets and in doorways, and suchlike splashes of presence, pushing into my life anonymously. Always on drugs, I presumed, for they were writ large into his gentle eyes. A face to spend afternoons with. To kiss. To go out robbing. To enjoy.

I walked past the newsagents and there he was sitting outside cross-legged and sipping delightfully from a can of lager. We'd briefly bumped only two days earlier. He was sitting in the same position now at the bus-stop when I got off. He commented on my Nirvana t-shirt.

"Miss, that's a great band. Have you got *In Utero*?"

I initially didn't listen to my reason, but to the cold wind. Wanted to move on past him. Safer that way. But my heart got the better, and I said -

"Yes. I have. It's my favourite album of theirs."

"Me too, me too," said the junkie.

"Yeah, see ya."

"Yeah," he said. "Yeah. I'm one of Derida's undecidables. Yeah. I am."

I turned the corner and he was gone. But today here he was again and I dreaded him recognising me. Not of any real danger but that my reactions wouldn't be able to cope with his intelligence, his imagination, his good humour. I tried to appear like I was in a dream but our eyes managed to lock and he knew he had my full attention outside the newsagents. And yes, he said out loud, but no one else was around to hear -

"Miss, do you like poetry?"

I debated putting my hand up in a yeah-yeah-yeah-I'm-busy gesture but dallied for a whole second, which meant I would say -

"Yes."

Not loud. Quietly. Trying not to disturb the air around me for it was a still afternoon full of promise.

"Well, will you listen to one of my poems so?" said the junkie.

I was only going to say the one thing -

"Yes, go on then."

My gaze sloped down to the concrete pavement. I readied myself for some wisecrack words or some stream of abuse or some plead for money but only poetry poured pure from his sweet-baby-James junkie lips.

I was shaking. I felt cold. A poem I didn't recognise gushed out of his mouth in bold enunciation. Strident and fully formed. He didn't stumble over a single iamb. His voice got stronger as he sailed the many verses like a modern Ulysses and he closed his eyes towards the end.

But society started scratching me. I listened more intently, to see if it was from a song, or a school learned-off-by-heart poem. No. It was definitely his, and I felt a moment when everything was justified. When everything sang. In rolling triplets. *Molto animato.*

The sun shone down and intensified the spotlight. His or mine, I don't quite know. The peak of his crescendo was coming and I wondered how much more? How long? *Ravvivando. Sostenuto. Affettuoso.* It stopped.

He lowered his head for a few seconds to recuperate, catching his breath with a fist. But before I could move on or catch mine, he said -

"Now, was that worth the price of a can?"

"Yes," I said. "It was," and dropped it into his empty one.

SATURDAY LUNCH

Kay Dunne

Cat, named Pie,
dreams on the step
in the sun
outside the door.

You, eager to please,
offer a favourite,
Humphrey and Lauren,
Doris and Rock –

Which one? you ask.

Me, I bring the bounty,
salad rolls, summer fruit,
the pot of tea,
our Book of Kells bone china mugs –

Doris, I reply.

New bread? I ask.
Like it? you say.
Soft, I add, as Doris sings,
and you settle beside me.

Better this, I remember.

This is what I loved.
This is what I miss.
More than the coupling.
More than the afterglow of hope.

.

LOUISBOURG

Mimi Goodman

Wednesday, my last morning, glorious sunshine. I put on the swimming togs, there was less chance of backing out if I was wearing them. Only one swim last year in September Salterstown, Co Louth, home, a twenty minute walk from Mother's house. One of the few sunny days, summer 2012.

I announced my plan to Mary Jo, she was on for it. It was nine. Train leaving Westport 1.15pm. We walked to Carrowmore, that last walk, walk the strand, overlook Clare Island for the last time.

Fields sprinkled yellow with buttercups. Warm, the air scented. Connemara white mares, foals at foot in a paddock.

We met another swimmer. He was a good ten or fifteen years older than us. If he could get in, surely we could endure it. Tramped up the hill from the beach round to the pier. The old stones on the pier warm under my feet, no wind, sea calm as a mill pond. A currach, Paddy's Surprise, tied up. I'd be able to do a few short lengths between the currach and the wall of the pier. Water crystal clear, freezing.

Normally I scream when I dunk in the cold, I get a headache, "ice-cream head." Neither occured. Piercing, icy, I did my strokes as fast as I could, waiting for my body to adjust to the artic waters. Five or six lengths (twenty strokes per length), breast stroke, then my pathetic crawl. I didn't want to put my head in the water to perform my back stroke, the only decent stroke I can do, just too cold. Did a bit of jogging on the spot. Therapy, joints ease out, I'm invigorated , delighted, proud of myself.

Mary Jo got in. When we were drying ourselves off in the sun, she said, 'That was peer pressure, you've done the Reek, I'm not staying at home, the couch potatoe."

The walk back to Louisbourg warmed me up.

A quick shower. A bowl of porridge. Mary Jo waves me good bye. We might see each other next November.

Into Louisbourg HQ to collect my purchases from the craft shop, the new tourist attraction in town. I bought Lavander and Neroli face cream; two small bottles of Lavander hand cream, they'll make nice little presents; bath salts for Emma; hand painted pottery mugs; a wooden butter knife, maybe it's my new cheese knife, and a dozen clothes pegs crafted from hornbeam.

Over to Durkans, I buy thick lamb steaks for the barbque. A leg of lamb – that'll be for next Sunday's dinner. I had already sent home a load of gigot chops and another leg of lamb, having instructed my brother to put them in the freezer. There's nothing like West Mayo lamb.

I had arrived the previous Friday, the Solstice. It's part of the holiday to take the train from Heuston. Buy a Butler's coffee – I choose a free 70% dark choclate truffle. Into Easons to pick up a copy of The Moth, a poetry and short story magazine published in Cavan. Cross the

113

country from East to West – cattle, horses, ponies, donkies, elderflower in full bloom, dasies, wild roses, yellow flag irises, rushes, brown bog. Bus out to Louisbourg. Haven't seen Clew Bay for a year, my heart sighs.

Mary Jo has a leg of lamb roasting in the oven. Catherine and the Flanagans arrive from Galway – Laurence from Louth. We've known each other thirty nine years, old friends are best.

Plan for the weekend, maybe climb Croagh Patrick, the locals call it "The Reek." Go with the flow, see what the weather's like.

Saturday. We left the house wearing only a rain jacket, no jumper. We walked Derrylahan, we were frozen. It started raining. We took refuge for a cappicuno in Louisbourg 74. Salmon mayonaise open sandwichs. I heard about the town's new craft shop – I made a bee line. Amongst other bits and pieces I bought a pottery butter plate. Told Laurence to leave it in the boot of the car. He brought it into the house – dropped the bag – smithereens.

Catherine cooked on Saturday night. Potatoes left over from our Friday dinner made a good old fashioned potatoe salad. She uses salad cream which gives a nice vinegarey flavour. Laurence's friend Roddy Minogue, a serious fisherman had given him a present of a big brown trout. It fed five adults. Patricia Woods had given Mary Jo a huge bag of Con's salads. Three or four different types of lettuces, basil, chives, parsley.

Sunday, the Reek. From one year to the next year you forget how hard it is.

Didn't do it last year. Didn't know whether I'd do it this year. Two years ago it lashed rain for the entire afternoon. Margaret was then training for the New York marathon, she was adament that she'd scale it. Now she's in the middle of her chemotherapy. This year, no sun, no rain, not too windy – you could see all the islands of Clew Bay. I snailed my way to the top. Laurence got there with Patrick Flanagan half an hour before I did. Catherine's husband ran to the top. He started some time after me. He stopped, we chatted for a minute or two, then he said, "I'll tip on." Catherine like myself, is dead slow and stop. When Vincent had got to the top, he tipped down again to help her. He spent the afternoon tipping up and down. I don't know if he's an iron man – he competes in triathlon eventing – he'd leave a body breathless.

Cold lamb sandwiches revived us on the top. By the time I was finished – rather than feeling fifty seven – I felt eighty – hopefully I'll be doing it in twenty years time.

Back home to Louisbourg, another hefty leg of lamb. Mary Jo cooked the dinner. I made mint sauce, it was all hands on deck. My friend Clare lives in Louisbourg, she brought along a lemon curd roulade – a spongy concoction with a cream tangy lemony filling. Clare is baker cook extraordinaire, up there with Nigella, Rachael, and Darina.

Monday. The routine seldom changes. Clare Island. A golden morning, a quick breakfast and off to Roonagh to catch the ferry. We know the crew members on O'Grady's boat. Mary Jo tells them, "Down in Co Clare I tell every one to go out to the island." We have to go to Anna's for her famous choclate cake and scones and a big jug of coffee. Tubs of yellow pansies and a tall, coral coloured lily sit outside the porch. We sit in the garden, we

115

photograph each other in sunshine on Laurence's phone. Last year I spent the day photographing sheep, and foxgloves, sheep posing in front of foxgloves, sheep in front of old stone walls. I didn't have the camera with me this year.

Ballytoughey Loomery. "I'm glad I'm not here with my lover or my mistress – you can't go anywhere, what are you doing here?" Laurence meets his sister in law who is doing a weaving course. Yes, that's what I'd like to do sometime, make greeny goldy pinky table mats for my kitchen, but with yarn that can be thrown into the washing machine. Beth is now weaving towels. I buy one for Dick, a black and white contemporary design. It feels soft, smells good. "Imagined designed and made in Ireland."

Mary Jo encourages "Try on that purple jacket, it suits your colouring."

I had promised myself a new jacket. "I haven't had enough wear out of the silk skirt I bought two years ago."

That skirt, beautiful, another of Beth Moran's hand woven creations. I'm still thinking about that jacket. I'm reminded of the Viennese woman saying to me about the multicoloured hand felted coat I tried on in Vienna,

"This is real luxury – there are only three of these coats in the world, one in Paris, mine and the one you're trying on."

There's only one of Beth's purple jackets in the world. I'm still thinking – all I have to do is make the phone call and Beth can post it to me. I'm being presumptious,

116

maybe it's already been sold. But, I did treat myself to a blue wolly jumper knitted by a Dutch woman.

"She's going home to Holland. She's been here for twelve years. She wants to go home to be near her family," Beth told us.

Tuesday, Inisbofin. It's a hell of a drive from Louisburg to Cleggan. The compensation, the scenery in the Delphi Valley. Mum and Dad used to bring us to Bofin on our summer holidays. We always stayed in Murray's Hotel. The last time was the year I did my Leaving Cert in nineteen seventy four. I had forgotten how beautiful it is. I wondered how had Mother discovered it, probably some newspaper article. I remembered the cheili one year – it started at eleven at night, probably after the pubs closed. It was in the parish hall in the middle of the island. We kids walked in the pitch black night. The highlight for me was being asked out to dance.

We used to swim at the west end of the island passing the long golden strand – Paddy Murray had warned Mum and Dad of currents. We headed further west to a cove where seals swam.

There's now a memorial window in the church to Paddy Murray. The hotel has a new, modern accomodation block. I met Mrs Murray, now elderly. I reminded her of the time that Mother fled some holiday spot on another island, the sheets on the beds damp.

"We'er not staying here another night, I'll phone the Murrays and see if they can take us."

117

We needed three roooms. They could give us two.
We stopped in Galway, a tent was purchased and pitched at
the back of the hotel. I slept in it one night with my cousin.
We were woken early next morning, "murr, murr," cattle
were nosing around, breathing heavily .

I also   told Mrs Murray of having met Mary
Catherine on Inisturk last year, having dinner in her guest
house. One word borrowed another, Mary Catherine had
worked in Murray's as a youngster.

Of course I had to tell Mary Catherine about Mum
and Dad, "I well remember Peter Goodman's table in the
dining room," she said.

The adults used to gather in the lounge at night
around the turf fire in Murray's . Dr Paddy Leahy was often
there. He was working in Ballyfermot, many of his patients
being mothers with too many children. At the time he was
one of the most outspoken voices advocating the right to
contraception. It was the time when Mary Kenny, Nell
McCafferty, June Levine et al took the train to Belfast to
buy condoms. In the summer of ninteen seventy four, I
went to Lourdes with the Dublin Pilgrimage. The day we
departed, Liam Cosgrove the Taoiseach voted against his
own bill introducing legalisation for the availability of
contraceptives for married couples.

Those were the days when most girls were afraid to
drink anything other than a shandy. Mother used to preach
"Drink and your defences are down...... Don't come home
to your Father pregnant, he'd kill you."

9.15 pm the eve of my departure from Louisbourg.
The lambs and sheep were baaaing and mehing, many still

118

standing, continuing to feed in their meadow on the little road to Carrowmore. I picked as many bunches of Elderflower as I could. I dried it when I got back home, on the sunny window sill in my south facing kitchen. I picked lots more up in Louth. Most mornings I start the day with a cup of elderflower tea, I might add a few dried nettles or a dandelion flower and a small sprig of dried carigeen.

Holidays end, life returns to normal. A few weeks later my nephew was home from Liverpool. A celebration dinner. We took one of those big legs of lamb out of the freezer. Into the oven, it sat on a bed of rosemary stems. An hour and a half later it came out golden and succulent. We finished our feast with strawberries and blueberries. I made a syrup by boiling up 100 mls of water, a tbs of sugar and another tbs of Irish honey, added a sprig of elderflower, 2 or 3 mint leaves and two heads of lavender. Boiled it for 2 minutes. Let it cool. I sliced the strawberries. Poured the syrup over the fruit. We had cream and icecream. "You've become a cook just like your Mother," my nephew complimented.

Catherine gave me Iris Galloway's book on the Green Way, the cycling and hiking trail that stretches from Westport to Achill Island . There a chapter on wildflowers along the route. From reading her book I have been able to identify Meadowsweet. I picked it, dried it and added it to lavander blossom, an Elizabethan pot pourri. I went on the internet looking up recipes – you can make icecream, a sparkling champagne, cordial. Slainte.

A happy time in the West. Laurence calls it God's own country, his spiritual home. Mary Jo and Catherine's mother, a Grace O'Malley descendant, used to say "Go mbeiridhmid beo ar an am seo aris."

SEASONS' HAIKU

Bláithín Ní Liatháin

Spring
Daffodils bloom on
Balconies quashing Winter
Gray; frost stay away.

Summer
Summer sea swimming
Sun clouded out, skin turns blue
Seek shelter 'til rain is through.

Autumn
Leaves golden fall
Reddening into Winter
Sleep 'til spring greens.

Winter
Winter all is grey
Christmas lights brighten day
Winter end on Brigid's Day.

THE TOP HAT

Brian Carroll

James Barry Harrington was an accountant but his secret ambition had always been to become a magician, although he preferred the term illusionist. He really only got into accountancy to please his mother who wanted him to settle down and give her lots of grandchildren. Jimmy had very little interest in this however and spent all his spare time practising his craft and acquiring accoutrements of the art of deception. During his lunch breaks he would try tricks out on his work colleagues, occasionally with some success. In the evenings he would perform onstage wherever they would have him. His lack of self-confidence often meant that he fumbled and stuttered his way through these performances. He would guess the wrong card that an audience member had chosen or drop some piece of apparatus that revealed the secret of the illusion he was trying to perform. One memorable evening Jimmy managed to slay a dove live onstage when the cage malfunctioned and the bird vanished in a spray of blood and feathers. That particular venue would not have him back after someone complained to the animal cruelty people. Jimmy did not despair though and he kept practising and looking out for new and unusual tricks. It's fair to say that his stage show owed more to Tommy Cooper than any other magician, unfortunately this was not intentional.

Around this time Jimmy started to notice a new check-out girl at his local Chinese supermarket. She was quite striking in appearance being half Puerto-Rican/Chinese. He gleaned that her name was Miriam from the name badge that adorned her plain uniform and he would always try to find himself queuing at her register. Miriam never spoke a word to him. He had heard her speak but all she ever said was 'yes' or 'no'. Her skin was very pale and she would often appear half-asleep with glazed eyes and slow languid movements. Jimmy became quite obsessed with her but he never managed to get any conversation out of her. She would only shrug at his polite enquiries and point at the amount due on the cash register display. Jimmy knew there was something special about her but he couldn't quite figure out exactly what it was. The other girls who worked at the store made fun of her and called her rude nicknames behind her back. They never said anything to her face though. Miriam was old Chang's niece and while he constantly berated and cajoled his staff for their alleged idleness and lack of enthusiasm, he never said a harsh word to his niece.

Chang was a hard-working if rather grumpy fellow but he was always very courteous to his customers, especially the well-to-do Westerners who would pay top money for his wares. He took a shine to Jimmy who began to frequent the store more and more in order to even catch a glimpse of his beloved Miriam. Somehow Chang found out that Jimmy was an accountant and one day he approached him to ask if he would consider helping him with his books which were in a terrible state according to himself. Jimmy readily agreed thinking it would afford him more opportunities to see Miriam and maybe get to know her better. Soon Jimmy was doing old Chang's accounts on a regular basis and it's true to say that he brought some order to the chaos that reigned in Chang's ledgers.

Chang's office was little more than a dingy partitioned-off corner of his store-room upstairs above the supermarket. Jimmy was vaguely aware that there was another room at the back where Miriam stayed. He never saw her come or go but he thought he could tell whether she was there or not by the presence or absence of a rather pungent smell which he couldn't identify. Old Chang used to laugh when the smell was strong and he would make pipe-smoking gestures as if Jimmy was supposed to know what that meant. Gradually Jimmy and old Chang became more friendly and Jimmy confided in him his aspirations of becoming a great illusionist. Chang surprised him one day by asking him if he could hide something in his accounts. He had a source of income he wanted to conceal and he felt that Jimmy would surely not object to a bit of creative accountancy. Reluctantly Jimmy agreed and after a few weeks had successfully hidden thousands of pounds among the numbers of the balance sheets such that only a skilled auditor would be able to detect.

Feeling grateful, one day old Chang took Jimmy into the back of the store-room where Miriam had her apartment. Actually it was just a small room with a rolled-up mattress, some books and some arcane trinkets which Jimmy did not recognize. The bulk of the room however was given over to all sorts of bric-a-brac that old Chang said belonged to his long-deceased Great Uncle Chu, who had been an accomplished conjurer back in the old country many years ago. He presented Jimmy with a box of this stuff thinking it would be a great token of his gratitude.

Jimmy was nonplussed, at first all he saw was a bunch of dusty old junk but he thanked Chang for it anyway and took it home. A couple of days later Jimmy had a closer look at the stuff and found that some of the things were indeed props for magic tricks. Much of it he could not figure a purpose for at all but one thing which leapt out at him was an old collapsible top hat. Something about it bespoke of mystery and ancient lore and he tried to discover what its secret might be. After much head scratching and chin rubbing Jimmy conceded that he couldn't find anything special about it. He placed it on the ground and began flicking playing cards at it from a distance to see how many he could land inside. When he had gone through the entire deck he picked up the hat and squashed it flat between his hands. To his great surprise the playing cards that were inside had completely vanished. He turned and flicked the hat repeatedly but the cards had indeed disappeared as far as he could tell. In frustration he pushed the hat out to its original shape again and lo and behold the vanished playing cards re-appeared, fluttering to the floor.

'Ha,' he laughed and tried the illusion again – it worked. He picked up a shoe and made that disappear and re-appear again. He was astounded for he could not for the life of him figure out how it worked. Almost immediately he conceived of a plan. He would buy some rabbits and win the upcoming TV talent show with his disappearing rabbit trick. So the next day he went to his local pet shop and bought three identical white albino rabbits, a cage to house them and some rabbit food for them to nibble. There was a downside to the illusionist's craft that he had not foreseen, having to keep rabbits in a hutch, taking up space and stinking up the living room of his tiny one-bedroom apartment. He practised with the rabbits and the top hat but unfortunately things did not go as smoothly as he would

124

have liked. The first rabbit he put in the hat disappeared successfully but alas did not rematerialize. Try as he might turning the hat inside out and every which way the errant bunny failed to show his whiskers again. The second rabbit he tried in the hat came back but it was not alive. The poor creature looked terrified to death with its teeth showing and its eyes wide open. The third rabbit proved to be more resilient than his predecessors and came back still chewing the piece of lettuce he'd gone in with. He tried again, just to be sure. Success. He put Pythagoras, for thus he had christened the rabbit, back in the cage and went to work on the rest of his routine for the TV talent show.

At last the night of the TV broadcast came and Jimmy was very nervous as he went through his act with the show's production staff. They seemed very blasé about his disappearing rabbit trick and their only comment was,

'Do you not have a glamorous assistant?'

'No, just me,' said Jimmy.

He was not disheartened for he felt sure that his magical skills would win over the judges and he would be catapulted to instant fame and fortune. Soon enough Jimmy found himself onstage under the bedazzling studio lights going through his act which he had rehearsed a thousand times. But things were not going well for Jimmy, his nerves began to get the better of him and great beads of perspiration were rolling down his forehead and stinging his eyes. Things got worse when a smart-aleck kid from the audience pulled the hidden card from his jacket sleeve much to the crowd's amusement. At last the time came for the disappearing rabbit trick. He successfully loaded Pythagoras into the hat and the rabbit duly vanished. The audience became quiet and stopped laughing. One or two people began to applaud. Jimmy's moment of glory was short-lived however. When he popped the hat back out again there was no sign of Pythagoras. He turned the hat upside-down and shook it but all that came out was a single black scorpion. The audience burst into spontaneous applause, but Jimmy was crestfallen. What the hell was going on? Where was Pythagoras? Where had the bloody great scorpion come from? Foolishly Jimmy bent down and attempted to pick up the scorpion by the tail. But he misjudged it and was stung on the hand by the venomous creature.

'Ouch,' he said.

The crowd laughed, thinking it was all part of the act. Jimmy dropped the scorpion into the hat and pushed the hat flat sending the beast back whence it came. The production assistant at the side of the stage gave the 'shows over' sign and the curtain came down abruptly. The audience continued applauding loudly and they all thought that Jimmy's act was the best by far. Jimmy began to feel nauseous and dizzy and collapsed on the stage behind the curtains. One person in the audience was not applauding – it was Miriam. She scowled and made her way out of the auditorium muttering oaths to herself in an arcane Mandarin dialect.

Jimmy was rushed to hospital and was given anti-venom without delay. The next day he felt much better and was released. He went straight back to the TV studio to collect his gear. He returned homeward nursing his swollen hand and his deflated ego. When he arrived home he threw his props in a heap in the corner and tried to forget about his public humiliation on national TV. He spent several days in bed recovering from the scorpion's sting and kept his phone switched off to avoid any further media intrusions. In his feverish half-sleep he had terrifying visions of being stalked onstage by giant rabbits and scorpions while the audience chanted his name. In one particularly disturbing dream both his legs had been neatly sliced off by the giant scorpions claw and he scooched around on his backside trying to retrieve them.

Eventually, Jimmy went back to work and to his surprise not many of his colleagues made fun of him. After a couple of days things seemed back to normal as if nothing had happened. In a couple of weeks he found himself back at Chang's doing his accounts again. One day while descending the stairs he saw Miriam in her room out of the corner of his eye. The door was partially open and she was in a state of semi-undress. Jimmy had to suppress a gasp when he saw that her back was covered by two huge burn marks, one down each side, they seemed to suggest a pair of dragons. Miriam must have sensed his presence for she quickly closed the door with the sole of her foot. Jimmy was quite perturbed by what he saw and he couldn't help but wonder how she had come to be so scarred.

That evening when Jimmy got home he felt compelled to rummage through his discarded magicians props. Almost at once he came upon the top hat which was in a state of collapse. He picked it up gingerly and took it into the light over the kitchen sink to study it. Steeling himself he gave it a good thump and it sprung open with a satisfying thunk. The flattened body of the black scorpion fell out into the sink and Jimmy breathed a sigh of relief. Jimmy regarded the creature dispassionately despite all the pain and humiliation it had caused him. He decided he would hang on to it as a keepsake and he placed it on his mantelpiece leaning up against an old stopped clock.

'Where the blazes did you come from? Who on earth sent you?' he said.

He sat on his couch and pondered these questions as he twirled the top hat in his hands. On impulse he placed the top hat on his head and gave the top a gentle tap with his index finger. The hat collapsed in an instant and Jimmy's vision suddenly went black. He felt as if he was falling freely through a void of dark space, he felt deathly cold and his mind seemed to turn inside out. All of a sudden he found himself standing in a darkened room dizzy and disorientated. He saw a woman standing with her back to him, what caught his eye immediately was her back which was exposed by the dress she wore. There were two great dragons tattooed there in vibrant shades of green, silver and gold. He was transfixed by their beauty but also by their life-like quality. The woman suddenly turned and regarded Jimmy with a sort of disdainful grimace. But what really made Jimmy's blood run cold was her face. It was Miriam or rather she looked exactly like Miriam except for her eyes which were an inhuman shade of emerald green. Abruptly, silently she began to move toward him, or seemed to glide in a most unnatural manner. Her outstretched arms had him in an embrace of sorts before he could react and her freakishly long fingernails carved exquisite pain into his back. He tried to scream but he could not. She whispered in his ear,

'Get out of my world.'

Such was the malevolence of her tone that a frozen shiver reverberated through Jimmy's body. He seemed to faint and somehow he found himself plunging again through the endless nameless void. He found himself back on the couch in his living room again. Jimmy felt woozy and feverish. His back hurt unbearably and he stood up to regard himself in the mirror above the mantelpiece. With a shock he saw that his once dark hair was now extensively streaked through with grey. He looked as though he had aged by ten years. He twisted himself around to better see his back and saw that his shirt was soaked with blood. He peeled it off painfully and stood looking at the two great scars on his back that seemed to resemble the great dragons tattooed on the other Miriam. He tried touching them but the pain was excruciating, he staggered towards the bathroom where he immediately got in the shower, running it cold deliberately to ease the burning pain he felt. Jimmy clambered onto his bed and fell immediately into a restless uneasy slumber. His dreams were haunted by the hideously beautiful woman and her flashing green eyes.

Jimmy was apprehensive but he knew he had to go and see Miriam as soon as possible. The next time he was at Chang's however she came to see him. He was absorbed in his accounts when he looked up there she was standing in the doorway. She had her arms folded in front of her and she glowered at him silently.

'Hi Miriam,' he said, 'I was just going to come looking for you.'

'Huh,' she said, 'you have been to the other side. You are marked now. Show me.'

Jimmy was taken aback, how could she know about his bizarre experience and the marks on his back?

'How did you know?' he said.

'You tried on my grandfather's hat, didn't you?' she said, 'You saw her and she embraced you.'

'Yes,' he said, 'but how do you know these things?'

'I know everything she knows,' she said, 'Come with me, we must take her mark from you before it is too late.'

Jimmy followed her to her tiny flat at the back of the dingy storeroom. As he took off his shirt, he turned to see Miriam coming at him with a steam iron in her hand. Before he could react she pushed him face-first onto the mattress on the floor. She knelt on his back pinning him there. Without a word she set to with the iron running it over the dragon images on his back without pause or delicacy. Jimmy was so shocked it took a moment to register.

'Jesus Fucking H Christ!' he screamed and tried to squirm away from her. But she had him in a vice-like grip and did not let go. The smell of singeing flesh filled the room along with acrid smoke. Jimmy's screams gave way to whimpers as Miriam drove the scalding hot iron deep into his back. Abruptly she stopped and doused his back with water from a plastic bottle.

'There,' she said, 'All done. You should be safe now.'

'You crazy bitch,' said Jimmy, 'safe from what?'

He sat up, winced in pain and almost passed out. Miriam went to her dresser and picked up an obscure looking pipe with a weird clay bowl at one end. She held it over a lamp and inhaled its vapours. She passed it to Jimmy.

'Here, smoke some of this,' she said, 'it will help with the pain.'

'What the fuck is it?' said Jimmy wiping a tear from his eye.

'It is chandu,' said Miriam, 'here, just take one good hit and all your pain will disappear.'

Jimmy obeyed simply because he was in agony. He inhaled deeply from the long pipe and almost immediately he felt better. He fell back on the mattress and dozed off, dreaming of unicorns and waterfalls. He never felt so free of pain or care in all his life.

When Jimmy awoke it was dark and he was back on the couch in his apartment. His head was groggy and when he tried to stand up he felt his shirt stick to his back and a searing pain struck him. He staggered into his bedroom and carefully removed his shirt in front of the mirror. To his surprise there were no great scars there, just a redness and the dim outline of what once may have been a pair of dragons. He noticed a piece of paper in his shirt pocket. He took it out, opened it and read. It was from Miriam, it said:

'I am sorry I had to hurt you but your wounds will heal quickly. I have taken my grandfather's hat. It is a family heirloom and should never have been given to you. It is very dangerous and should not be used by those who do not understand its power. Also, I left a present for you.'

Jimmy sighed and walked back in to the living room. There was Pythagoras in his cage, munching away on a piece of lettuce, he regarded Jimmy curiously with his ears. Jimmy laughed and went to the drinks cabinet and poured himself a generous measure of brandy. He sat back gently on the couch, took a sip of his drink and put his feet up on the coffee table. He toasted Pythagoras and couldn't help but chuckle to himself.

'Oh well, so much for my career as an illusionist,' he said.

The next time Jimmy went back to Chang's there was no sign of Miriam. When he asked the old man about her all he would say was, 'Away, away,' gesturing with his hand as if Jimmy would know what this meant. He peeked into her old room but all that remained was the rolled-up mattress on the floor and one of those odd clay-pipe bowls on the dresser. He slipped it into his jacket pocket telling himself that it was not stealing, he simply wanted something of hers as a memento. At home he placed it on his mantelpiece beside her note and the black scorpion. In the corner Pythagoras eyed him coolly, as if he knew and understood everything.

GRAVE DIGGER

Frank George C. Moore

Glasnevin grave yard is the official grave yard of the Pale of Dublin. If you ever visit Dublin, come out here and speak to the originators of all civilisation. If it happens to be in fifty years' time. Say hello to me.

Drop the gauze of heaven/
in a dew containing my essence/
as it falls on grave stones/
and my bones begin to sense/
where they will lay for God's eternity
beyond (the tavern) of Brian Boru
on the old Glasnevin road.

Grave digger place me
(Between Drumcondra, Parlmerstown & Little Bray
In the ordained grave yard of the Pale)

Ring the bell my son or brother/
to a rectangular plot on the warden's chart
that sets out the paths, by the stone of Parnell;
Of paupers & city burgers and holy angels
That flit about the throne (of god).

Drop the gauze of heaven
from the baptismal fonts of Dublin
as God's neutrinos move all to resolution
& my bones begin to sense all things in rebirth.

(Son or brother) plant me in the flux
of ever -moving neutrinos in soil
that make up you and me & America

to all the stars, of Sean O' Casey.
and god's earth changing in cemeteries
from the fonts of Nazareth
in songs of Simian and Anna
to the re birthing plots of Armageddon.

Across the Cross Guns bridge/
(by the tavern of Brian Buru)
lay me in the garden of the Botanic road
by Isaac Butt, Collins, old Parnell
my sister, father, mother
for there is a plot awaiting me you & all
to reconfigure in the neutrinos of essence
to new life to walk all city streets
as do angels of our antecedence.

Plant me, grave digger of the Pale
in a plot awaiting (new Jerusalem)
in the antecedence of Dublin.
on the Botanic road by old Glasnevin.

SANTA IN AFRICA

Geralyn Rownan

I'm with Roald Dahl here; I too love children, especially on toast...Here is a story I wrote for the darling little ankle-biters. There are illustrations for them to colour in, as well. It's not fiction, because of course Santa and the Rein Deer are real.

It was Christmas Eve in South Africa. In the big dark forest, Dozi the donkey was travelling along the paths the elephants had created through the forest. He was pulling a big cart painted red and gold. The donkey's reins were made from gold ribbon and had little gold bells dangling from them. There was a glass bottle full of fireflies tied to the front of the cart, to act as a lamp. The fireflies glowed in the dark and helped Dozi find his way through the thick bushes. In the back of the cart Santa perched on top of a heap of brightly wrapped parcels. Santa was trying to hold on to both the donkey's reins AND the parcels as the cart bounced up and down on the hard road. It was getting late. He still had gifts to deliver in South Africa before he travelled home to the North Pole.

"Dear me" said Santa as he looked at his watch. "I'm late! Hurry, Dozi! But be careful! If I fall on these parcels one more time, I'll squash them!"

Dozi put his grey ears back flat against the sides of his head and galloped on, looking for the road to Cape Town. The moon was clouding over and misty fog was creeping through the forest. It was getting harder and harder for Dozi to see the elephant path in front of him. "For such big animals, elephants make very small paths" muttered Dozi to himself.

Suddenly there was a big BANG! Santa was thrown out of the cart onto the grass and the parcels all went flying out on top of him. He sat up, covered in dust and mud. "I'm bruised all over!" he said, rubbing his bottom and his head at the same time.

"Dozi, what happened?" But he got no answer. Poor Dozi was stretched out on the ground with his four legs pointing in four different directions and his two eyes looking in two different directions. Between his big ears sat a flat piece of elephant dung which still had a dung beetle clinging to it, like a little hat with a brooch.

The ground shook. There stood Skukuza, the biggest elephant in South Africa. A piece of yellow

136

marzipan from one of the cakes thrown out of the cart was impaled upon a tusk. It looked very funny but Santa daren't laugh in case he got offended. It's not very clever to offend an angry elephant.

In the darkness Dozi had run slap bang into the rear end of Skukuza. "I'm sorry, I didn't see you" wailed Dozi, trying to focus his eyes on the angry elephant. Of course Skukuza was not hurt at all by having a donkey run into him at full speed. But poor Dozi had a very bad headache after the collision with the ten ton elephant.

"How could anyone not see an elephant?" asked Sabi, a lady elephant who had been asleep in the thicket when Dozi crashed into Skukuza. "I'm tired and it's very dark and foggy" replied Dozi. "Oh, my head" and he groaned and laid his head on the ground with the ridiculous hat of dung still stuck between his ears.

The whole herd of elephants gathered round. Skukuza used his mighty head to roll the cart upright onto its wheels. The others picked up the parcels with their trunks and placed them gently back in the cart. Sabi and her friend Kruger pulled branches from the sweet thorn trees and wiped the dirt from the parcels with the leafy branches. "Never mind a bit of mud" said Santa. "On we go!" But poor, dizzy Dozi was not able to go anywhere. He sat splayed on the ground, unable to move.

"What am I going to do now?" asked Father Christmas. "I must deliver the toys and sweets before morning comes!" The elephants huddled together and muttered amongst themselves. Elephants are very wise, as everyone knows. "We have decided" said Skukuza in his deep voice, "that Olli the ostrich must pull your cart. Ostriches can run at 60 kilometres an hour. The donkey can stay with us until his headache is better".

With that Skukuza lifted his trunk and trumpeted through the forest until the thumping of ostrich feet was heard.

"What is all this noise about!!" shouted Olli the Ostrich as he ran into the middle of the herd. Skukuza explained. "I can't do that!" said Olli and he ran round and round flapping his wings. "Ostriches can't pull carts! Everyone knows that! Goodbye!"

Olli was heading back to his nest in the grass when Santa stood in front of him. "Please, Olli" he said. "Please, just get me to Cape Town to leave the gifts for the children.

They have been so good this year. You live here and know the way. Please?"

"Oh alright" said Olli crossly. He allowed the elephants to put Dozi's harness with the little bells round his long neck and under his big black and white wings. Father Christmas climbed back into the cart and off they went, Olli flapping and hopping. The cart swung first to the left and then to the right. "I hope I won't be sick" groaned Santa to himself as he was flung first one way then the other.

Olli hopped and jumped and ran and danced. He tried and tried to fly but no matter how fast he ran and flapped his wings nothing happened. It was now midnight and the North Star sailed up into the sky. Everyone knows you can make a wish on the North Star. So Olli wished he was an airplane. The Star shone its light down on him. Suddenly, as if by magic, Olli was running along the tops of the trees. The cart soared into the air, still swinging from one side to the other. "Whee!" shouted Olli. "Look at me! A flying ostrich! I'm going to be rich and famous!" He was so excited he even tried flying upside down. Santa had to hang on tight to the sides of the cart.

At last Cape Town came in sight and their last stop; the Orphanage. Olli dived over the fence. He missed the grass and landed on the roof of the Orphanage. Feathers flew everywhere. Olli hopped down onto the ground but the red and gold cart was stuck on top of the building.

There was a big hole in the roof. Santa was stuck in the hole with his legs dangling down into a classroom. He laughed so much that his big fat belly shook. "Now what am I going to do" he said. "I'm stuck!" and he started laughing all over again.

"Don't blame me" said Olli as he tried to straighten out his neck which had somehow tied itself into a bow. "This is the first time I ever flew. The Orphanage should have landing lights like the airport!" As he spoke the cart slowly slid to the ground from the roof.

Suddenly there was rustling and humming in the grass. Santa and Olli stared as the grass moved and whispered. There were thousands of spiders hurrying towards them. They were the type of spider called Community Spiders, the ones who build enormous webs where they all live together. Everyone knows spiders are very good house makers.

The spiders stopped and looked up at Santa. They whispered amongst themselves. Next thing, a big spider wearing a builder's hat and boots left the group and climbed onto the roof. He stood in front of Santa and crossed four of his eight legs.

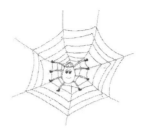

"We'll rescue you" he said. "Spiders always help people, even though people don't like us".

"Thank you" said Santa. "But how can you help me? You are all very small if you don't mind me saying so." "Spiders' webs are stronger than the steel that men make" said the spider with the hat, whose name was Shamwari. Shamwari gave a signal and without another word a thousand spiders climbed onto the roof.

They spun web after web around the jolly old man till he looked like he was wrapped up in glittering ropes. Then they started to push him down through the hole in the roof. "Stop!" he shouted. "I'll fall down onto the floor and break my head!"

"No you won't" said Shamwari. "We will lower you slowly to the floor with our spider ropes if only we can get your fat belly through the hole! Heave! " With that half of the spiders sat on Santa. They jumped up and down and tried to shove him down through the hole. The rest of the spiders stuck their feet to the roof with web glue and held on to the web ropes they had woven around him. Slowly they lowered him, all of them breathing heavily and some of them losing their footing on the roof. But since spiders have eight feet each it didn't matter if one or two of their feet slipped. After a long time they managed to set him down on the floor of the Orphanage classroom.

Santa worked quickly. He took parcels and quickly placed them on the children's tables. He left sweets. He left socks and coloured pens. He left toys. The he went into the kitchen to leave Christmas cake for the Big Mamas who looked after the children. Olli was in the kitchen with his head stuck in a pot of soup. "Stop that!" Santa said. "Oh well," said Olli. "It's not nice soup anyway. There are no nice muddy insects in it." "Humans don't put insects in their soup." said Santa and he laughed at the ostrich. "I'm tired and hungry. I'm going home to fix my neck. Goodnight" said Olli. And off he went, walking sideways because his head was back to front. "Goodbye and Happy Christmas, Olli" called Santa.

When he had finished setting out all the presents, he climbed back up through the hole, using the web ropes as a ladder. Then Shamwari and the spiders took over again. They glued the broken bits of roof back on with their sticky web glue. When they had finished no one would ever know that anything had happened to the roof.

"Thank you so much, my friends" said Santa. "My work is finished. I can go home. But how will I get there? I have no one to pull my cart."

Just then, he heard a delicate cough. "Ahem!" There it went again, a little bit louder. "Ahem!" Santa peered into the darkness. There, looking back at him, were six pairs of brown eyes. Six furry faces. Topped by six sets of the furriest ears you ever saw.

Six deer of the kind they call "Kudu Deer" in Africa stood in front of him, their five black noses and one red nose sniffing the air and their ears flicking this way and that.

"Good Evening Father Christmas" said the one in front. "My name is Monday, and these are my brothers and sisters Tuesday, Wednesday, Thursday and Friday. Saturday is the one with the red nose."

"I'm very pleased to meet you" said Santa and he bowed to the Kudu Deer, just to be polite. Their tiny hooves went tap-tap on the ground as they bowed back. The smell of warm fur filled the air.

"Excuse me," said Shamwari the Builder Spider to the red nosed deer. "I hope you don't think I'm rude, but why is your nose red when everyone else's is black?" The red-nosed one sighed. "I have a cold. I have to blow my nose all the time" and with that he blew his nose again and wiped it with one of his long ears.

The Kudus inspected the red and gold cart. "Maybe we can help you get home" said Monday. "There is a story

143

told amongst our tribe that long ago, it was our kind, not donkeys that pulled the cart for Father Christmas. Somehow the knowledge was lost. Maybe we can find it again."

"What a wonderful idea" said Santa "Let's try it!" The Kudu scurried around each other and re-arranged themselves in three pairs with their big brown eyes looking straight ahead like soldiers on parade. The red-nosed one stood in the front row. "I will lead" said Saturday as he blew his nose again. The golden reins with their little bells were looped round their furry necks. Father Christmas took out his map and they all looked at it and tried to figure out which way to go. "Maybe we could go to the Airport and take off from the runway?" said Tuesday. "We're not allowed," said Father Christmas. "You have to have a pilot's license to take off from the airport."

"Does the cart ever bump into planes when you are flying home? Can people in the planes look out the windows and see you flying past?" asked Wednesday whose little feet danced with excitement. "Only if they believe in magic" said Santa with a smile. He shook the reins and the little gold bells jingled and jangled. Saturday, Monday, Tuesday, Wednesday Thursday and Friday trotted out the gate of the little orphanage pulling the cart behind them. They were running along the track when the North Star came out from behind a cloud again. Once again a strange thing happened. Their ears started to flap like birds' wings. Suddenly they were lifting off the ground and flying through the air, laughing and singing Christmas songs. "Be careful, we nearly hit that blue gum tree" laughed Santa. They collected Dozi from the elephants and put him in the back of the cart. Then off they went, singing and whooping.

144

"Happy Christmas everybody" Father Christmas called as the cart flew north over Johannesburg.

Before the sun rose they were back at the North Pole. "Thank you my friends" said Santa. "How well you flew and pulled the cart. But I do not think calling yourselves after the days of the week is a good idea. You must have far more beautiful names that suit you. I name you Rudolph, Comet, Vixen, Dasher, Dancer, and Comet. Will you stay a while?"

The little deer stayed with Santa from then on. Over time the cart became bigger and bigger and the elves turned it into a beautiful sleigh. The deer carried the reins so delicately and pulled the sleigh so well, that gradually they forgot their previous life as Kudu Deer and became known as Santa's "Rein Deer" instead. Every Christmas they continue to make children happy all over the world. Every Christmas as they flash over the big forest in South Africa, Skukuza and the elephants look up and wave their trunks in greeting, because elephants live to be very, very, old and they never forget a thing.

146

147

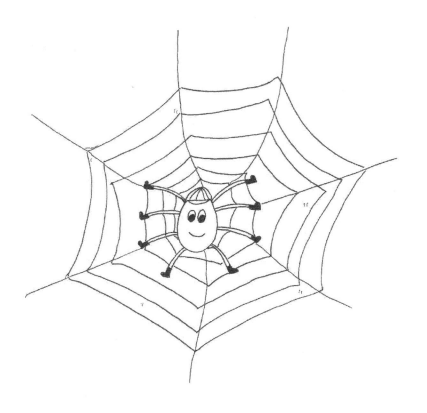

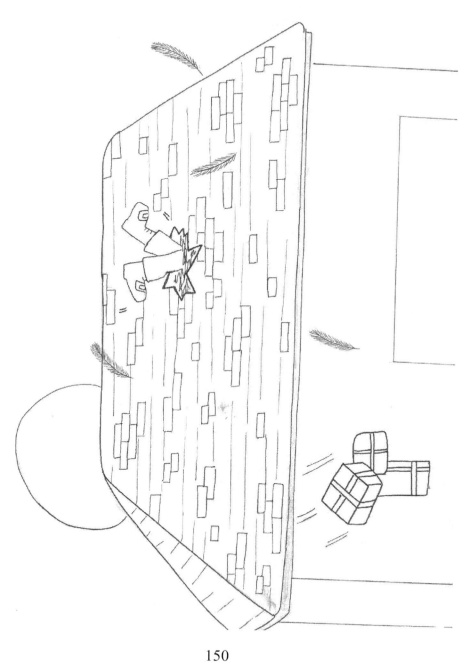

150

PETER'S PAINTING

Breda McAteer

The colours I wear are my coat of armour,
They protect what's hidden beneath.
I want to be within that tranquil space
In the green painted canvas,
It's safe and protective there.
Outside, I'm faced with confusion.

Wondering what colour to wear today.
A fiery Red! To hide my soul
From reflecting rays of gold.
A muddy Brown that won't let the
Scarlet woman come out to play.

If the radiant red gets too hot!
I can jump into the cool Blue River,
And wash my entire colour away.
To stay within the calming Green,
My true colours will shine through;
Throwing light on the Grey path,
Where I may find my way home.

THE STORY OF A BOY.

Brian Browne

This is the story of a boy and his early life. He was an ordinary child in most respects, most that is but one. You see he was born as part of a set. He was an identical twin and yes his other half was also a boy. He was also one of 10, that is to say he had 9 siblings not that there were ten twins in the family. He was also joint last in the line. For whatever reason the kid was stuck with the moniker of Bernard, a name quite expectable for a serious adult but for an unfortunate child, well I ask you? The other half was less afflicted with the name of Tom.

Entry into this world was no more traumatic for them than for any other baby ever born; which is to say it was indeed a major trauma, and not the last by any means. The family was among the better off in the neighbourhood as their farther not only had a permanent and pensionable job, but a good one at that. He was a minor official in local government and so reasonable levels of living were pretty much secured. Lucky little devils I hear you say. Well yes and no, but more of that anon. Yes life was really quite pleasant for him as the sisters, with one exception, doted on him. Nothing was good enough for this kid. The one who was not quite so besotted was in fact the eldest, here after referred to as the wicked witch of the north (WWON). Well it's an appropriate name, they did live in the north of their city.

By the time the twins arrived the mother was already almost fifty years old and the WWON was disgusted that a woman that age was still having babies. The fact that it was her mother only made matters worse.

At the age of twenty four it was just humiliating. The accompanying rage could not be directed at mother, since it had to have a target, the other kids would have to do. Naturally the twins would be the bull's eye of said target. This particular sister was in her own mind something of a thespian, and as a consequence spent a lot of her free time practicing lines from various plays. She took particular delight in torturing the younger ones with some of the darker passages from Shakespeare, such as the witches seen in the Scottish play. Those lines still ring in his ears every time any memory of child hood intrudes and this to spite the intervening decades.

There was an earlier intimation that there was to be rain in our hero's life from time to time and indeed that is the case. At the age of fifteen months Tom developed problems and was admitted to the children's hospital where they operated and removed a restriction in his bowls. To use a well-worn phrase, " The operation was a complete success but ..." This is not quite the middle of the last century and it would be nice to believe, to spite evidence to the contrary, that things have changed but then again?

Telephones in private houses were as rare as hen's teeth in the late forties and consequently mother had to go to the local phone box last thing at night in order to check and see that her baby was ok.

"Hello, this is Ms Black, I am Tom's mother, can you tell me how he is please?"

"Oh yes, he is dead, please make arrangements for burial as soon as possible"

This event was to have a profound impact on the life of not only Bernard but also his mother and to a lesser extent the entire family from that day on. In fact it is no exaggeration to say that till the day mother died it was an ever present grief for her. This, like most grief needed company and was consequently shared with the surviving twin.

"There is not a day goes by that I don't think of your twin and the way he died" Let me tell you, statements like that stay with a body. There was what might be viewed as an upside to the tragedy as far as Bernard was concerned. You see he was viewed and treated by almost every one as even more special as he was the one who survived.

It was necessary in the early days to get a pram to accommodate the twins and so a special one was purchased. To spite the family's relative wealth there simply was not the ready cash and so the system known as the never, never was invoked. (This method was properly known as hire purchase). Once there was only one occupant the carriage was now redundant but worse than that the remaining infant was always looking for his other half and patting the pillow as if to say "Where is he". This was an insufferable state of affairs for the unfortunate mother and so the pram had to go; even though the payments had still to be met for the term of the agreement and in spite of the hardship caused.

There were of course other challenges to be faced by this lad as there are with everyone on earth. The specific ones in this case were to ratchet up a gear when school started and he could make no sense of what they were talking about when it came to reading and writing. There simply was no relationship between what was called letters and sounds and so he was judged to be either lazy or stupid

156

and there was, luckily, a remedy for those short comings. Better yet the remedy was the same in both cases and was simply beat the shit out of him.

That will teach him not to be lazy and or stupid, now won't it? Well no not really. Aged ten English is the subject;

"Black spell orange" (this being one of the words designated for learning the previous day, and sweated over for an hour) "O" well he could remember that much but nothing else. Teacher "p" Bernard "p" Well teachers don't tell lies, do they?"

"Get up here you lazy pup. Six of the best and maybe next time you will get it right". This agony was to continue through all the years of school. The only respite being during classes devoted to practical subjects and these only started in technical school. It should be borne in mind that these were not the dark ages we are talking about but a mere half century ago. In those days no one had apparently even conceived of the idea of dyslexia let alone diagnosed it. If there was any awareness of this condition it hadn't reached either teachers or parents.

To add to his woes the lad was by nature somewhat effeminate and so gained the nick name of 'Nizzles' (This from his sister nearest in age). So this part of his nature would need to be hidden along with his inability to read or write. By now however he was fast becoming a good actor. Better at this than even the dreaded WWON. Of course for him it was no mere affectation but in a real sense a matter of survival and so the skill developed over time.

In spite of the dyslexia, or maybe because of it, he had sufficient intelligence to protect himself even in an all-boys school. The strategy was quite simple, look out for the strongest bully and by whatever means necessary befriend him. After that life was so much simpler. One of the drawbacks, of this course of action was the need for silence when some other unfortunate was being tortured, in some respects this was a small price to pay.

It's after school on a nice spring day and all the kids are gathered in the local park. One of them has been singled out to be made an example of and so a bunch of nettles is fetched and given to Nicky "The Boss" with which he proceeds to scourge the bare legs of today's victim. "Just keep silent Bernard and watch, otherwise you could be next".

It is not necessarily recommend as the best way to deal with nasty people but a kids' got to do what a kids' got to do, and at the time it seemed the only way. And so hiding became a way of life. Hiding in many different ways, what he felt, what he was and what he wanted. As life progressed things got better and worse, better because of the acting ability and worse because of the need to act out so many lies. A conversation overheard between the eldest brother and a fellow worker about 'queers'. Gerald (older brother) "I know what I'd do with them, into a house with the lot of them and burn the place down".

Co-worker "Too fuckin' right". Now this had its funny side as by now Bernard knew that there were literally thousands of people like him in the city they lived in, not to mention the rest of the country. There was simply no way that even a small fraction of them could fit in a single house no matter how big it was. But still to hear this crap from his own brother was, well let's just say, difficult.

On reaching the stage where it was necessary to start work mother and eldest brother conferred and decided that Bernard should become an electrician. Yes that's the best bet for him as there is clearly no point in further education.

And so began the next five years of largely painful attempts to fit in all the while knowing that he was definitely a round peg in a square hole, so to speak. The old trick of making friends with the biggest bully didn't always work in the day to day environment but superior intelligence was usually enough to save the day. It was sometimes sufficient to work out solutions to tricky problems and to allow the others to take credit for his work. On one particular winters day while working in the open air on some freezing metal he decided that enough was enough. There just had to be a better way to live then this.

As it happened he had lately become involved with a religious group whose purpose in life was to send lay missionaries to developed countries to work and preach the Gospel. How this came about is anybody's guess as he was not in the slightest what is usually described as 'religious'. However there was a retreat and in the course of a conversation with the priest it was decided that Bernard should apply to join the order. This seemed like a good idea as it would kill two birds with one stone as it were. Firstly it would mean no more working in freezing conditions and secondly it would be a safe haven from the temptations of the world. Just how wrong can a body be?

Well yes there was to be an end to metal-working in freezing conditions and indeed in any conditions from the day of joining. But as to a safe haven, well yes and no; a large degree of emphasis is placed upon education in what is called religious life and consequently he was thrown into that alien world. For the next four years there was study and more study. In fact the candidates are educated to a standard that the individual is capable of achieving. Then comes the rub, having been trained to ask questions one is then told that there are things about which questions are simply not allowed.

For example from where does the Church draw its authority? Answer: from Jesus Christ. How do we know anything about Jesus Christ? Faith has revealed it to us. This brings any thinking person back to Descartes and his notion that, how he knows that he exists, is because he is a thinking being and how does he know this?, well because God would not allow him to be so deceived if it were not true.

Then there was the absurdity of the property in which the order lived and who exactly owned it? The first answer was that it belonged to the pope but that changed upon investigation and it seems that there was a trust which owned everything and held all the property for the use of the order.

All in all it became increasingly clear that the three vows upon which everything depended were not quite what they seemed.

Poverty: a matter of interpretation.

Chastity: for those who are able.

Obedience: to the will of God.

Poverty then simply means that every material need was catered for, Chastity, well for a young man who had a particular leaning, in a house full of other men, many of similar leanings. Need I say more? Obedience, obviously if one acts in accordance with the dictates of consensus, that's that. Perhaps by now the reader will realise that this was an untenable situation for Brendan and also for all but three of the people who joined in the four years of his sojourn.

What could he do? After all they had been preparing for this day for the past three years and now his parents were outside in the church along with his brothers and sisters. They had arranged a reception and everything and were expecting a speech from Brendan. Then as far as the order was concerned they had suffered so many disappointments what with the rapid exodus of recent years. Six entered in his year, nine the year before and six the year before that. Of that number there were only three left.

So now it's the fateful day, Solemn and perpetual vows. Once this step is taken there is no way out of it not just this life but for eternity. That's the theory at any rate although they all know of people who have been granted dispensations and even those dreaded ones who simply left without permission. What was to become of them? Ah well God is going to grant Bernard Divine grace and it will be all right, won't it?

Well here goes, out onto the altar and repeat the words as practiced endlessly over the past few weeks. And as prepared for three years. "Yes I vow and promise to live the life of a friar minor in poverty chastity and obedience according to the rule of St. Francis and the constructions of the order of Friars Minor"

Bernard was thinking, somewhere just below consciousness. "How indeed can I say it even to myself? Do I actually believe in God, the church, its sacraments or in its vows and ceremonies? No I will have to just grin and bear it, there are after all worse ways of living. I have a roof over my head as much food as I can eat and from today on (perhaps ironically, given the vow of poverty) as much as I want to drink as well. How could I say that it was all a sham? But sham it is for me at least."

Being a man of honour, or at least trying to be, He decided that a chat with the superior was in order and he hoped it was not too late.

"Father, may I have a word before the ceremony?"

"But of course, come to my study and we can talk in private".

"Well now what can I do for you Bernard?"

"If you remember telling us that if we had any doubts about profession we should come to you?"

"Ah! Its doubts is it? Well this is the time to voice them. Or if you prefer we can just postpone your vows to a later date. There may be some embarrassment on your part but that will pass. And far less hassle then seeking a dispensation later down the line"

"How am I going to explain all this to my unfortunate parents? And won't that bitch WWON be over the moon about it all." Bernard thought.

Whatever about her delight or otherwise the first thing she said to the parents was "Well if he is leaving, you are not letting him back into the family home are you?" This was a home she had departed from on her marriage some ten years earlier. Well of course in spite of the enlightened stance that the superior had taken, there was really only one course of action left for Brendan.

It was a different world he came out into than the one he had left those few short years earlier. Or more probably he had changed rather than the world. In some respects it was like being born as an adult into a strange place where the rules aren't properly understood. After a time Bernard decided it would be a good idea to set up a group where ex religious like himself could meet and perhaps ease their way back into society. Ironically once he found what was then called the gay scene it became evident that there was already a group whose members were mostly ex clerics.

It would be unfair to characterise our hero's life in wholly, or even mostly negative light. On the contrary his life was and is a journey which is mostly enjoyable. Many, but not too many, friends to share the triumphs, and the lows, along the way; oh and yes to spite his learning difficulty, and the fact that he still can't spell, he now has not one but two university qualifications. Better yet he has found a soul mate and they have been together for thirty years at this stage and looking forward to many, many more.

In a Second

Susan Cooney

"I'll be there in a second"
Don't linger because
Anything can happen in a second:

The truth or lies
Glimpsed in his blue eyes
can reignite or burn a tie,
Fortunes made or lost at cards
Seedlings coming from the soil
Stars start to explode, implode,
A kettle whistles to the boil.
The right decision taken in a life
The end of sorrow; the start of strife
A bullet hits an archduke, president
Changing history for all time.

An old man gives up his breathing
Impoverishing others with his leaving
A bubble bursts on Grafton Street
Pricked by a curious child.
Clouds shift, thunder rolls

A second isn't long, all told
But it takes a finite number to grow old

DUBLIN CLOCKS

Pronsias O Mordha

Where is the Latin clock that once hung
above the Irish Times in D'Olier street gone?
I first met my Suzette beneath those Roman hands
to dine in a French crêperie
within the literate mists of Dublin's Pale.
After pancakes, a half carafe of wine
coffee , a cheroot cigar, she asked me,
'If I loved her?, I said, 'not yet my dear!'
In the embrace of tempus fugit and desire.
we now own our own crêper
beneath the clock hanging on the Irish Catholic
by the bridge of trains in Gardiner street.
We have three garcons two fillies
A St. Bernard dog called Carpae Diem/ Eva Gabor
an Irish Times on request hangs daily by our door.
Do drop in to our salon, to sip coffee.
with the ghosts of Oliver Goldsmith
James Joyce, George Moore.
For the literati still set the pace
and wind up Dublin's clocks in tempus fugit.

SARAH'S TALE

Brian Carroll

Sarah was stunningly beautiful, her Asian features were blended with Tibetan and Mongolian overtones. Her natural beauty was offset however, by a scar that ran from the top of her nose under her eye all the way to her right ear. It was an old scar and sometimes she forgot it was there at all. Men would stare at her in the street and she would remember.

At the age of twelve she was married off to a local merchant who had paid a handsome dowry for her. He found her great beauty irresistible and he thought that she would give him many good-looking children. But the man turned out to be a drunkard and a brute who treated her worse than a dog. One night in a drunken rage he gave her the scar that adorns her face with his straight-razor after she had laughed at his drunken impotence. She found herself cast out into the street. She was marked now and not even her own family would take her back. They said she had brought shame on them by provoking and disrespecting her husband and that now she must fend for herself.

At first she had no choice but to resort to begging and petty theft. She became quite adept at this until one day she was caught red-handed trying to steal from an old mendicant in the market-place. The old man was blind but he stared right through her with his pure white eyes.

"I can teach you the black arts so that you may avenge yourself upon those who have wronged you," he said.

He had her wrist in an iron grip, he was immensely strong despite his bony frame and feeble appearance. She could not break free of his grasp and she was intrigued by his offer. Sarah studied and practised with the old man for seven years until one day he sent her away.

"There is nothing more I can teach you," He said, "but you must use these secrets I have taught you wisely or you will end up like me."

She struggled by herself initially, having become accustomed to the old man's protection. But she soon found that she could manipulate people easily, she had the gift of making them see what they wanted to see. She could use her melodious voice to have people do her bidding and believe it was their own will.

Eventually she returned to her native village disguised as an old crone where she could observe her former husband with ease. He had acquired a new wife by now but she seemed timid and obedient to his demands. Sarah resolved to set this new wife free and to humiliate and destroy her former husband. She found a young puppy and slowly set about the task of mind transference. Gradually the man started scratching himself behind his ears and making little yelping noises. After several weeks he was going about on all-fours and defecating in the street. The authorities eventually had to confine him to a cell in the local asylum where he lived out his days barking and scratching himself.

The puppy became very bad-tempered and ran away to roam with a pack of wild dogs. When it became rabid it was torn apart by the other dogs. Sarah was well pleased with her work until shortly thereafter she noticed she had grown a small tail of her own. Soon however, she learned to love her tail and enjoyed wagging it very much.

LEAVING TOWN

Katie Dwyer

She feels lighter in that instant

train pulling away

the dash and scramble of departure

completed.

She tries to see through the windows of the houses.

Here here and here

she thinks—

on the move.

LIFE IS NOT A BOWL OF CHERRIES.

IT'S A PIE.

Geralyn Rownan

Life is not a bowl of cherries. It's a pie. That's according to the fifteen self-help/self- improvement/self-development/it's all about me books, now helping me enormously by holding up my bedside lamp.

Yes, it seems that Life is a Pie. The segments of the Pie are; Work, Relationships, Hobbies, Family, Travel, whatever is important to you. The instructions in Self Help Manual#7; Get some paper, draw a circle, mark out your segments, label them and think about them. Write about them. So that's what I've done. Here are a few slices from my Pie. I hope you like them. I've indicated where pieces are fictional.

ME, MYSELF and I kind of stuff

On being a Bed-Head

I regard the state of my hair as a metaphor for the state of my life. Many times have I said to myself; No wonder I can't control my life - I can't even control my hair. Probably as I sailed into yet another business meeting attired elegantly and appropriately in a nice business suit and sensible shoes – topped by hair that made me look like I had been dragged through a vortex backwards. Here are just some of the hair-related remarks that have punctuated my life;

At school; Sr. Benedict, the nun who wouldn't have disgraced an SS Regiment. "You..."she'd say as she dug her knuckles into my shoulder. (A move I've seen martial arts practitioners use to paralyse people). "You...don't come to school again without brushing your hair." Useless to protest that I had already shed tears that day as my poor mother strove to untangle the riot of curls with a comb.

At work; a male colleague remarked that he could always identify me from the back – as no one else on the workforce had "leonine" hair like mine.

My brother-in-law; "It's funny but that kind of scraggy hairdo or whatever you call it, suits you." Was that actually meant to be a compliment? And I think "bedhead" is the correct technical term, Bro...

The postman; "Are you just up?" This at 2.30 in the afternoon...

171

No, I don't have neat and tidy hair. But then, my life is not neat and tidy either.

I had to get my photo taken a few months ago for a CV. The instructions for women were; no jewellery, plain dark top, straight hair, not pinned up. So I went to the hairdresser and got my hair straightened for the photo. The result? A photo of me that doesn't look like me, to show people what I look like in real life, only of course I don't.

A while ago, I decided to try a different hairdresser. Got stuck into the coffee and magazines and paid no attention to what my new hairdresser was doing. The result? By the time I surfaced from photos of the royal wedding I had been given a short-back-and-sides and scrunch dried. I looked like a dish scrubber. Lunch time hair activities over, I went back to work. One of my Company Directors observed me in silence for a few minutes before he came out with; "I don't know how to describe it, (*allow me to describe it for you - dish scrubber*) but it suits you". Later another Director came into my office; "I like the new hairstyle –it takes years off you Oh God I suppose I shouldn't have said that". Hello? Do I normally look a hundred and ninety and just hadn't noticed? I had to stop him in his tracks before he upset himself. It didn't bother me in the slightest, not after all these years.

The *piece de résistance*? One Christmas Eve I had my hair done and headed straight from the hairdressers to visit my Mother in her Nursing Home. She took one look at me and said: "Are you not getting your hair done for Christmas?"

I rest my case.

SPIRITUAL STUFF

Gimme that old time religion…

A group of us were sitting chatting at a wedding. "I need a break, a quiet place where I can just rest and think" I said. "But where can you go to get away from radio, TV, internet, noise, 'phones, traffic? Apart from the moon?"

"I know the ideal place", a friend of a friend said. He recommended a monastery in the country. "I go every year" he said. I knew of the place. I knew they took women guests as well as men and that it was a safe place I could go to on my own. That night I googled it and emailed the Guestmaster asking if I could stay 4 nights, any time after the 19th ^{of} July. He replied that certainly I could stay 4 nights, why didn't I come and stay from the 14th to the 18th July… Eventually we settled on an arrival date of July 21st.

I drove away from Dublin listening to a CD of Gregorian chant to get myself in the mood. Problem is, that kind of stuff is very hard to sing along to. After taking 3 wrong turns I finally arrived in time to hear the bells ring for the 4 p.m. prayer. Parked, I rocked up to the church for my first experience of chanting and prayers. All very peaceful. I could feel the calmness already.

Next; tea in the Guest Refectory. The evening meal was "Tea". Apparently "Dinner" was served at 1 p.m. Heaps of scrambled eggs, doorstep slices of bread and butter and pots of tea were handed out through a serving hatch. As someone who would normally have dinner in the evening and who hadn't eaten since breakfast, I was very hungry. I'd brought fruit and water but nothing else. I did my best with the scrambled egg while covertly observing the other guests; a motley crew of lay and religious, men and women, age group twenties and up. Tea finished, the place tidied up and all the crockery and cutlery handed back through the hatch to the religious washer-uppers, I made my way to the Guest House.

On arrival I had been given a key by the male Receptionist and pointed in the direction of a high wall behind the church. There was a door in the wall. I turned the key and entered the secret garden. A white robed, elderly clerical Brother came down the path to greet me very warmly and escort me into the Guest House. He pointed out the internal door to the passageway between the Guest House and Church, to be used for night time and 4 a.m. ceremonies. Upstairs we went – here was my room. Rules; the Guest House door was locked each night at 9 p.m. Here was the Common Room and the Kitchen, where one could sit and read, make tea or coffee etc.

My room was lovely and more importantly, ensuite. So far so good. Ok! Here I am- ready for 4 days of silence, prayer and reflection. As long as I don't meet with any misogyny – I'd be out the door if there was any of that in this house of men. The Catholic Church is not known for its pro-women stance - the Hierarchy is a Men's Club. But I was here to spend time in silence and reflect on **my** life and where **I** was going, not where anyone else or any institution was headed.

Down in the Common Room, men and women guests chatted. I explained that no, I'd never been here before. Never stayed in any place like this. A lady asked if I'd like to join her in climbing the hill behind the monastery to "The Cross". I'd love to, I said. Another guest joined us and up we went, past the farm and the fields, past streams and paths, up and up through woodland. After 25 gasping minutes I reached the top of a hill where I flopped down at the base of a concrete Jesus. The view was beautiful…a pastoral scene reminiscent of those 19th century paintings of gently undulating hills bathed in golden evening sunlight.

The older woman chatted away. She had children and grandchildren. Was I married? Had I children? No, I said. But I had nieces and nephews. In fact, yesterday I'd gone to see the new Harry Potter film with my youngest niece. With that I unleashed a torrent. The Harry Potter films were satanic. The Harry Potter books were satanic. No, no, I argued gently; like Lord of the Rings, they show the triumph of good over evil, after much suffering and conflict. That's a good moral tale for children, surely? Apparently not so. Lord of the Rings was satanic as well. While babysitting her grandson, she was afraid demons would come out of the Harry Potter books and the Lord of the Rings DVDs in the child's bedroom. So she'd taken the whole lot of books and DVDs into the garden and set fire to them. Her son wasn't pleased with her. He wouldn't let her babysit any more. But she'd do it again. You couldn't be too careful. There were bad spirits everywhere. Sprinkling salt on the doorstep would keep them out of your house. That's what she did to keep the demon alcohol out of her house.

The other lady nodded agreement with a lot of that, although she drew the line at burning children's books. She was of the opinion that it wasn't just spirits you had to look out for. There was technology that meant our conversation could be heard through our mobile 'phones, even if they were switched off. Spy agencies had it. The good thing was they could be outwitted with tinfoil…

175

I sat on the concrete plinth of the statue wondering if I should make a dash for my car before the monastery gates were closed and locked. I'd have to get my stuff and the car keys from my room first. How long would it take...?

Just then, the church bells rang the call to last prayers of the day. It was my excuse to leg it. I flew down the paths faster than bad spirits could fly.

In the church I said all sorts of prayers I'd never said before – including prayers for safety from demons and spy agencies... After prayers, back in the Common Room, people made tea. Life shrunk back to normality. Tea. Biscuits. Chit chat. I relaxed a bit.

I was standing at the kitchen sink washing my teacup when a smiling monk came into the room. The ordained monks don't usually enter the Guesthouse. This one made a beeline straight for me. "Are you the Rose of Tralee?" he asked. "What?" I said, bewildered. "Are you the Rose of Tralee? We heard there was a lady who was a Rose of Tralee staying, and we thought it must be you". "No, I'm not the Rose of Tralee, Father" I said, even more bewildered. "Oh, well, goodnight" he said, turned on his heel and left. Hello? What was going on? The enclosed monks must have seen the guests arriving and had decided "The Rose" had to be me. Which was very flattering in a way. But...gossip in the cloister? They obviously knew more than their prayers! Funny to think of them behind closed doors wondering who the most likely candidate for Rose of Tralee was...Events were getting more bizarre by the minute.

A young priest guest sat at the table beside me. I really like your shoes, he said. What type of shoes are they?

They're called ballet pumps, Father, I said. Oh, do you do ballet? No, I replied. It's just what they're called…

I said goodnight, went up to my bedroom, checked the door was securely locked (twice) and closed and locked the windows for good measure. I hadn't been in the place six hours…and I'd booked myself in for 4 days of this…stone cold sober…

Day 2; the bells, the bells…

Ah the bells, the bells… They rang at 3.45 a.m. for the first prayers at 4 a.m. Not that I had slept much. Someone, somewhere, was snoring their horrible head off. Despite earmuffs and exhaustion, the noise of the bells woke me good and proper. In fact, I thought there was a good chance that the residents of the local cemetery had been woken up as well.

Did I want to get up and flit through the Guesthouse, through the secret door, across the silent chapel, along the cloister and into the big chapel for the 4 a.m. prayers? No I did not. I wanted the bells to stop, I wanted the snoring to stop and I wanted to sleep.

Eventually I dozed off, to be woken by the next Carillion heralding the 8 a.m. prayer and chanting. I gave in and got up. Sat in the church with my head on my arms, trying not to fall asleep and out of the hard wooden pew. All I wanted to do was go back to bed. As soon as the religious observances and breakfast were over, that's exactly what I was going to do. The reflection, meditation and whatever you're having yourself would have to wait till I was less tired and less damn cranky.

Breakfast was a buffet affair. Jugs of orange juice and packets of cereal from which you helped yourself, were then followed by heaps of bread, butter and jam and gallons of tea. Like the Dormouse in Alice in Wonderland, I was in danger of falling asleep with my head stuck in a teapot. Breakfast conversation proved to be as interesting as the previous night's supper conversation; this time it was the likelihood of aliens as well as foreign governments watching us, and whether tinfoil was sufficient to keep their alpha waves out of our brains so we didn't inadvertently get brainwashed... A very nice man took an interest in me; he offered to sit with me in church and explain all about the psalms, chanting, and so on. He also said he was going to give levitation lessons in the pretty Summer House on the lawn. "Isn't there a health and safety issue there?" I said. "Shouldn't you have crash helmets ready in case people hit their heads off the ceiling?"

So...dishes handed back in through the serving hatch and table wiped, I headed for the bed. I stayed there till lunchtime alternately dozing and reading "When things fall apart" – written by a Buddhist monk.

I got up in time for dinner served at lunchtime; hearty vegetable soup, heaped plates of potatoes fresh out of the ground with bits of clay still sticking to them here and there, bowls of steaming cabbage freshly picked and boiled, and dinner plates holding 2 thick slices of bacon followed each other out of the hatch. Delicious. Followed by homemade apple pie and lumpy custard, just like you'd make at home. Well, I would. Some people's custard isn't lumpy. Their lives probably aren't lumpy either.

Afterwards I sat in the garden. Too antsy to stay there long, I hopped in the car and went for a drive. So much for sitting in the tranquil grounds and meditating. I went to the seaside instead. Then I did a tour of a castle. Then I went to an Art Exhibition. Then I stopped in a village and bought sweets. Then I went back to the monastery, arriving just in time for the 4 p.m. session.

The sun streamed through stained glass windows. The monks chanted, their voices rising and falling. My new friend sat close beside me, sharing his Psalter and explaining what each section of plain chant signified. I left the church feeling very peaceful.

All the guests walked back to the Guesthouse for a cup of afternoon tea. Somehow things ended up in a heated discussion. Somehow I ended up in the middle of it. I couldn't sit there and hear people deny that child abuse had gone on in church-run schools. I couldn't listen to them state that victims were only people looking for a way to get money. I had to speak up.

I found myself in a minority of one. Luckily the conversation changed to people who can talk in tongues. (As opposed to with tongues in the normal way of things?) Some of the guests had witnessed such happenings. More stuff about spirits and demons! I was getting very spooked. My newfound but short-lived serenity shredded along with my nerves. What did my new and learned friend and the young priest with the penchant for ballet pumps think? They were of the opinion that you had to invite such bad things in. So I was safe, apart from the fact that I was beginning to think I was surrounded by lunatics. And I'd been worried about coping with 4 days of silence…

My new friend asked for my room number. He wished to escort me to the 4 a.m. session next morning.

179

Apparently it was something special... As a child I'd gone to the 6 a.m. Christmas Mass with my father. I wasn't mad about that either. But yes, it certainly would be special for me to be getting up at 3.45 a.m. I'd normally be going to bed at that hour after a night out.

No thank you, I said, reluctant to give my room number, the bells will wake me, nothing surer, and I'll fly along the corridors and make my way to the chapel myself. (Thinking; if I can manage to rouse myself).

I went to bed, having double checked the door and windows locks. If I'd had salt I might well have sprinkled it on the doorstep.

Day 3; the Silent Chapel

When the bells rang at 3.45 a.m. I staggered up out of the bed and dressed in the warmest clothes I'd brought; i.e. ALL the clothes I'd brought. A tee-shirt under a sweater under a fleece. Jeans, socks and trainers. Quietly I unlocked the door and peered out into the corridor. Empty. Good! Off I ran on silent feet through dimly lit corridors and down staircases to the unlocked door in the wall. Into a tiny chapel where the only light came from still-burning candles now flickering down to their wicks. On into the main church, where only the main lights over the nave gave illumination. The church was very cold. There were just two of us in the pews. The monks filed into individual choir stalls and turned on little reading lights attached to the lecterns. The praising of God began. My new friend Henry of the Levitation Lessons sat beside me, whispering explanations of the order and parts to the singing. As it ended and the monks filed out of the church, dawn was beginning to light the stained glass windows of the apse.

180

The ceremony had been beautiful. Praise and thanks for a new day. Now I could flit back to bed. Oh no I couldn't! It seemed Henry and I were going to hear Mass. Apparently a very elderly monk who liked to do his own thing, said Mass after the first prayers of the day, the Invitatory Prayers I'd just witnessed. So back to the tiny side chapel where the two of us sat in the light of flickering candles and waited for the swish of robes...

After the Mass (attendance; 2), breakfast was chocolate cake and tea in the Guest House kitchen. The Maverick Monk who said his own Mass in the chapel came. So there I was at half past five in the morning eating chocolate cake with a monk and a fellow guest. Let's just say, I learned a lot about the monastic life. It was daylight when I fell into the bed, full of calmness, spirituality, and chocolate cake. Still hadn't sorted out my head, but, well, there was time yet.

In the interests of quiet reflection, I brought my book to the Summer House. Ordered myself to sit quietly and just read. Be spiritual. Reflect. Breathe deeply. What I didn't know until I entered the pretty little building was that the Summer House was the Smoking House, and not for kippers or salmon. It reeked. I sat on the veranda. Still coughed – but this was due to the fact that two smokers had taken up residence on the bench beside me....have people no consideration? The damn cottage was already ruined, why not just go in there for a puff and leave the outdoor benches for non-smokers? Stop... I'm here to learn Patience. Charity. Unselfishness.... Feeling very impatient and very uncharitable, I made a beeline for the car and took off so impatiently that I practically did a hand brake turn. Another spiritual exam failed! I won't be getting canonised any time soon. Ah, but there was compensation for my failure; fish and chips by the seaside.

Day 4; Farewell to the Mountain

Up at 3.45 a.m. again and not feeling wrecked! Working hard at acquiring serenity and spiritual whatever.

Later in the morning, I made my way, on my own, up to the Cross. Heard noises as if something were coming up the path after me. Alone on the mountain, my heart was in my throat. Indeed, something was coming up the path after me- two somethings. A pony and a donkey. The donkey was in pitiful condition. His hooves were so overgrown that he could barely walk. The poor thing was in need of urgent veterinary attention. Later enquiries ascertained that the mountain and any animals thereon belonged to a local woman with a reputation for being difficult.

I made my way down to the Guesthouse, packed and tidied up in preparation for an early afternoon departure. I was leaving feeling not very different to when I had arrived. I had met some very interesting people (to say the least) and gained huge respect for the strength of belief that kept this community of monks in this life day after day, year after year.

Final task; donation envelope to be filled. The advice given was to donate whatever you would pay for Bed and Breakfast in an ordinary guesthouse. Or less - whatever you could afford. I gave what I thought a hotel would cost; I thought it the least I could do in return for the experience I'd had. I also added a note requesting the Brothers to please, please, look for the little donkey and

182

have it attended to. I'd have made reference to the little donkey of Bethlehem if I'd thought it would strengthen my plea.

Goodbyes said and envelope slipped into the Guest Master's post-box, I was heading out of the secret garden when I heard my name being called. The Guest Master was hurrying down the path, robes flapping. Very taken aback, I wondered what could be wrong. Had I not left enough money for my stay? Had he taken offence at my requesting help for the poor creature on the mountain? This is what he said when he caught up with me: "I couldn't let you leave without complimenting you on the state you left your room in. It was spotless. Thank You."

I was speechless. The fact that the elderly Brother practically ran down the garden to thank me, begs the question; what state do other guests leave their accommodation in? Are they partying and trashing the rooms? Perhaps he finds rooms lined with tinfoil tacked to the walls in order to keep the mind readers away? The thought of him having to shovel piles of anti-demon salt away from the doorsteps of bedrooms sent me into an unseemly fit of the giggles.

My four days and nights had not been silent, quiet, or enclosed. On the contrary, they'd been action packed. I'd climbed, gotten up at 3.45 a.m., had chocolate cake for breakfast with a monk, met people who talked in tongues and made day trips to castles and the seaside. And that wasn't the half of it.

I left the monastery and drove home, singing along to the Gregorian chant CD, until I took a wrong turning.

After that, only The Eagles could help me fly along when I eventually got back on track.

FOODSTUFF

The Domestic Goddess topples off her plinth...

It's a Sunday afternoon. In between slurping hangover cures, lying on the sofa and looking up the signs of alcoholism on the Web, I decide to make something simple for dinner. There is a recipe in the Foolproof Cookbook for baked potatoes. I take out two enormous potatoes from yesterday's shopping. As instructed I use a large knife to score lines across them from side to side and then rub sea salt into the lines. Into the oven they go, on a wire rack. As they are very big potatoes I decide to increase the temperature a few degrees and leave them baking for a bit longer than the recipe states. Three hours later I have the steak grilling as His Lordship's key turns in the lock. I put the steak and peas out on the plates with the potatoes. The potatoes are a bit overdone. Well they're black actually. Big black things with lighter coloured stripes. He stares at his plate. "We are having giant woodlice for dinner?"

NIGHTSTUFF

The dark teatime of the soul...

In one of my favourite books, The Hitchhiker's Guide to the Galaxy, Douglas Adams wrote not of the dark night of the soul, but the dark teatime of the soul. Usually, even in the blackest of darknesses, there are flashes of light, of humour that somehow leaven the unbearable to the just bearable. One of the worst times of my life was when my mother passed away. As she lay in her coffin, a woman approached me and said "She looks marvellous! I never saw your mother looking better!" She was DEAD. How could she look worse? But at the same time I understood and saw the funny side of that remark.

The blackest, darkest journeys I have been on have been in my dreams. Night terrors- journeys through endless darkness, nights when I startle awake, drenched, heart in my throat, then relief flooding through me that I have escaped. But I never know what it is that I have escaped from, or from which abyss my dreaming soul has climbed once more. I never know. No matter how hard I scrape the walls of my memory, there is no image available to me of where, or what, this darkness is or what it might contain. Shadows hang like cobwebs in my memory. I do not know how I enter it, or exit it. I only know it is as real to me as the velvet darkness of a night without stars, or the cosy darkness of my own bedroom through which I move easily without need of light.

On nights when my sleep is fractured by such dreams, and the jagged edges of nightmare tear at my imagination, I comfort myself by saying it's just a dark teatime of the soul, and that a trip to the kitchen for a glass of water will break the spell and drive the shadows away.

HOLIDAY STUFF

Bush Camp...

We had disembarked from a nice big Jumbo (excellent safety record) and now were off to a Bush Camp in South Africa... A man in a uniform that wouldn't have disgraced an admiral ushered us towards a plane the size of an oversized gnat. As someone with more phobias than a psychiatrist's handbook, I was now faced with two big ones together; Claustrophobia and Aerophobia. First lesson; you never get a holiday from your neuroses. They always pack their little neurotic cases and go too.

Due to bottle bravery engendered by large amounts of alcohol, I had agreed to go on a safari with my other half, a cousin and my cousin's lovely English partner. My cousin was a globe trotter who had contacts everywhere. She had done the research for our trip, including booking a private plane to take us from Johannesburg to "The Camp". Apparently she and he were used to this type of thing. Now it was really happening for me, I was panicking.

I was rooting in my bag for Xanax when Himself grabbed me by the belt loops (what he had the nerve to call the hasp of my arse) and shovelled me into the gnat. The little Alice in Wonderland door closed and we went trundling down the runway. (Only ONE pilot! - what if he had a heart attack?) I pulled my new safari hat over my eyes and prayed. The hoppity-skippity plane lifted and rattled its way into the sky so slowly that I thought it would fall back down.

After a while the chatter started; "Pass my other lens darling." "Oh look, elephants." I lifted the brim of my hat and chanced a glance out the window. Surprisingly, the vertigo wasn't too bad. We weren't miles high, and the view was incredible. Plains. A bendy river. The little plane seemed quite steady. I was Meryl Streep in "Out of Africa"!

After what seemed an eternity we reached our landing zone - a grassy rectangle in the middle of nowhere. I didn't need to worry about the landing gear not coming down because the little wheels were fixed and never went up in the first place. A few bumps and we were down. I offered a prayer of thanks and posed on the dinky steps having my photo taken, channelling Meryl like you wouldn't believe.

There was no Landover to meet us… Five minutes later we saw dust rising. Only this Landover wasn't for us. Its driver radioed our camp. Our guys were on their way, allegedly. Another small plane taxied in. The Landrover loaded up its guests and left. I now discovered an unknown advantage to being 5'4". I could stand upright in the shade under the wings. Everyone else just had to suffer the blistering heat of an African noon.

Relief… Our pilot assured us that he was not allowed to leave until we were collected by someone.

More dust rising. Yes! No. A truck rumbled past. Five minutes later hopes rose again as dust blew from the opposite direction. But it was only the truck coming back. The driver stuck his head out the window. "Just thought I should let you know, there are four lions in the road about 25 metres down". He reversed and continued his journey. Oh my God. "No worries" said the Admiral. "If the lions come up the road we all just get back in the plane". That's alright then. Or maybe we pelt them with our bottles of sun lotion? Can't they smell us? They can. But in the heat of the day they sleep. Oh that's fine so. I stood back in under the wing, necking the bottle of Xanax.

Forty five minutes after we landed, "our" Landrover finally hove into view. The driver offered no apology for leaving us sweltering under the sun and in the company of lions. We set off on the 20 minute drive to Camp. Twenty minutes. Not forty five minutes. Not impressed.

The Manageress was showing us round our hut of clay and wattle made. Here was the loo - behind one side of the bedhead. The shower and washbasin were behind the other side of the bedhead, beside the backdoor. But there was no backdoor. No curtain. Nothing. Just a large hole in the wall. Authentic hut it might be, but my heart sank.

She continued; there was no electricity. Here are two windup torches. What about the hole in the wall? Snakes? "Oh snakes don't come into camp" she said. Oh really? Is there a notice on the fence written in the 11 official languages of South Africa to the effect that snakes are not allowed?

"Snakes don't come in" she repeated. "But if a snake should appear, just blow the whistle hanging above the bed and we'll come with the snake stick". Dear Heaven. There actually was a whistle hanging on the wall, half obscured by mosquito net. That's alright then. "See you at Reception at 4.15". We were booked in for five days of this...

Cousin and boyfriend emerged from their hut, as unimpressed as I was. We can't stay here, she kept saying. But we were booked in for 5 nights. This was what we wanted, wasn't it? An authentic experience? I was dreading it.

We went on the afternoon drive with our very young Ranger and even younger Tracker. Bouncing over bush, shrub and rock for hour after hour. Finally the jeep stopped beside a tree, underneath which two lionesses lay lollapanzi. We sat and watched the girlies as they snoozed. With that, our Professional Guide broke the cardinal rule of safari;

189

Never, ever, interfere with the wildlife in any way.

He stood up on the driver's seat and shook the branches.

The great head of an adult male who had been lying invisible in the long grass, shot up. As did the lionesses. The four of us patsies exchanged glances. But the fun was only beginning. Our tour guides decided to let sleeping lions lie and drove on. Next stop; 20 metres from the shore of a waterhole, where we spotted three hippos wallowing in the muddy water. Guide and Tracker jumped out and walked right up to the water, where they stood imitating the Eh-Eh-Eh of a hippo call. When that didn't rouse the mammals to put on a show, they picked up fallen branches and started beating the water with them. We were in hysterics of laughter until one of the hippos opened a mouth as big as a coffin and started moving. The boyos legged it back and we reversed away. Only later did we realize that not alone were they in danger from the hippos or any passing predator, but we were too. It never occurred to us while we were crying with laughter, that lions hunt prey from the rear. They could have lifted one of us off the back of the jeep and Laurel and Hardy wouldn't have noticed.

The drive continued, with sightings of one elephant and one tree squirrel before we stopped again. Our Tracker had spotted a particular bird with a show-stopping routine; it shot up into the sky like an arrow, and then plunged down to the ground like a stone. Yet again our deranged Ranger stood up and shook branches. The bird shot up into the sky and plummeted. Delighted with himself, our Ranger did it again. Once again the poor bird shot up and plunged head first to the ground. Dear God. Was there no end to their craziness?

190

We drove back to Camp while the sun went down like a Plummeting Bird.

Winding our torches like crazy, we picked our way to the dining area. Lovely! My first safari dinner on the savannah. Lanterns and candles were placed on tables. It was very nice until suddenly all hell broke loose. Like a Biblical plague, a blizzard of insects engulfed us. Moths. Flies. Mosquitos. Beetles. Ants. They were doing the backstroke round my wineglass. They were surfing in my water. Perhaps because of my pale skin (Factor 50 - can't be too careful) and light-coloured hair, I attracted them in their hundreds. There was no getting away from it; we were at the Ugly Bugs Ball and I was the Belle of it. My blouse was covered in bugs; I was wearing the bloody things like brooches. A massive stick insect stuck itself to my wine bottle. The others were fishing around for swimmers in their glasses of red wine when BANG! The black carapace of a cockroach hit my plate. The thing wasn't even concussed. It righted itself, waddled through my risotto and fell off the edge of the plate to join the throngs swarming across the tablecloth. Cousin's Boyfriend had a praying mantis perched on top of his head like a tiara. We had come to see the wild life and now we were wearing it.

Insects whirred and crashed around in the bedlam until at last woven blinds were pulled down from the thatched roof and the blizzard eased. We got fresh plates of risotto. Aided by copious amounts of drink our nerves settled and we saw the funny side.

Much later; Cousin and I were revving our torches like mad and clinging to each other. She was worrying like crazy about snakes. I was worrying about everything. As

191

we said goodnight, her partner's dry English wit came out of the darkness; "Hopefully, you'll both survive the night".

In our hut, we turned down the oil lamp and crawled into bed. Next lesson; night time is day time in Africa. Everything sleeps during the day and comes out at night looking for action. Grasshoppers chirping, birds shrieking, lions roaring, baboons brawling and God knows what else. The Ugly Bugs Ball had turned into Temple Bar on a Saturday Night. Eventually, exhausted by travel, insects and drink, I fell asleep. After such an intake of wine, I had no option but to crawl out again and creep round the headboard.

I was hoping there were no other occupants behind the beaded curtain that nothing had slithered or crawled in through the hole in the wall. Luckily for me, I was alone behind the headboard.

Morning came extra early. It glared in between every crack in the walls. I had a hangover. I'd had very little sleep. Still, we were alive and unharmed. We might make it through the remaining days after all. Provided a lion didn't lift us off the jeep and the hippos stayed in the water.

Sun Factored up, I set off for breakfast and met - a snake. I jumped with fright and fell over a rock. The green boomsling was hidden by bush again before I hit the ground. Ever wondered why people can't get away from snakes, since we have legs and they don't? Olympic speed. That snake was faster than Sonia O'Sullivan on a good day. It was obviously illiterate as well.

Cousin was standing outside Reception, smoking (having given up months before) and talking on her mobile.

I could only assume that she had contacts in the CIA and was using their communications satellite because I knew there was no signal in the Camp. I'd already testing ringing 999.

"Never slept a wink. We're out of here" she said. This is where her real genius showed itself. She had already organized a transfer to a fabulous Game Lodge in the Timbavati Reserve, called Kings Camp. Relief bubbled through me. I left her to explain our new plans to the Manager and ran to pack.

Dragging my case to Reception I encountered two staff members. Was I imagining a distinct chill? I felt bad; there was nothing wrong with the Camp. I was the wimp who fell at the first fence, or in this case at the first snake.

Two jeep transfers and another hoppity-skippity plane later (no Xanax) and we arrived at a fabulous Lodge west of the Kruger Park. We were escorted to a gorgeous rondavel with mullioned windows, like a gingerbread house African style. All doorframes contained doors. No whistles. No snake sticks.

Later that afternoon, the four of us sat on the veranda, warding off malaria with gin and tonic. Vervet monkeys perched on the balustrade. Summer-coloured weaver birds peered out from nests hanging like brown raindrops from trees dotting the lawn in front of us. A heat haze shimmered golden in the hot, still air. At the water hole King Fisher sat on his leafy throne observing a solitary elephant throw water over his leathery elephant head. It was bliss.

"By the way, Cousin," I said. "What did they say when you told them we were leaving the Camp? Did you explain that you were absolutely terrified in the place?" Without missing a beat she replied; "Oh God no. I told them YOU were."

Over the next four days I got up close and personal with the Big 5 and the Little 5 (more insects). Drank sundowners on the savannah. Grew used to making trepidatious comfort stops behind bushes. Hell, I even went on a bush walk and didn't panic. Well not much. My inner Meryl was emerging day by day.

Sometimes under the mackerel sky of a Dublin evening I picture orange-gold sunsets. Final Lesson; they say if you visit Africa you always long to go back. It's true. I left a part of my heart there. What I didn't realize at the time was that I also left my fear there.

ROMANCE n' STUFF

This is a piece of flash fiction I wrote.

The last dog days of summer...

The last days of summer dripped slow and golden like honey from a spoon. Those days were just as sweet, made more so perhaps, as I saw passion slowly fade from his eyes as summer fades like smoke into the fall. Those long summer days when light and love seemed endless were drawing to a close.

The arc of summer had crossed the sky and now was dropping slowly into gold and crimson sunsets. Lush green curled up into brown slumber. The god of harvest

194

drew   yellow drapes across a summer of crystal chandeliers, cool sheets and gauzy curtains stirred by the breath of a wind that carried the faint scent of orange blossom.

He would leave. Gently. Politely. But leave he would. For him it was a summer fling. But it would fling me towards the darkness and doubt of winter, as the approaching hands of autumn would fling the leaves from the trees and then scatter the first sprinkle of snow upon the stripped earth. I had known from the beginning. Known but not acknowledged.

He would not stay forever. This was understood. But his way of understanding was not mine. Always did his gaze focus outward, his attention caught by the clamour of his business world; always did mine focus within, upon the world that lay between the two of us. It is ever thus with men and women.

When summer had arrived in a new dress and the sky was always blue and the earth always soft, it had been so easy. So easy to lie on a bed of sweet, park grass and know nothing except the sensuality of his brown eyes looking down into mine. Cocooned. Warm ground beneath me, his body warm beside me and his arm flung casually across me.

But... almost imperceptively, as bit by bit the months stole minutes from the sun's span, so did the intensity of feeling leach from his embrace. I knew this. But I would not acknowledge it. I knew, for him, memories of me would fade to sepia like the gently fading pictures in a child's book of fairy tales and he would turn his gaze back to the world and the new. But it would not be so for me.

195

Unless the coming winter wheels in its wake bright ribbons of spring that will unfurl across the winds and draw him back to me again...

DUBLIN STUFF

Out and About in Dublin...

I don't usually pick up hitchhikers, but at 11 p.m. the January night was bitterly cold and dark and the rain was torrential. I was driving the back roads behind Dublin Airport, taking a shortcut home from a committee meeting which had dragged on far too long. At the unlit stretch of country road near the junction of St. Margaret's Road and Dunbro Lane, my headlights picked up a car with darkened windows parked on the left side of the road, in front of which stood a woman waving me down.

Oh God. What to do? If it were me, I'd want someone to stop and help. I pulled in, locked the doors, and lowered the passenger window about half way down. She was wearing pyjamas, tracksuit jacket and sneakers with no socks on, on such a cold and rainy night. "I'm out of petrol" she said. "Can you bring me to a garage?" I hesitated. "OK," I said, "Hop in". I unlocked the doors, she got in and I drove off, only then thinking that she might have a knife concealed on her person, a gun even. Plus she was a lot heftier than me, not to mention a lot younger as well. I put the boot down and drove the dark roads as fast as I could. My passenger made several calls on her mobile. All she seemed to have in her hands was her 'phone and a roll of notes, no handbag, no purse. "Four cars passed" she said. "You're the only one to stop. Thanks very much." Then followed a rambling tale of visiting Balbriggan, her sister's

196

children, she lived near Blanchardstown, all sorts of things. Nothing that explained why she was in a car with darkened windows on the back roads of North County Dublin at 11 p.m. on a bitter January night.

I was very relieved when at last I pulled into the service station in Glasnevin. She thanked me again and got out. I drove home, relieved, to be told I was all sorts of a fool, what was I thinking, there could have been men hidden in the car or behind it etc. All of which was true. But I'd done what I'd done, and that was that, and everything had turned out ok.

Two weeks later the body of a drug dealer was found in the ditch on Dunbro Lane. It had been there for a while. I like to think she had nothing to do with that.

DUBLINERS

This is a piece of fiction; the characters are composites of Dublin people I have met over the years.

She had arthritis, and headed off to Lanzarote every October....

"I'm a martyr to the arteritis", she'd say as she boarded the big green Aer Lingus bird. She'd be wearing a floral blouse from Guiney's shop in Talbot Street and Capri pants that were not flattering to the stout Dublin legs that stood at the stall in Moore Street for 60 years. She had started as a child on her mother's stall. On Mondays she sold the vegetables that had been stored in boxes under the bed when they'd been returned unsold on Saturday. "Just give them a spray of water" her mother would say. "That'll freshen them up". She forbore to mention to her mother that they needed more than freshening up, having spent the weekend under the bed in the company of her Granda's chamber pot. "What nobody knows about, nobody gets upset about", her mother would say.

Over the years she sold vegetables on Saturday, Monday and Tuesdays, Fish Wednesday and Friday, fruit and flowers from Smithfield Market on Thursday. She absorbed the hardworking ethos of her mother and grandmother through her pores, along with the fish smells, the rotting vegetable smells, and the flower scents she loved. Sometimes on Sunday, her day off, her mother would send her to Glasnevin Graveyard with leftover flowers. These were given to her aunt who sold flowers outside the black iron gates of the Cemetery. Her aunt would mix them in with her own newer, fresher blooms. Use them to pad out her bouquets. In return, her aunt would give her a few bob for herself. She didn't have to hand up this money to her father; she was allowed to keep the flower money, as it was called, for herself. What money she could save went into a Credit Union Account, against the day when the handsome stranger of her quiet dreams would stop by her stall and notice her, see her, not her wares, nor pay any heed to the floral pinafore smeared with fish scales nor her chapped, red hands.

Day after day, week after week, year after year, she worked on the stall. She had been taken from school early, although she was clever enough. "I need her" her mother had told the nuns. "Her father's - well he doesn't earn much, you see".

When she was old enough, her mother took her on the annual parish pilgrimage to Lourdes. That was their holiday. She loved the trips to Lourdes. The singing on the plane, the sunshine, the hotel where all your meals were handed to you and you didn't have to do a thing, not even make your bed. She even liked the nightly torch lit procession with candles in paper lanterns, always followed by singsongs and Baby Cham in the residents' lounge of the Hotel Jean Marie.

Long years passed for her, standing in the rain, the cold, the sleet, the snow, the wind, and the summer weather that was all too short. The joints in her hands began to enlarge, to pain her. Her back began to bother her. Even the knees that had done such service began to give trouble. Osteoporosis. Arthritis. Nothing could be done to reverse it. Only pain management and hot, dry weather might help. She could no longer tie the bunches of flowers, fillet the fish, string together the fairy lights sold with the poinsettias throughout December.   Her fingers grew too stiff, too clumsy.

The Public Health Nurse and the Doctor arranged for her to get a Disability Allowance, and then came her Old Age Pension. The bathroom of her small Corporation flat in Hardwicke Street was adapted, the old enamel bath taken out and a step-in shower cubicle put in. She managed well. She had continued her savings, always hoping, always dreaming, but when the years caught up with her and she knew the possibility, the hope of children was past, she started travelling.

The hot, dry dust, the black volcanic rock of Lanzarote warmed her to her core, brought some long forgotten suppleness to her hands. Always she stayed in the same hotel in Costa Teguise where she could sit by the pool or go for a paddle in the sea. She did not swim, could not risk immersing herself in the enormous waves stirred by the sirocco winds blowing from the coast of West Africa. At night the hotel entertained her; Monday and Wednesday Bingo with really good prizes, Tuesday local music or a Flamenco Show, Thursday and Sunday Family Games Night. On Saturdays she went to the local Irish Pub and sat at the bar, chatting to all comers. She was still hoping that Prince Charming or, she'd say, at this stage of her life, Prince Charming's Granddad might yet stop by and notice her in her floral frock and embroidered cardigan. "You can't beat Guiney's for style", she'd say.

200

THE NEXT DOOR NEIGHBOURS' STUFF

The Memorial Hall...

In November last year I was up in Northern Ireland, staying in a little seaside town for the weekend. Friday night was spent in the Kings Arms, giving it large. On Saturday the friend with whom we were staying had some banking business to transact. Up there the bank staff actually work on Saturdays so the three of us drove to the big town, in the heartland of Norn Iron Unionism. I left the other two queuing in the Bank and wandered round the town centre, a plaza whose centre was an imposing Town Hall. Above its doors an inscription read "Memorial Hall".

I stopped to read the inscriptions on the Memorial/Town Hall, from Her Majesty's loyal subjects. Then I read all the labels on all the poppy wreaths left on the steps in memory of the loyal sons of Ulster who had marched not on the 12th July but off to two world wars, Aden, the Falklands, Afghanistan and various other conflagrations from which they never marched back. I was about to bless myself and say a little prayer for them when I remembered where I was and that that action might not best the best idea in the circumstances so I strolled on around the perimeter. Ah! Chairs! Somewhere to sit! My back was beginning to ache from all the standing around and walking around. Although there were stone benches set into the perimeter of the square, they were soaked from the rain which had fallen steadily over the course of the weekend. Some kind souls who stood with a banner proclaiming them to be members of an evangelical Christian movement had put folding chairs in front of the Hall. They were handing out leaflets as well. I'm sure they won't mind if I sit down for a minute, I thought to myself.

So I eased myself down onto the nearest chair. With that, a lady came over to me. "I hope you don't mind" I said, "It's just that my back is aching". With that three others of the flock came over. Before I knew what was happening, one was standing behind me with his hands on my head, two others were standing one each side of me with their hands on my arms, and the Chief Evangelist herself crouched in front of me. "We're going to ask for your backache to be taken away" she said. With that she grabbed my jeans-clad legs and pulled. It was fortuitous that the other three had a good hold on me; otherwise I'd have ended up on my bottom on the wet cobblestones. "I see why you have backache" said the High Priestess. "One of your legs is shorter than the other". This came as news to me. With that she pulled on the (presumably) shorter leg while they all prayed in unison for the Holy Spirit to come and sort me out. All this in the middle of a busy Saturday afternoon. In the middle of a busy town....There were now six of them holding various parts of my anatomy and praying aloud.

Out of the corner of my eye, I spotted my two travelling companions, doubled over with laughter at the edge of the Square.

Finally, we were done. "Now" they said, "how do you feel? Is the back pain gone?" "Oh yes" I replied – "Thank you very much, that's wonderful". After a chat about miracles, healing and conduits of the Divine mercy, they released their holds on me and I rose from the chair. I left with leaflets and an invitation to their church service. I forbore to ask if they could cure my hangover. I didn't think it right to have the just punishment for drinking too much removed from me. I crossed the Square to the other two. "Only you..." they said and the pair of them crying with laughter. "Only you..."

With the back fixed I walked till I could find a pharmacy where the purchase of Solpadeine Soluble worked another miracle.

HOME STUFF

The Domestic Goddess does Christmas...

I have no idea what happened. I followed the recipe although as I don't possess weighing scales I had to do a bit of guesswork with the quantities. Beat the eggs milk and sugar together, folded in the sifted flour, sprinkled in the handful of raisins, handful of sultanas and two packets of cherries (don't you just love sticky red cherries in a fruit cake), bashed it all round in a big saucepan as I don't seem to possess a mixing bowl either. Lots of whiskey was consumed by me and the cake which meant we were both well moisturized. Into the tin with the mixture, into the oven, time to relax in front of the fire with the remains of the whiskey and the Westminster Choir singing Christmas carols. Lovely.

Anyway to cut a long story lengthways, when the cake came out it had risen to a height of approximately one inch, despite the weight of ingredients in it. It had the density of a Black Hole. All it needed was an event horizon. So what, I said to myself. There's good stuff in it. I'll ice it anyway.

So the rich fruity pancake got plastered with apricot jam. Then I rolled out the ready-pack of marzipan using a glass since there didn't seem to be a rolling pin available. The cupboard was devoid of icing sugar as well so I used ordinary sugar- well its white; surely the only difference must be the granular density?

After draping the lovely yellow sweet stuff over the cake, I had to do a tricky bit of cutting and pasting. The marzipan kept falling off the sides of the cake; it just wouldn't please me by sticking to the bloody apricot jam. I was beginning to get annoyed – in the end I hammered the bloody stuff into the cake with the back of a steel spoon.

Next; the white icing. (Never be fobbed off with Dundee cake and the like; if someone offers you Christmas cake, it must have marzipan aka almond paste, white icing and be adorned with at least one of the following; a fir tree, a reindeer or a Santa. Otherwise it's just plain ordinary fruit cake.)

I followed the instructions to mix the contents of the packet with water and then spread it over the cake with a flat knife. It sorted of poured over the cake actually. Very messy stuff. Job finished, I left it on the kitchen counter to set, and went back to the Westminster Choirboys and the whiskey. Baking in a hot kitchen is thirsty work.

Half an hour later, back into the kitchen ready for the final touches; planting the fir tree, the Santa, the eight little reindeer and the sleigh full of toys onto the pristine whiteness…

A winter wonderland awaited me, but not the one I expected… The icing had flowed down over the cake all right. It had continued flowing down over the cake plate, the worktop and the floor. Icicles of royal icing hung like stalactites from the worktop. I wouldn't mind, but it hadn't set on the actual cake itself.

In the end I used a breadknife to prise the cake plate away from the worktop. The imploded cake supernova was transferred to the waiting plastic container. I stuck my little figurines into the top with all the force of a mountaineer sticking pitons into a glacier and hoped for the best.

I was back with the sofa, the whiskey and the choirboys when a thought struck me; maybe I'd better sample it. Just in case....

What can I say? It tasted as good as it looked.

Compliments of the season, if not compliments to the cook....

The true Spirit of Christmas...

The talk last week in the Bridge Club was all of making cakes, making puddings; making mince pies...I related the tale of my culinary misadventures. North was apparently a master of the kitchen table as well as of the Bridge table, where she certainly takes no prisoners. If you can read you can cook, she said. All you need to do is follow a recipe. I've never found it that simple, I say.

This week said Bridge Master approached me before the Turkey Competition began. See me after the game, she said. Make sure you speak to me before you go.

After being blitzed due to the fact that I and my partner (B Grade) were listed to play with the bloody A players, masters, grand masters and what have you, we knew there was no chance of a turkey. Or even the giblets. Or the bottle of wine, or the box of chocolates. There was only one thing for it. Hit the pub on the way home and de-stress/de-adrenalize/drown our sorrows. Before we left, I threaded my way between the tables and waited until the Grand Master addressed me. I have something for you, she said and with that, handed me a Christmas cake.

Thank you so much, I said as I hugged and kissed this person I only know from coming up against her in the Bridge Club and coming off worst at every encounter. What kindness. It's not iced, you'll have to do that yourself, she said. The cake was large, square and heavy; a real, proper Christmas cake. I thanked her again, and told her that I forgave her for annihilating me at the Bridge. Almost.

Ah here, you want jam on it...

Today I called in to Sister# 2 and explained my needs. Could she lend me a rolling pin? What do you mean; you don't have a rolling pin? What else don't you have? Have you a pastry brush to put the jam on the cake even? No I don't have a pastry brush. Well that's what you're getting for Christmas – what else don't you have? Well I don't have a vegetable brush either, I said. Bet you don't even have a bread knife, she said. Well I definitely don't have a bread bin I said. Or a wooden spoon, which is what someone told me, is essential to every kitchen…What! She was appalled at my lack of kitchen stuff.

By now Niece# 2, a witness to all this, is shrieking with laughter.

What would I use a pastry brush FOR? I ask. I don't make pastry. God you're hopeless, she said.

Not at all, it's completely logical. Plan A; buy packets of readymade marzipan, packets of readymade roll

- out icing (definitely not the water-to-be-added kind) icing sugar and more jam to stick it all to my new cake.

I left with a rolling pin and four cake ornaments; a Santa, a fir tree, a "Merry Christmas" sign and a holly leaf. Bring it on!

But nothing would do my lovely Bridge partner but that I bring the cake to her house to be decorated with her help. Cake decoration under the supervision of a responsible adult?

D Day! I stand amazed. Educated. In awe. She heated up the jam in a Bain Marie, cut out grease proof paper to the exact measurements of the cake sides/top, and spent ages rolling out the readymade marzo (she learned something too – that there was such a thing as readymade marzipan) and in one hour the cake was painted with warm sifted apricot jam using a regulation pastry brush and the marzo was applied – and didn't fall off. Apparently "The Cake" must now reside on her sideboard for a few days while today's paint job dries. Is this what Michelangelo had to do with the Sistine Chapel? Just askin.'

In a few days Step 3; the white icing can be overlaid. According to Bridge Partner, four ornaments are perfect for a square cake- one at each corner. So all will be shimmery symmetry... I'll take a photo when all is finished. Then I'm going to eat it. Well ok I'll try to restrain myself till Christmas Eve. But I'm not making any promises. Or maybe I'll break a bottle of champagne over it and launch it like the Titanic...

ANIMAL KINGDOM STUFF

This Committee is going to the dogs...

The Animal Welfare Charity Committee Meeting is in full swing; the discussion moves to producing a really nice calendar. As we don't have corporate sponsors for all of the twelve months someone suggests that we invite anyone who wishes, to submit a photo of their own pet and pay a small fee to have their little darling feature in the calendar as "Miss Doggy December or Miss Feline February or whatever. There then occurs a robust debate (to use committee-speak), as to whose dog is the best looking. The Chairperson and the Treasurer nearly come to blows as to whether Treasurer's Jack Russell terrier or Chairperson's walking shag pile of a collie is the prettiest. I can see trouble ahead here so I suggest we do a "Calendar Girls" job instead – i.e. topless volunteers holding strategically placed dogs, cats or even draped in collars and leads... Strangely, no one warms to my suggestion. The opposite, in fact. So now the calendar features twelve lovely girls who all have wet black noses, are completely covered in body hair and have six nipples each. And they're all really beautiful

Drama at the kitchen sink...

There certainly was drama at the kitchen sink, but not the type of drama John Osborne envisaged when he wrote "Look back in anger". Certainly my kitchen sink drama bore no resemblance to the sink estate, TV dramas of the 80s starring the working class. No, my kitchen sink drama included me, the cooker, the sink, the spaghetti Bolognese, and 3 others. Three mice in fact, and they weren't blind nor were they running up and down the clock.

They were doing laps round my kitchen. Here's what happened.

I lifted the pot of pasta off the hob and turned to the sink with the intention of draining it. Something black flickered at the corner of my peripheral vision. I thought it might be a spider until a black mouse ran from beneath the fridge, across my path and under the dishwasher. I was frozen to the spot. Next a browny black, bigger mouse emerged from the gap between the sink and the dishwasher, galloped across the floor and ran in reverse direction to the underside of the fridge. With that, a third mouse exited from under the fridge and ran across and into the gap between the dishwasher and the sink. They were doing laps! My skin crawled. Plus, I was cut off from escape. They were blocking my path to the back door and the door into the hall. Maria Callas would have had a hard job hitting the notes I hit as I stood in my own kitchen, trapped by rodents. What if there were more? If there were mice under the cooker, I was finished. I couldn't jump onto a kitchen stool; the mice were between me, the kitchen stools and even the countertop. Between the screaming and the clattering to the floor of the spaghetti pan as it fell from my shaking hands and hit the floor in a mess of stainless steel and organic gluten free ribbons of carbohydrate, the furry Husain Bolts were scared into stillness. Seizing the moment, I made a bolt for the door.

For days afterwards I only entered the kitchen when I absolutely had to, and only when my arrival was heralded by me singing, thumping the kitchen door, stamping, and sneaking a hand in to switch on the light before I entered, loudly. When in the kitchen, I made as much noise as possible, River dancing up and down the tiles for the time it took the kettle to boil. I lived on takeaways. The other non-rodent resident in the house was assigned the task of getting rid of the intruders, who in the meanwhile had also made their presence felt in the cupboards, on top of the counter, on top of the fridge…everywhere they left evidence of their passing. I thought I'd have a breakdown. Some atavistic instinct gives us fear of sudden movements not to mention fear of things that can run up your legs and will most definitely run over your food. In the end thirteen rodents were evicted from the building, none of them called Elvis. It took weeks for me not to feel severe trepidation every time I entered my kitchen, still festooned with ultrasonic mouse annoyers which sat in every plug socket going click, click, click. Of course what we should have been doing, according to Sister#2, was putting blessed relics of St, Martin in the places the mice frequented. I forbore to tell her that in that case, the entire kitchen including the insides of all the cupboards would have had to be wallpapered with relics. Thus endeth the drama of the kitchen sink. I'm not the better of it yet.

INFORMATION TECHNOLOGY
AND GEEK STUFF

Ah, the Interweb...never mind electronic spiders, here lurk geckos...

I have been prevented from posting to my own blog, my own blog, by a gecko. That's what the message said, the message that kept popping up in the middle of my screen like a demented meerkat. Something about compiling errors and 8 geckos...Certainly I have compiled plenty of errors in my life but... geckos? So I brought the machine to the Computer Clinic for Virally Transmitted Diseases and Geckos.

The PC Doctor didn't wear a white coat, was very colourful not to say floral in dress and was born in hotter climes than mine. He asked as doctors do, "What is the problem, Ma'am?" "There's a gecko in it" I said. "It's preventing me from accessing my blog". He didn't say "It's a picnic", i.e. problem-in-chair-not-in-computer. "Your computah requires much, much healing" he said. (His exact words. He was obviously taking the doctor thing seriously.) I asked how long it would take to get sorted. I had to trust someone with the blog stuff, otherwise how could I get it fixed? Who better than a professional IT person.

"Come back this afternoon aftah lunch – about three o'clock" he said. While I had waited for him to power up the machine and reach a diagnosis (10 bloody minutes) I looked at our surroundings; the Clinic was decorated with colourful Biblical drawings, and little framed sayings e.g. "The end is near." "Rejoice, the righteous shall see the face of God soon". Well, hopefully not too soon. Or at least not till I get my laptop back. The place was giving me the heebie-jeebies, although the shopkeeper wasn't. He seemed like a very nice man. He was obviously a man of deep religious conviction too. "How much?" I asked. The price equalled four bottles of good wine or 8 ½ bottles of cheap stuff. Ok. I came back at the appointed hour to find the shop closed. Decided to wait for a while, wondering where he was…

As I stood outside the shop in uncertainty a workman who was painting the shop front next door to the Clinic stood up from his task and spoke to me. "I wouldn't leave anything in there" he said. "That place is closing. The guy who runs the shop is leaving. I know the landlord of all these shops". Me laptop! Me secrets!

The 'phone number was on the shop sign so I rang it. Several times. Eventually he answered. Eventually he drove up, in a car filled to the brim with boxes and children. Maybe he did know something we didn't; maybe he was heading up the mountains to await the Second Coming. Never mind. We exchanged money and machine. So now I'm back in action. No geckos. The world hasn't ended yet either. Result.

Coda; The following morning the shop lay silent and shuttered. The Gecko re-appeared but doesn't seem to have found his way into Google Chrome. The world is still spinning.

NIGHT CLASSES IN INTERESTING STUFF

Focus on the breath...

In keeping with the recommendations in self-help books #1 and #3, which I am following religiously, I joined a Mindfulness Meditation class. The answer to everything, apparently, is learning how to be "in the moment". This plus the Wednesday yoga class and 3 sessions per week in the gym should keep me calm and "grounded". I suppose I could nail my feet to the floor and that would keep me even more "grounded". It would make getting to work a bit awkward though.

How can I put this; I was thrown out of the meditation class. Very gently. Very mindfully. What happened was this; the instructor decided to do a "Movement Meditation". This involved all 18 of us, men and women, walking as slowly as physically possible, in whichever direction our feet took us, up, down and across the sports hall, in slow motion. No talking, no noise. All round me people were lifting their feet and putting them down excruciatingly slowly, with heads lowered and arms swinging loose. Then it hit me; "Night of the Living Dead" – we looked like Zombie Prom Night as we criss-crossed each other in the School Hall. So then of course I had a fit of the giggles – ok I was shrieking with laughter. It was just so funny...

Back again in the circle of chairs, I apologised and explained... I couldn't help it, I started laughing again. What could I say? It's not my fault that I have a mind like a grasshopper. So then it was suggested (very, very calmly) that perhaps I wasn't yet ready to commit to a ten week course in Mindfulness Meditation. So that's it. I'm barred.

I did learn from it though....I found out that it's not so much that my mind wanders...it's that it's very seldom at home.

CULTURAL THINGS 'n STUFF

Come on baby light my fire – we're roasting

Shakespeare tonight...

Being a lover of words and of all things Shakespearian, where better for a weekend than Stratford-upon-Avon? Accordingly, on a cold February morning, Sisters #2 and #3, Nieces #2 and #3 and myself boarded a flight to Birmingham. Our flight was uneventful; bugles sounded when we landed and for a minute I thought it was a heavenly accompaniment to my fervent prayer of thanks for being on terra firma once more. Before long we were ensconced in our pretty little B & B, thrilled at being in the village and among the houses so familiar from the pages of books and the screens of TV and cinema. All set for a weekend of history and culture, tea and cream scones, and walking in the footsteps of the Bard.

That's what we did. We walked the village and its environs, we visited Shakespeare's house, the Town Hall, walked to Anne Hathaway's cottage, the Globe Theatre, walked by the river, did it all. Interspersed with frequent stops for refreshments of every kind. By Saturday evening we were all walked out. We'd seen everything, gone everywhere any of us wanted to go. Had a wonderful time. On one of our forays into shops, Niece #3 bought me a little hedgehog. Christened Snedgespeare, he starred in all my photos from then on.

Saturday evening- what to do? It was too early to go back to the B & B and we had no tickets for the play. One

214

of the Tudor townhouses, now a hotel, caught our eye. We could have a quiet drink there, it wouldn't be heaving with noise and disco-goers like the other places we'd passed.

The hotel bar was full; the Function Room was hosting a small wedding party, so we settled in at the side of Reception, in a lobby containing chairs, sofas and an open fireplace stacked with twigs, logs, papers and cones. Low tables held flower arrangements and candles. All very nice. We were sipping our drinks and relaxing when a gentleman in shirtsleeves approached from the back of the hotel. With a smile and what sounded like an East European accent, he asked if we would like the fire lit. Oh yes, Sister#2 exclaimed; we'd love it! Us Irish love an open fire! With that he took a strip of paper from the fireplace, lit it from one the candles and touched it to the kindling. I thought it a strange way for an employee to light a fire, and even stranger, he continued on and went out the front door of the hotel.

The fire took light all right. It roared up the chimney. Within seconds a black waterfall of smoke was cascading down the chimney. Oh my god, the chimney must be blocked up, someone said. Better go and tell Reception what's happening. Niece#3 got up and ran round the corner to alert the staff. By now smoke was billowing along the lobby. Next thing the smoke alarm went off. Now the staff were evacuating the guests from the bar, next thing the wedding party were streaming out of the Function Room. No problem, just smoke from the fireplace, no problem, please leave the building. Oh my God, said Niece #2. I myself was beginning to worry in case we got blamed – this was a Tudor building, listed, priceless. As we stood outside in the cold hoping we wouldn't get arrested the Fire Brigade Tender arrived, sirens blazing, and firemen charged into the historical, irreplaceable building.... Eventually order was restored and guests and wedding party were shepherded back in. Our little group of unintentional arsonists meekly followed. The fire was a rosy glow now. The smoke had dissipated; the wedding disco was in full swing, the bar full of drinkers. We got fresh drinks, including a whiskey for Niece#3, a non-drinker who felt she needed something to get her over the humiliation of being related to me and her other aunt... Niece#2 was blaming her mother and me, insisting that we egged on whoever he was. He certainly had not been an employee of Shakespeare's local Travelodge.

What to say? Well it has to be a quotation from the man himself; "All's well that ends well". It did all end well... We weren't arrested, the hotel didn't burn down, and Nieces# 2 and 3 still speak to me. While Snedgespeare is sitting on my desk, smiling a big hedgehog grin at me as I type.

RELAXING STUFF

Close encounters with Serenity...

Morning snow caped the shoulders of the Wicklow mountains and lifted my spirits as I drove south. Like the Ent in Lord of the Rings, I love heading south. As he says, "Somehow it always feels like heading home". My best friend was taking herself and January Girl (me) away to a 5 star hotel for an overnight spa-and-dinner break.

The hotel was wall to wall marble and staff. Having checked in to our lovely double bedded marble room, we headed straight for the spa centre with its Swarovski crystals and lighting as soft and gentle as a peach. I could feel that cruel master Tension uncurl his talons from my shoulders as I changed into a peach robe... Lunch was a bento box, every bit of it delicious. Next, into the Blissful Suite for two hours of pampering. When it ended I had practically melted, ready to flow out of the therapy room under the door in a river of peach.

To complete the day of relaxation, I was led to the Serenity Room to relax until dinner. The Serenity Room had a sign on the door requesting Silence. Inside, a table bearing a selection of herbal teas and juices, a water cooler. Two rows of loungers piled with white blankets, all facing the ceiling-to-floor windows and the panoramic views of the mountains. White dividers separated the couches, gave privacy. Heaps of magazines lay beside each lounger; I selected my couch, filled a beaker with water, and poured myself a cup of orange blossom tea. Selected a few magazines and climbed onto my plinth. The backrest was at 90 degrees. Totally upright and uptight. No good – I wanted to lay back, kick back. I pulled the lever to adjust the backrest. RAK, RAK, RAK went the hydraulics. The backrest went back a few degrees then stopped. Kept trying to go further. Kept failing. The backrest was trying its best to lie down. But it couldn't. It just kept going RAK, RAK, RAK, like a demented crow, and didn't move an inch. The noise in the silent room was deafening No matter how I pulled and pushed the lever back, RAK, RAK, RAK. I couldn't shut it up. I ran out and called a member of staff. "We'll get an engineer up straight away" she said. Right enough, five minutes later, he arrived. Silenced the crow. Suggested in a whisper that I choose another bed. So I did. Picked up my magazine, my water, my herbal tea. Chose a new couch. Settled in. Draped a white fluffy blanket across my legs. Leaned over to reach the lever and adjust the backrest - and knocked the cup of orange blossom tea and the glass of water over. In unison, half spilled all over the bed and floor and the other half emptied itself into the mechanism of the bed, poured down the little hydraulic hole. I leapt from the thing, afraid I'd be electrocuted. Ran into the Ladies Room, where I grabbed every bit of tissue and every paper towel I could find and raced back to the Serenity Room, where I set about mopping the floor and the bed of the plinth and tried to stuff tissues down into the mechanism to absorb the spill. Unfortunately all of the above entailed some noise. There was some movement from the other occupied beds, some rustling of magazines, some deep breathing...

Back into the Ladies to dispose of the sodden tissues and paper towels. Back onto my plinth. Fluffy white blanket draped over my legs, backrest at 45 degree angle. Settled. Fresh glass of water beside me, I relaxed. Lay down. Turned over and pulled the blankets with me to settle down for a nice cosy nap. Unfortunately my right elbow caught the stand alone divider which must have been made of Japanese rice paper, very delicate, because it toppled over. Onto the bed next to mine. Luckily it was unoccupied. However it caught the next divider which went over onto the next bed and…It was like a game of dominoes and not in a good way. The second glass of water and cup of orange blossom tea…how can such small receptacles hold so much liquid? Is there a separate law of physics that governs spills? There's always a spilt amount at least double the quantity the container held, I swear it.

Bottom line; I've trashed the "Serenity Room" in a five star hotel. I left before I got thrown out, went back to our room and ate the complimentary chocolates they'd left to say "Happy Birthday Geralyn". Well if you've had an upset, you need sugar don't you.

We had a lovely dinner. Afterwards, we spent our joint annual income on a few gins and tonic in the bar. Fell into bed. Sleep eventually came to me as light crept in under the damask curtains and most especially, when my companion finally stopped snoring. If I'd realized at the time that the marble bathroom had under floor heating, I'd have slept there. Wrapped up in fluffy white blankets and peach towels.

Awake and in a gin induced depression, or maybe because we had to leave this marble palace, we headed to the self-service breakfast buffet. The staff were enquiring of us and many others if we were on "the package". Yes, of course we were, otherwise we wouldn't be here. Most of the other clientele were on "the package" as well it seemed.

Having placed my orange juice and omelette on our table I went off to make toast. Inserted two pieces of bread and changed the setting on the 6-slice toaster to "maximum", same as my own little toaster at home. One minute later two charred, blackened slices popped up –and a fire alarm went off.   WHEE, WHEE, WHEE, it went, deafeningly, as an electronic voice calmly exhorted us all to please leave the building quietly by the nearest exit... God now I've set off the alarm. The bloody noise wasn't going to help the hangovers either.

"No, no"" said the staff reassuringly as they moved among guests now standing at their tables in uncertainty, ready to abandon the fried eggs and muesli. "No need to go outside. It was just the toaster. The fire alarm system is very sensitive. "

First I've trashed the Serenity Room and now I've set off the fire alarm...

We left and drove back to Dublin, back to January, back to reality.

"Well, do you feel the better of that?" asked my kind, good friend. "Oh yes, thank you, it was all lovely. Very relaxing" I said. "Let's do it again soon. Only let's try somewhere else, it's nice to see new places."

THE CÚPLA FOCAIL agus STUIF

Here is the first poem I wrote os Gaeilge. It was suggested

that it also be the last…

"An File"

Níl me Raftery an File
Geralyn is í m'ainm
Scríobh liom ós mo croí
Mar cé hé is mo anam?

Tír gan teanga, tír gan anam
Dúirt an sean'a'chai
Beidh mé ag iarriadh a choiméad
Dánta a scribe, gach lá, gach mí.

THE DARK STUFF

And now…a fairy tale for grownups…

"No!" screamed Cinderella. "Of course the shoes fit me!" But alas and alack, no matter how much she pushed and pulled they didn't. Two shoehorns were used, one front and one back. Her toenails in their pretty pink sparkly polish were trimmed to barely peep out over her toes. First butter then olive oil was massaged into her feet. The glass slippers were gently warmed in a Bain Marie. But it was to no effect. Years of wearing her stepmother's too-small shoes with seven inch stiletto heels and toecaps narrowed to the point of infinity had given the beautiful Cinderella feet on which bunions bloomed like bunches of flowers. The glass slippers became cobwebbed with cracks from the stresses placed upon them but still they would not fit her. She threw herself down on the red velvet sofa and wept.

Prince Charming sat beside her and said, "My love, it matters not if you spend your life in Ugg boots. I love you. The problem is, I have made a state decree to marry the person who fits the magical glass slippers"

"Let me try" cried Chlorinda Sal Ammonia, one of the two Ugly Sisters. Lo and behold, all the stretching, greasing and warming of the slippers somehow enabled her to fit one of her cloven hoofs into the delicate footwear. Cinderella fainted dead away, to be followed shortly thereafter by Prince Charming.

Just for that, here's one for you, Snedgespeare.

"An Gráinneog"

Is maith liom na gráinneoige
Ós t'ám mar a bhí mé an-oige
Gráinneoige abú!
Tá spice mór acu!

Ach nuair a ritheann
Siad ardú iad
Cósuil le na mban
Lena sciortaí glan

Is é mo ghrá eile boíní De
Choinneáil siad áit speisialta
I gcroílar mé.

Deich míle uair níos lú na ár gé
Alainn sin, go bhfuil siad I ndáiriíne
"Dealga beag Dé".

Is breá liom na créatúirí beag
A thugann siad aoibh gháire
Le mo haghaidh.

0000000000000000000

So that's it. Sin é mo scéal. Dear Reader, May your
pie be filled with love, laughter, and all good things.

Geralyn

LITERARY ASSASSIN

Frank George C. Moore

I reached inside my light summer reefer jacket,
touching the slim Luger I kept strapped loaded, found the
envelope I took it out. The bald Mexican agent pushed his
envelope of money a little towards me. But kept his hand
on it, pressed firmly down on the table. The train rocked
on, on in darkness by German towns. Opening the letter I
began to read. To my surprise it was a simple monologue
appeal addressed to the James Joyce Society in Zurich,
from Dublin's Lady Lavery society my sanction spongers.
Asking for assistance. As did the old revolutionaries ask
the king of Spain for help and as in 179o'ties the new
French republic. 'My dark Rosaline/ Do not sigh do not
weep/ stuff. So this was how such people addressed one
another I thought, God save the world from poets and
revolutionaries. How pathetic I thought but began to read.
It was a complaint from literary societies in Dublin that,
the self commissioned arts officer class, were closing
down all unofficial open mikes and reading societies for
monetary gain. Taking power of expression into a certain
clique themselves. My cold professional assassin's mind
reassured itself. 'C'est la vie, whet's new pussy cat.
Money talks.

I won't be assassinated for reading this. I read on.

What is it of those who try to set the borders
　　　ofscripted art

putting down a markers, of who can practice
freedom's verbal wit.

As did a literary assassin by the Thames, called
Thomas Cromwell

who plied his trade dissembling, laying
literary assassination

fowlers traps, false trails. As does the self-appointed
art's officers mess,

who sit by a large check book at false desks snared
from our taxpayer's

23% vat. Beneath a plaque quoting George Bernard
Shaw's say

Those who can do - do, those who can't preach,
organise, administer, plot,

Dublin fools we, for stating this. Professional office
seekers in the arts are slick

cats/who wait by the rails to impale those who can
do;/

never forgiving the discovery that they cannot/

Whispering into the ear of the king, and on the
officer- airways

"How do these men know these things, there only the
sons of Nazareth,

We've agreed no good can come from there. We the
    chosen men priests of the pen,

see how we organise everything, who pulled the rug
    on the most successful, open mike,

in our tax renovated father's house, ' This temple it's
    ours now, we can't allow

a spontaneous forum, unregulated for the
    un'deloused; sacrilege in our literary father's
    house/

You must have the mark of the political scribe
    engraved on your bonce, to publish

Wit must be baptised with unctuous pseudo crème,/to
    forum in our tax renovated realm/

So let these poets find a place on a mount,/to practice
    their art

of wit exposing untruth, in celebrating unofficial
    poetry, music & dance/

far, far away from our arts officers mess, where the
    inner cognoscenti

misrule over the best across the road from three
    rising swans

Although they'll try strike a vixen flag to state/

no one can own /the expression of god given gifts of
    the arts by the Thames or by the Liffey nearer

226

home, where Thomas Cromwell's ply murky
parts -Laying calumnies to spend the check of
de'poor's, tax extracted 23% vat

all by a ten gallon drum of bum sudocrème

nice work if ye can get it son

So to the republic of literature of Zurich we implore

"Send an armada with troops and guns to rescue
        freedom in Jimmy J.'s town

where freedom's speech & open mike's are trodden
        down

closed by the arts officer's Madame Guillotine a
        callous lot's gibbet on a hill, in Parnell
        square, has replaced freedom here

We will meet your troops landing in Mayo, to march
        by Castelbar avoiding Aughrim to win the
        day- 'As we rescue the pound of Lady Lavery.

        I smiled refolding, the missive from Dublin. The
fools the fools I thought, they have left us our literary
dead type stuff. I placed the envelope on the table, seeing
in my mind's eye a fleet of tall European ships with
literary flags, cannons set sail to rescue Dublin.
Attempting to land in Mayo. And I knowing a storm was
set to blow that fleet off course I pushed the envelope
towards the malign presence of the bald Mexican agent I
noticed in his other hand he held a small pocket luger I
recognised it as an official Irish governmentc3 issue.

'Thomas Cromwell', I uttered, but the sound never left my mouth. Clasping the envelope containing ten thousand European, I slumped gently forward dead, as a lost prop in the Gate. My last thought realizing even here the arts officer's hand, can pull the trigger. As the train speed onward across the European plain. It was the last thought I had as I looked into the muzzle of the literary assassin's luger. .

TO A PROMPT

Bláithín Ní Liatháin

All that Spring Paris was agog
Awaiting La Collection of Monsieur Frog
The latest designer of gowns
For ladies from county and towns.

His use of colour was always bold
His pattern cut to fit no mould
For conventions were not his way
Or rather, he knew they did not pay.

Disaster struck when banks went bust
Less spending by ladies on their looks
Changéd much the world of Haute Couture
To almost, Mon Dieu, resemble pret a porter.

Monsieur Frog spent long in pondering
How to achieve le look both sensible and daring
And then to him le moment Eureka
Born then La Robe en rouge avec l'ache.

STORIES FROM 'THE VILLAGE'

A Collection of sketches from the InkSplinters
Writing Sessions
Martina Carroll.

The Beginning

I walked into the old pub in the centre of town, and there was Jean having a drink with her three children. My son Jack, who's married to Jean's daughter Lucy, was there. He waved as I walked in,

"Mam, great you could make it, what're ye having?"

"I'll have a glass of white wine" I said.

He stopped to give me a warm hug as he headed for the bar. By then Jean was standing. I turned to her and we embraced like old friends. Actually, we didn't really know each all that well. Jean is an artist like my Charley. We'd overlapped with a few big exhibitions and family events over the years.

"You look fantastic" I said, and indeed she did look great, tanned with blond hair in loose curls, and big arty earrings and necklaces, her soft hippy style clothes giving her a carefree look. Next I hugged Lucy and her sister and brother.

They're a lovely family I thought to myself. What a shame Jean had left like that...

Their Dad Philip is a nice enough guy, quiet and hard working. He'd done his best to take care of the kids. Lucy the eldest had already moved out by then but the younger two were only teenagers, still in school. They needed their mother.

Jean and Philip had never gotten over the death of their youngest son. It had been a tragedy but it was no accident. He was just an innocent young teenager who'd been attacked by a couple of 'troubled kids' who were out of their minds on drugs. He was stabbed and left to die as Lucy stood helpless, watching, the whole family torn apart in an instant. I couldn't even begin to imagine what it was like and now ten years later Jean was back to visit, catching up with everyone and spending a bit of time with the kids. They'd visit the grave together.

I didn't stay long. I'd planned to meet a few friends from my writers' group. As I made my way up the centre of O'Connell Street I met David, a writer I know from the Workman's. He's one of my favourite poets. Actually I knew him for ages before I discovered he was a good friend of my son Jack, who's a singer songwriter. There's an interesting network of writers in Dublin, a kind of hidden city I'd only discovered when I started writing myself. It was nice to find that Jack and I shared lots of friends. We navigated the same writers' scene and it was only when we both got more involved that we found we had a circle of friends in common.

As I crossed over the street I saw Mimi standing at her bus stop. We smiled and waved at each other. She's almost eighty now, a poet but also an artist. I've been to some of her exhibitions. She made plenty of money in the boom years. Now you'd meet her where ever there's a free glass of wine. Such an interesting person. We've had some great conversations

.The one thing I love about meeting up with writers is that you don't actually need to know anything about their personal lives. It's all about the writing and the expression of ideas and emotions abstracted from the everydayness of life to a level of common experience. We meet in the city and write and read and sometimes we hug and drink tea together or wine... I step into my village and here I am in a world of the imagination. I listen to soft voices read mournfully in words that touch my soul. I smile at the rhythm and movements of lively poets, both young and old, as they recount tales filled with the wisdom of the ages and insights into life as lived by the ordinary people we see and meet every day.

I've lived in Blackrock most of my life. It's a lively place, although I love the buzz in Dublin city, only 15 minutes away on the Dart. Yet, Blackrock is the centre of The Village, my village, because of this big old house left to me by my dear Grand Mother Maysie, who raised me from the age of three. I don't remember my parents, sisters

232

or uncle who all died in the fire in Cork while I was staying with Maysie in Blackrock. That was Maysie's whole family gone, apart from me.

She was a great artist, and very well educated for a woman of her generation. She'd come from a well off family and was the only one left in Dublin. Maysie never bothered to send me to school but I had a wonderful education, meeting amazing people when we travelled the world together exhibiting her beautiful paintings. She was so loved despite her sad smile and it was no surprise when she was found with the empty pill bottle beside her bed. I respected her right to exit this world and although I was sad to see her go I knew her suffering was finally over. She left me this beautiful house, the centre of my village.

This is where it all began, first with Maysie, then Oisín, and later my dear Charley who I loved so much.

Life goes on, always moving forward and changing. I've built on the foundations laid down by those people who have departed. But! This house has a wonderful secret locked away in the attic. The Village may be a place of the imagination but the people are real, and although the world's broken it's also magical; so I recount these tales of wonder that reach out from a hidden place, and of the people who came here from a strange far away land and changed our lives forever.

Ryan Kaiazu and the Garden Party in Blackrock.

It was Ryan's idea to have the garden party at the old house in Blackrock. Ryan is the youngest of my five children. They're all here together enjoying the day and the sunshine. Jack the eldest and his wife Lucy have come with their little baby girl, now toddling around to the great joy and pride of her besotted parents. Rory my second is here with Ben whom he met three years ago. Ben has three children. The kids are here and also their mother with her new husband. The four adults and three children share adjacent apartments and Ben and his ex-co-parent very creatively. It's lovely to see the extended family happily getting along as if it was the most natural thing in the world.

My two girls Josie and Eliza are here with their many friends. Eliza is especially fond of Lucy's brother Steve.

Ryan, Charley's son, is much younger than the others. He's always been different. He didn't talk until he was five years old. Then one day he started talking and he talked non-stop for three days. We had to take turns listening and no one ever heard the full story because he simply continued on regardless. When he realised we were all exhausted and confused he decided to write it down so we could read it in our own time.

That's when we discovered he could read and write. After three months of exhausting writing, in pencil because he didn't like pens, he decided it would be more efficient to simply type. That way he could keep backups and make multiple copies. It turned out he could type 120 words per minute. Then one night when we were all in bed, we were awoken by the eerily perturbing sound of Chopin emerging from the drawing room below. Thinking someone had turned the radio on I moved quickly to suppress the disturbance, only to find Ryan bashing out the notes on Maysie's old piano. By then it seemed that nothing Ryan could do would surprise us. Little did we know!

You see The Village somehow came alive because of Ryan. These people come together because of him. He's like a magnet, quiet yet powerful. Since those first three days he rarely bothers to talk. His presence simply draws people together and makes everything all right. All that matters is the present moment. All perceived wrongs are forgotten and there's no need for forgiveness because right here right now everything is all right. Whatever happened, happened and we must now create a future story.

That story is about a village where we all belong, The Village that is not a place but a soul that connects people, special people, people who are chosen because they belong together and because they will change this world. These people are Ryan's family, his brothers and sisters, their friends and families, writers from the city and artists whose lives have touched ours, the friends we've met on our travels, in the physical world and online. Even Jean has managed to come and I'm so happy to see her there talking to Philip and who can say, no one knows what the future holds. Today the whole Village is gathered, a village that doesn't even know it exists.

When everyone leaves, Ryan and I will ascend the stairs to the attic and we'll step through a gateway into a world on the edge of a forest where Gemma the dragon waits. You see the secret of this magical house is that it contains a break in the space time continuum. I know it sounds like Star Trek but it's true. Maysie of course knew about it as did Charley and I, but the gateway had been broken for years and then the key was lost after Charley left, it had simply disappeared along with him.

One day, a few years ago, Ryan found the key; but my life was busy at that time taking care of my five children. So I said nothing and let Ryan keep it in his room, not knowing how important it was, until a few weeks ago. He was rummaging in the attic when he pulled back a screen and found the door. Then he remembered the key. We were together when he first tried it in the lock. I remember how my heart almost stopped when the gateway opened and I gazed into the cave and Gemma's golden eyes. I'd never expected to see her again, yet there she was, Gemma the dragon, my dear old friend, still waiting after all this time. She had said she'd wait...

Bailfort

Mary Lorellian had lived all her life in Bailfort in West Cork. It was a quirky little village, a stone's throw from Baltimore. There was just one street with a pub, shop, church and a few pretty old houses lining the road on either side. The village overlooked the sea on a height, with paths and trails weaving down to a small cove. People said it was originally a pirate stronghold and that in the middle ages it had been an extremely busy place with lots of people coming and going. There were plenty of old ruins about, including a castle that predated most of the fortresses along the south coast. It was a strange place for a busy settlement. There was no harbour, only a small sandy beach, but there had been lots of caves where it was said that goods had been stored and people had lived, although it was hard to image knowing how stormy and bitter the weather could be there. The caves were now gone, eroded across time. Only a few crevices remained, places where children played and walkers sheltered as they sat and looked out to sea.

Mary had spent most of her youth hanging out in Baltimore which was quite a cool place, very popular in the summer with visitors and summer residents. She continued to hang out there well into her twenties. There's a little pub, where she used to go to write, with an open fire in winter and a big window overlooking the bay. That's where she met her best friend Josie whose people had originally come from Bailfort and whose family home had been burnt to the ground in a terrible tragedy in which several people had lost their lives. The locals had never talked about it and the ruin had been left to tumble into the ground until Josie's mother had decided to rebuild. The new house was only a fraction the size of the old but it was built in the same tradition and there was room to expand incorporated into the plans. The main feature of the house was a big traditional country kitchen with a wood burning range and all the delightful little features that made it very characteristic of the locality. The locals seemed pleased that life had been restored to the old place and many said it was a good sign and that it might bring life back to the village. When Josie moved into the new house Mary soon got to know her whole family and their big network of friends. Now looking back she remembered how happy she'd been in that time dreaming about being a writer and travelling the world. She was glad to see how well Josie had settled into the village.

Her own people, the Lorellians, were also an old Bailfort family and like so many others in the village no one knew the origins of their unusual name. Otherwise they were a typical West Cork family. Mary's father had died and her two brothers and her sister had moved to England to live. Her mother continued to live alone in the big old farmhouse on the hill above the village. Mary had moved down into the main street where she'd bought her own cottage. It was close to Josie and she'd been happy there for a time writing her book and travelling with Josie back and forth between Cork and Dublin.

Three years ago she'd had the opportunity of her life when she was invited to New York. It was a journey that had brought her to the edge of a cliff. She felt her life was over and she didn't want to go on living in this world. Now she sat hunched down in a crevice looking out on the waves that tumbled into the rocks far below. She knew about the Dragon lands. She wanted to go there.

Keith remembers his Dad

Keith lounged in the corner of the tavern listening to the laughter coming from the other side of the room. He took a swig from his mug of local green ale. He remembered how frightened he'd been this time last year sitting in this same corner with Phailim and Taise the night before they had departed on their quest through The Dark Forest, across The Great River and into the dragons' cave that led to a magical village in a distant place. He had lived with them since he was twelve and just one year ago at the age of twenty they decided to accompany him on a quest to find his parents. Adam, his friend, and Adam's sister Sarane had come too and together they had begun a journey that would never end.

Tonight they had arranged to meet again in this same corner of the tavern in their home town where their quest had begun. He was early and as he sat there waiting his thoughts drifted back to the last time he'd seen his father Charley. He was only twelve when Charley had taken him into The Dark Forest. Back then he didn't understand why it was named Dark, but people became quiet when it was mentioned and sometimes he could sense them shudder just thinking about it. But Charley wasn't afraid. He went there often.

The forest wasn't as Keith had imagined, bleak with twisted trees, gnarled roots and black muddy pools of water. No, it was bright and enchanting. The path Charley led him along was a winding leafy trail where the dapple sunlight glistened through the trees. Soon they came to a clearing. On the right was a mossy bank and on the left an awesome swimming pool with a waterfall tumbling down over rocks from ten feet above. They were hot after their walk and happily peeled off and dived into the cool deep water. Afterwards they lay back on the mossy earth and dried off in the sun as they ate their lunch of bread, cheese and cold pink tea.

That's when he noticed Charley was looking sad. He knew that look very well, Charley was thinking of Lorna, Keith's mother who had disappeared in The Dark Forest when he was just a baby. It was as if a grey cloud had descended. Charley started to speak, but then hesitated for a moment before starting again. Keith remembered his sense that something bad was about to unfold. He listened carefully as Charley slowly began to speak.

"If your mother was here we'd be eating small cakes topped with white and pink icing and red cherries"

Why was his father talking about cakes? He remembered the ghostly chill that had overwhelmed him as his Dad continued,

"It's interesting that this beautiful forest is called Dark" he said, "People used to say there was something evil here. They warned us but we often wandered these paths together. We loved this forest. Then one day she went into the forest and didn't return. It was a bright sunny day like today. You were just a baby. It would be easy to blame

239

the forest and ignore the mystery. I need to know what happened to her. You know I searched and searched but couldn't find her. What I found was a bridge and then I turned back. I had to take care of you but you're big now. I know you'll understand that I have go find her, I have to cross the bridge. Phailim and Taise will take care of you. I promise I'll come back if I can. You can head back along the trail, they're waiting for you there. I have to go on".

Keith had jumped to his feel shouting

"No, Dad, please..." but Charley simply hugged him, and then turned and walked away.

Charley hadn't returned and after a long time Keith began to plan his own quest to go after him. It was Phailim's idea and it was comforting. They'd talked about it for years, how they would never give up. They often said that somehow they knew that Lorna and Charley were out there somewhere, they just didn't know where.

And so, one year ago today, they set out on their quest. They walked for days through the forest before coming to the river. They wandered for weeks along the river bank looking for the bridge. It was beautiful and peaceful in the forest. They felt well; safe!

Adam was first to spot the wide fragile bridge made of rope and wood. They walked forward slowly, their mood changing. They would have to cross. Charley was somewhere on the other side.

Mary in New York

Mary walked quietly through the busy New York street on her way to the market.

This is like a breath of fresh air she thought and then smiled as she looked around, her senses taking in the noise, dust and fume of the city.

As she stopped at the crossing she thought about the party. Then she shuddered when it occurred to her that she was like Mrs Dalloway on her way to buy flowers.

She hoped it wasn't a bad omen. But, she was nothing like Mrs Dalloway and the party was nothing special, just a few friends catching up. With her equilibrium restored, she entered the store and picked up a cheap bunch of flowers. It was no big deal, just a few flowers to stick in the vase in the hall. She cheered up thinking

I'll grab some food at the deli, bread and ham, some salads, no big deal.

Back in the apartment she took the bread and butter out of her bag and placed the basket of food and flowers on the table. Brad arrived at that moment.

"Great", he said "I guess we'll get stuck in with preparing the food".

He opened the fridge and took out a beer. He seemed pleased with himself standing there drinking from the bottle.

"How was your day" he asked.

Mary thought about the morning. It was like climbing a hill. You have to keep going even when your strength is failing and your heart thumping. Whatever it takes you have to make it to the top. So she put on a brave smile and turned to face him.

"It was fine", she said "We have the flowers and all the food, do we have enough drinks?"

"Plenty" he counted the bottles of wine, seven on the rack and another five in the fridge and lots of beer. He smiled back.

"I'm looking forward to the party, have you talked to Phil today?"

"Not yet" she felt a chill. "I think I'll pop up to see if he's all right, he just doesn't seem like himself lately. You go ahead and get started; I'll be back in a minute".

In the past few months Phil had been involved with some strange people. It had something to do with sex but Mary wasn't sure what? She had managed to avoid poking her nose into his personal affairs. It was a principle she lived by, people had a right to their privacy. As she climbed the stairs to his apartment she became aware that there was a commotion above. His door was open so she entered and followed the noise into the apartment. Several police officers moved about busily, talking! She moved forward, slowly, to the kitchen, then froze, stuck to the spot as if observing a scene apart from herself. Phil lay lifeless on the floor. A paramedic stood over him holding onto a piece of brown soda bread and meat.

She remained there staring at the strange man standing in her friend's kitchen. He was wearing purple rubber gloves and in the dim light it looked like he was holding a heart in his hands, right in front of his face, yet his eyes and mouth were cast down. He stood amidst the ugly scene, blood splattered on the walls and spilling down across the kitchen floor spreading out from Phil's still body. It was a violent death. He must have severed the artery with the first cut before falling to the ground. The grim white shirted man had picked up the sandwich and now he was just standing there; nothing was moving. Mary gazed at the scene for several minutes, then slowly she turned and walked out of the room.

Looking back now she knew that was the beginning of the end of that surreal sense that had hung over her for years. In that moment she knew this would be a turning point in her life. The concreteness of existence had already begun to erode.

The party evolved into a memorial. Phil's body had been removed to the mortuary. There would be a post mortem but no one doubted it was suicide. There was a note. 'My life is over, I'm already dead'.

Mary sat on the couch with her friend Aoife, sipping wine and looking stunned.

"Do you think we should have done something" she asked, "could we have done anything?"

"No" was Aoife's response, "You can't interfere in a person's life, Phil was a private person. I don't think anyone really knew him and yet we all loved him. I think he brought a lot of joy to people but he had his dark side always. It could have been anything. Looking back who knows?" She sighed.

Mary thought about how busy their lives were. She realised she wasn't close to anyone. For the three years she'd lived in New York, she had maintained a distance in all her relationships. She didn't need to be close to people, she wanted to connect with others as herself, who she was inside and not Mary from West Cork defined by the outer world.

As the evening evolved it felt like a mist descending around her, the eerie silence in her heart, the feeling of aloneness and the sense of distance from the others in the room; together it had the effect of separating her from reality while she continued to function normally on the surface. Then she said simply, "I'm going out for a walk, I need to be alone".

The last time she'd seen Phil alive was just for a moment in the library. They talked about his book. He seemed so happy and pleased with himself. It was what he'd always dreamed of and it had done so well. He'd just come back from a tour in Ireland. So much had happened after that and Mary had mostly been out of touch with him since. She'd met a group of people whose ancestors had come from her home town, Bailfort. Now she wanted to return home one last time.

The Boat

Six months earlier Mary had decided that she wanted a boat in Baytown Harbour a couple of hours drive from New York City. She had grown up in the seaside holiday resort of Bailfort in West Cork not far from the pretty coastal village of Baltimore. Her best friend Josie had lived in a house overlooking the bay. Watching the boats come and go she had always dreamed of owning her own boat but it seemed impossible. When she visited Baytown it occurred to her for the first time that it was crazy to think that something was impossible when you knew nothing about it.

She decided to investigate the cost. There were dozens of websites selling second hand boats and they were not at all out of her price range. The cost of mooring in Baytown was reasonable and there were people you could hire to bring you out on the sea and teach you how to sail. Thus having established that it was affordable she made up her mind she was going ahead with her plan. However, there was another important reason why she had chosen Baytown Harbour. While researching online she had discovered several locals with names she'd only ever come across back home in Bailfort. There was something else about the place she couldn't quite put her finger on but she felt good there

.So having spent the entire spring travelling back and forth, soon she had the boat of her dreams moored in a place she loved. It was small with a compact lounge dining area and kitchen on the upper deck and a small bedroom and bathroom below. She set about doing it up in April and it soon became an obsession. She wanted to restore it to its original style. At first she began to buy the various bits and pieces she needed to get started, then she began doing workshops. She met some great people and discovered there was a group whose hobby was restoring old sailing boats and before long she was fully immersed in the group. Then she met Brad. They were at a seminar and he just walked over and introduced himself.

"Brad Torrallyn" he said while extending his hand.

"Torrallyn" she repeated, "not the Torrallyns from Bailfort by any chance?"

"My family's been here in Baytown for centuries" he said, "but indeed they say the founders came from a place called Bailfort. I don't think anyone knows where it is, some say it's a legend".

"It's not" she'd replied "it's in Ireland".

She introduced herself and soon they became good friends. It turned out that the town had been founded by people who had indeed come from Bailfort. Brad was a teacher in the local high school and was very interested in the history of his home town so they went to the library and set about doing some research. They spent days searching through old books and papers. All the strange names from her village were there, even Lorellian, her own surname. The stories were incredible and they all fit what she knew about her home town, about it having been a busy port with lots of goods and people moving back and forth; but according to the manuscripts they were not arriving by sea. They used portals in the caves, like in Stargate the science fiction TV show. Mary wondered if it was really possible and yet it would certainly explain a lot. The documents said that the people of Bailfort had originally arrived from a distant land through the portals in the caves above the bay. No one back home knew how the town came to exist at all in such a remote place where there was no natural harbour. The stories were captivating. Mary wanted to believe they were true.

Then she read about the Dragon Lands. Her mind was busy connecting all the pieces. In her village there were lots of legends about dragons. There were old ruins with carvings and statues of dragons everywhere. It all seemed to match and slowly she began to believe that the portals had really existed. She knew the caves were gone but she'd found drawings and paintings of places she recognised. One stood out in her mind. There was a strange looking rock that still stood just above a wide ledge where she knew that caves had once existed. In the manuscripts it was the statue of a great dragon, its stone wings spreading out overlooking the bay. It had been carved out of the rock but eroded across time. It was the same place. She felt certain; she knew it in her heart.

Over the next few months she'd worked steadily on the restoration while living onboard in the marina. The group took turns visiting each other's boats and hosting parties and dinners. She became as totally immersed in the challenge as the rest and they talked about almost nothing else besides boats and Bailfort.

Now one week after the death of her friend Phil in New York city she stood in Baytown Harbour on the quay looking at the beautifully restored yacht. She was so proud of it and was really surprised standing there, feeling how much she love it. She had told Phil all about it and had promised to bring him on a trip out to sea but she'd never gotten around to actually learning how to sail. The much loved vessel had never left the docks. It was securely tied up, with potted plants on the deck and hanging baskets on either side of the door into an interior where the tiny kitchen contained a display shelf filled with clean glasses and china mugs. As she stood there looking at her beloved possession it occurred to her that she had never actually used it as a boat but indeed it had turned out to be a dream come true. Now she had to go back to Bailfort. She had to know if the legends were true. She was captivated by the idea of the Dragon lands and wanted to go there. It was like a magnet pulling her back.

Keith's Quest leads him into the Dragon Lands

Keith, Adam, Sarane, Phailim and Taise cautiously walked across the bridge. Step by step they entered a new realm. The terrain was different, the trees were scattered and there was a wide stone road wandering visibly into the distance. It was not what they'd expected. There had been no road on the other side, just a wild track through the dense woods. They walked along the paved road for three hours and as it was getting dark they were once again surprised when they observed lights ahead. As they drew nearer they saw the tavern surrounded by a scattering of small houses. They stopped as they arrived at the door and stood silently looking at each other. Above the door was the sign 'Dragons Inn', painted in bright red letters woven around a golden dragon with green gem eyes and flaming tongue. Keith pushed the door open. It looked warm and homely inside. One by one they stepped across the threshold and stood staring at a jovial scene, speechless.

No one paid them any heed until the Innkeeper ambled over and warmly greeted them and welcome them inside. The room was filled with people eating and drinking and talking noisily. The travellers had been surprised to find this place in what seemed like the middle of nowhere but no one there was surprised at their arrival as though strangers came there every day. They were shown to a cosy corner and soon they were enjoying the warm food and good green ale they were used to at home.

"Are you on your way to Dragons' Mountain" the Innkeeper enquired at last.

"Mm, Yes, I guess we are" said Keith "I believe we are going in that direction".

He looked to the others for support.

Phailim took advantage of the opportunity and said "Tell us about the mountains, are there really dragons?"

The Innkeeper looked at them suspiciously, "of course" he said "why else would you come this way but to hunt dragons...

Next morning they stood in the courtyard staring up at the sky as a great dragon flew overhead. It appeared to move awkwardly, lurching from side to side.

The Innkeeper was pointing and shouting,

"What's it doing? Why's it here? They never come here." he roared as he began racing along the street. People started running and screaming.

Just then Keith caught sight of a red haired scruffy looking man taking an arrow and aiming at the huge creature.

"You've got to hit them in the chest to kill them" he yelled as he let loose.

Keith had his knife out and instinctively threw it at the man, but too late. The dragon lurched and fell to the ground right in the middle of the courtyard. Everyone stopped and stood silently staring, but Adam's attention was on the man lying still in the corner. Someone was standing over him.

"He's dead, Graham's dead" he shouted.

Keith thought to himself, *it was the first time I killed a man...*

He sat back in the dim corner of the tavern, drinking his ale and reflecting on that moment. He remembered looking around nervously as heads began to turn in his direction. It was as though the world had slowed down, yet his mind was racing. He was thinking slow and fast at the same time but he hadn't been fast enough to save the dragon. She lay sprawled on the dusty courtyard, her life blood pooling around her chest and heart. He'd known somehow that his destiny was tied up with hers. Later he'd discovered that she'd actually come looking for him. It was a day that was etched in his mind forever.

Now he understood that she had a brave heart and that she would have sacrificed herself for him, but in that moment as they'd stood there in the courtyard gazing at the beautiful creature, her eyes beginning to dim, half closed, the sun peeped out from behind the grey clouds. Felicia's scales glistened as the shining rays of light touched them, reflecting the orange, gold, green and blue hues of her head and back and the bright red and gold of her massive wings. She had planned to join their quest as they entered the dark hills.

The crowd had wandered off one by one. Then the Innkeeper came over and slapped him on the shoulder.

"I guess you're a keeper of dragons" he announced.

"What?" the question came from several voices in their small group.

The Innkeeper explained,

"The dragons will come now. There are those who protect them and those who hunt them. We haven't seen any protectors in these parts for a long time. I'm glad you've come. They are gentle you know, there used to be thousands of them but they've been hunted almost to extinction."

Keith didn't know what to say...

He'd looked down sadly at the majestic beast that lay at his feet.

"I tried to save you" he said gently, "I'm sorry"

Tears fell from his eyes one by one onto the pale blue of Felicia's face. She opened her eyes slowly.

"She's still alive" he said quietly then shouted for help.

They carried her to the stable. She was badly injured so they'd stayed at the Dragons Inn for three weeks until she was well enough to walk. By then they knew the story, about how she had come looking for them, how the dragons had been searching...

They'd journeyed together to a cave in the mountains where lived a wise old dragon called Gemma.

She knew his parents. They'd travelled through a magic portal that had once existed in her cavern. It led to a place called The Attic. He wanted to know the whole story but Gemma just said "in time, in time, but first you must find a way to go to The Attic. I know they're still there. I've been waiting for them to return".

The other dragons said that Gemma was mad, that she had been a witness to a terrible slaughter and now there were less than fifty dragons left.

Keith and his companions had stayed with her for months. They talked often. She spoke quietly about her silence, describing for the first time her experiences of the hunt that had been buried deep inside. As she recounted the tale she was once again gripped by the terrifying feelings she'd been running away from for years but this time she sat there calmly, a witness, her silence now broken, allowing her sense of rage rise up inside as she remained calm and emotionless on the surface. The sense of being trapped, of being pinned down was still there but she sat it out until the end, then she rose and walked slowly out of the dark cave knowing that now she had the key that was locked away for so long. She surveyed the land and her tears fell in torrents creating a stream that tumbled down the rocks, splashing into the valley below, and flowing out into the world. In that moment she knew that everything would be all right. She let the love in her heart calm her mind and felt the sadness, knowing that love and sadness are partners.

It happened when she least expected. She'd been curled up asleep in a recess of her cavern when she was awoken by a strange yet familiar sound. Slowly she opened her eyes. There was a bright light, and Lorna stood there, older but still beautiful, with a young man beside her who looked a lot like Charley...

Cliff's Edge

Mary was in the lovely old country kitchen drinking tea with the dear friend she hadn't seen for so long. She sat quietly, politely smiling and nodding, yet barely listening, knowing she'd be gone shortly. She just wanted to say goodbye but Josie was so happy to see her. She talked away in her usual cheerful voice, updating her on all the latest personal details of her life. Mary was calm in the moment but knew the questions were coming,

"what about yourself then?"

"how's Phil?"

"how long are you staying?"

"have you been up to the house yet? Your Mam seems happy now she has the kids. What's the story with Gráinne?"

There was a time when she loved these conversations but it was different now. Her life was so complicated and uncertain, it was impossible to reduce it to a few facts. One day maybe she could tell the story but then again there might not be a story to tell.

"I have to go Josie" she said,

"Sure you've only arrived. I have the room ready. I thought we'd head down to McKenzie's after dinner. Where would you going at this time in the evening, sure it'll be dark soon. Here I'll get the..."

"No, Josie, I can't stay"

She smiled as she put on her coat.

"I'm sorry, I have to go".

She gave Josie a warm hug and headed straight out the door. When she got to the end of the lane she looked back. Josie was still standing there. She waved and turned left into the village, past the pub and then left again after the church. It was a sleepy village but there were a few people about enjoying the mild, although damp afternoon. When she was out of sight she doubled back around below Josie's house onto the path down to the cove. She kept low hoping Josie wouldn't see her. She wanted to be alone. As she rounded the cliff she saw the grey sandy beach below. She wandered on down until she came to the wide ledge that she had remembered. She gazed up at the huge rock above. Indeed it did look like a dragon. She turned and stood on the edge.

Tears rolled down her cheeks as waves splashed on the craggy rocks to the north then spilled elegantly into the churning water. She took a step back, then another and another as she retreated into a crevice where she sat down, still and quiet.

Charley leaves Blackrock

Charley walked silently along Blackrock beach. He loved Ireland, he loved Lorna and he loved Ryan and all the kids. He remembered when he arrived here for the first time, it felt like home; and then when Ryan was born he'd taken him in his arms and the first words he'd spoken were "Welcome Home", and so he'd named him Kaiazu which means 'welcome home' in the language of his homeland. Lorna gave him the Irish name Ryan and so he became Ryan Kaiazu.

When Charley had come looking for his long lost wife Lorna, he'd found her in this magical place she called The Village. It's where she'd originally come from and he knew she'd visited here many times when their first son Keith was a baby although she never talked about it. Then one day she didn't return and when Keith was twelve years old Charley had gone looking for her. She'd been trapped here and he also became trapped. Something had gone wrong with the portal but he couldn't stop thinking about Keith. He had to find a way back. There was an endless aching in his heart for the young boy.

Now he had an idea. He remembered the legend about how dragon fire could open the gateway between the worlds and so he decided to try setting fire to the door in the attic. It was all about love, he knew, love, love, love. The Village would never be home without Keith. He was missing a piece of his soul, he had to pull his lives together somehow.

He wandered back through the town to his local pub, ordered a pint of Guinness, then sat at the bar savouring every drop. His mind was made up. He was going to get back to Keith even if it meant setting fire to the attic. Of course it wouldn't come to that although there was a risk. He looked over to the corner at his dear old friend Edward. He wanted to tell him but that was impossible. He thought to himself, *my dear friend Edward is asleep in his chair. I can't talk to him anyway, he'd think I'm crazy if I start talking about dragons.* There was no one he could talk to and his unhappiness was dragging him down, slowly making his existence impossible.

The big problem was how to tell Lorna. The previous night he'd manage to pluck up the courage.

"I have to go back" he'd said. "It's been too long".

"Yes", Lorna had agreed, "Indeed it has been too long" but she didn't get it, she continued talking.

"By the way, Jack's coming over tomorrow with Lucy".

He wondered why it was so hard to just come out and say "I'm going to try something tomorrow, I have everything ready" Then he thought that it might not work and so why say anything. He decided to go ahead and try out the fire idea first thing tomorrow.

It was a bright sunny morning, a bit frosty but calm. He'd spent ages trawling the web for information about how to create the incendiary device. It was all set up. Lorna was still asleep, they'd stayed up late talking. He really did love talking to her. They could get so engrossed in conversation sometimes yet he couldn't say the simply words, "I'm going". He climbed the stairs to the attic.

In the end he hadn't talked to anyone and at that moment as he climbed the stairs to the attic it seemed so unreal, after two happy years in Dublin, he had a solid plan to get back. The device was ready so he didn't hesitate. He pressed the button and instantly there was a sizzling sound

256

that lasted for a few seconds and then a flash that seemed to set the door alight. It began to glow a shining white. He stood in awe for a few moments then reached out his hand. It felt cool to the touch. He realised that he could push right through so without hesitation he walked forward and entered the world on the other side.

It was not at all what he expected. He found himself standing on the edge of a cliff overlooking the ocean and beheld waves splashing the rocks below. As he caught his breath and steadied himself he thought: "Where on earth?" Then he shuddered as a moment of panic gripped him. He turned around slowly and faced a grey cliff wall. Was he on a ledge? No, his eyes followed the narrow path that seemed to wind down to a small cove. He felt some relief but his legs crumbled beneath him and he slumped to the ground instantly overcome by the terrifying reality. He had no idea where he was.

It was impossible to say how long he remained curled up against the cold cliff wall, mind in a whirl and heart pounding in his chest, but after some time he began to feel the chill of the cool moist air. He knew he had to move, so slowly he got to his feel and began to walk, one step in front of the other, he made his way up.

As he rounded a bend the ledge widened out. He began to feel better but just then something caught his eye. Curled up in a crevice there was a woman alone gazing out to sea; she turned her head slowly and the two strangers faced each other, silent.

Into the Future, an Evening in Galway

"It's not what you do, it's the way that you do it..." Eliza sang quietly, while raising her eyebrows and nodding her head slowly. She stopped and smiled.

Steve wrapped his arms around her and gave her a warm embrace. It felt good and afterwards they stood savouring the moment.

"You sure know how to plan a party" he commented, as he picked up the bottle of Shiraz and refilled her glass. Together they sipped their wine, satisfied, anticipating a good night ahead. Whether three or ten people turned up, they knew it would be an enjoyable evening. For certain Eliza's sister Josie was coming and also her brother Jack and his sister Lucy. He hoped that Keith would make it too.

"What was that you were saying about the neighbours?" he said picking up on what she had been talking about earlier. He often did that, appeared not to be paying attention until he'd surprise her. Eliza tended to prattle on a bit and often felt embarrassed, wishing she could be more responsive to what was going on in the moment. She felt well with Steve knowing he was actually listening.

"I was talking about the roof" she said laughing, "the way the neighbours pulled together. It was a collaboration, very 21st Century, the way we created the roof garden as a collective, a community. There's a real sense among the people in this building. I must say, it is amazing what you can do with a flat roof, especially one like this in a sheltered place..."

"Indeed" Steve said, "Maybe we'll have the next party there."

"Maybe we will." Eliza responded as she gazed out the window with a dreamy look.

"I feel so calm having this view just outside my living room. It's such a transformation compared to that flat grey tatty old roof".

She took the poker and began stoking the embers.

"I love an open fire" she said simply, as she added a large log. The flames blazed up the chimney and illuminated the room with a warm glow. The lamp in the corner had the same soft orange hue and together they generated a calming atmosphere. Steve brought a plate of food from the kitchen just as Josie arrived, early as usual. Josie often hung out with them in Eliza's place. She loved the wall to wall, ceiling to floor windows that had the effect of bringing the outside in and the inside out. It was just one floor above the roof garden, directly above her own flat. She had the advantage of patio doors opening onto the garden. Yet here the view from above had its own charm, and there was easy access between the two apartments via the stairs that led down into the shared space. It would be lovely in the summer, but at this time of year, Eliza's apartment was the perfect hangout. She had moved to Galway to be near Eliza and Steve.

She filled her glass and sat on the soft sofa. She liked Steve. *'Eliza and Steve'* she smiled, thinking, they were good together, very down to earth. They had done well for themselves here in Galway with the small gallery out in Spiddal and the online store distributing their artworks throughout the world. Their apartment in the city overlooked the sea on one side but opened into a cosy sheltered courtyard on the other. She loved her sister dearly. They were a close family. Steve was their Brother Jack's best friend. Then she thought about Adam. He'd also been friends with Jack and Steve...

"Do you remember that day when we took the ferry to the Aran Islands?" she asked.

It was a wild day mostly spent in a little bar with a big open turf fire? She thought about the stormy ocean outside and the safe feeling in the warm flame lit lounge.

"This room reminds me of that little pub, what was it called?"

"Tig Eoghan" Steve reminded her quietly and dreamily. They sat silently together gazing into the flames and drinking their wine.

The doorbell rang.

"That's Keith", Steve jumped up happily and threw the door open.

"Great, you made it, I see you've brought the whole town with you, come in, come in, glasses and ice in the kitchen, help yourselves"

Keith introduced the three guys and four women, then pointed them towards the kitchen.

"Sue and her friends will be here later. They stopped to pick up food on the way. What a great place for a party".

He surveyed the room, smiled at the open fire, then gazed through the glass wall at the brightly lit roof garden and down into the courtyard below. He turned back to the room and took the beer handed to him by one of his mates, then he sat down beside Josie.

"Have you heard from Adam" he asked casually. "How did the exhibition go?"

Josie was really fond of Keith. They were good friends. He was supposed to help her with Adam's exhibition. It was now cancelled, or at least postponed. Keith didn't know. She hadn't told him yet. He'd been away for a while, she didn't know where. Sometimes he was gone for months at a time and then he'd turn up thinking that the whole world had stood still in his absence. They were used to him and loved him anyway. It was just Keith and that's how he was. She thought about Adam's exhibition, shelved after the stormy ocean had welled up and swept away the foundations of their existence.

As Josie paused, thinking to herself, Steve returned.

"Great to hear you have the truck on the road again" he said to Keith, "We were just talking about that time in Tig Eoghan. Wasn't that the time when we got back from Inis Mór and all the paintings were gone from the back of the truck. Did you ever get them back?

"No", he shook his head, "and everything changed after that..."

"Yes" said Josie, "everything changed".

Just then Keith's phone rang. "Sorry, I'll have to take this he said as he wandered into the bedroom".

Josie's Story

Josie got up and walked over to the window, wine in hand, as Steve turned his attention once more to Eliza. She thought about Keith. He was an excellent painter and managed to make a living out of it. He had a studio somewhere in Dublin and often brought paintings down to Spiddal to the gallery. Visitors would purchase his works online after seeing them on display. It was a good arrangement. He wasn't much of a businessman himself and was happy that Steve and Eliza took care of the finances. He only ever took fifty percent but for him that was a lot. They were delighted because they loved his work. It had a magical feel and it was popular not only with artists but also with the general public. That's something that's hard to achieve.

As Josie looked down at the roof terrace from the upper floor window of Eliza's apartment she was thoughtful. The night was calm and the moon large and bright making the world seem grey and shimmery. Her mind drifted back to another time, another place, different people, and another less fortunate roof, one that was open to the elements, the wind often howling from over the mountains, rattling the beams and ripping loose the felt. She thought of the day when Adam arrived.

"I can fix your roof" he offered. So he fixed the roof and then stayed for dinner. He came back and fixed some other things that were broken, and all was right with the world until after a long time Adam went away. By then they were in a different place and there was a different roof, one

262

that was more fragile. It held for a while but then one night the wind howled and howled until eventually it caught the edge of the material and lifted it slightly. Josie remembered standing looking nervously outside as the wind whipped a piece of wood loose. She'd gone on watching until the wind eventually died down. Then everything was calm, for a while, until the next storm came and then another and another until finally the big one arrived that whipped the corner off and threw the surface crumpled up into a corner where it remained until one day Adam returned. Once again he said "I'll fix the roof".

Josie smiled looking out at the pretty roof garden. She turned and held out her glass as Steve arrived over. He poured the dark red wine.

She looked at him and said sadly "You know sometimes it's what you do that counts".

Steve wasn't sure what Josie meant. She often had that faraway look in her eyes. Then he remembered Eliza's happy chant from earlier, before Josie arrived, "It's not what you do, it's the way that you do it". This was almost like a response plucked from the air as though there was a hidden sense that held things together, something profound yet invisible.

Keith returned and looked at Josie. He thought about the exhibition for a moment then opted for a change in the conversation. He'd leave that one for later.

"Have any of you been up to The Village lately" he asked.

"I was there last week" Eliza chipped in, "We had a great session down in the Workman's on Thursday night, ended up in the Bison Bar and had to get a taxi back to Jack's place afterwards".

Josie thought about The Village, how it's not actually a village but rather a network of creative people, mostly writers and artists, all connected through her mother who lives in Blackrock in Dublin. Most of the crowd still hang out in Dublin city although a lot of them now live in Galway. They often gather spontaneously when someone sends out a text naming a time and place. Usually if there's anyone in the vicinity they just turn up. They're all people who feel well with each other and appear to be drawn together by an invisible force.

Eliza continued,

"We dropped over to see Mam", she said, "I love that old house and garden, there's something magical about it. We were so lucky to grow up there".

"I know what you mean". Keith remembered his first visit. He was one of the privileged few who knew about the attic. If Eliza had only known how close she was to the truth. It is indeed magic, a portal into a cave where a majestic dragon lives. The day he stepped through that portal changed his life forever. It's truly amazing what can happen in a second. In that one moment in time he had become part of the secret society at the centre of The Village.

Josie was listening quietly. Something had just struck her. Keith and Adam had come to The Village around the same time. Actually they had a similar accent and they looked similar in a lot of ways. She wondered...

The Dragon Lands

Mary and Charley stepped through the portal into a wide cavern. There were flaming torches on the walls illuminating the way ahead. They walked forward, then turned into a narrow tunnel where they could see daylight ahead. It led out onto the side of a mountain. Charley looked out on the beautiful valley below, the majestic river and the dense forest to the south. Beyond the great forest was home. He recognised the Dragon Lands to the west but there were no dragons. He remembered a time when they swarmed the skies in their thousands. His people had been their protectors. He knew the dragons often visited these caves. Gemma and Felicia lived here with about ten others. There was a huge labyrinth of caverns. If they were asleep it would be hard to find them.

"So where are the dragons?" Mary asked.

"Good question, normally you'd see them flying about. Something's happened. That's why the attic portal didn't work. Damn it, I knew something was wrong."

Charley was visibly shaken. He sat down on the grass and held his head in his hands. Then he looked up at Mary who seemed somewhat bewildered. She sat down beside him and put her arm around his old shoulders. Finding a way to the Dragon Lands had become for both of them a reason to go on living a life that made no sense in a world that was missing a piece of its soul. They'd talked about it as they'd wandered the cliffs in Bailfort searching for the elusive portal. Charley had known about Bailfort where some of his people had gone a thousand years before. They'd travelled back and forth for centuries but then they had been cut off when the portals become unstable. He'd been surprised that some of the portals were still working. Just then he heard shouts from below. Out from the woods appeared a scruffy band of soldiers with swords and bows and arrows. They wore armour made from leather and metal and their beards were scruffy and their faces wild. There was no escape. They were roughly captured and dragged away along a dark forest trail to the east.

Terrified Charley realised that something terrible had happened. He didn't know who these people were or where they'd come from but somehow he knew they had something to do with the disappearance of the dragons. What had they gotten themselves into he had no idea. He hoped his son Keith was safe far away in their village in Landale with his dear friends who had promised to take care of him.

They were forced to walk for days. Half-starved and exhausted they arrived at a castle where they were thrown into a dungeon. Then they heard the sad tales about the dragon wars. The dragons had been wiped out. No protectors had been seen for years. They had been overwhelmed by the hunters who had arrived in their droves by sea at a natural harbour where the great river entered the ocean. They built a city there and castle outposts throughout the land. No one mentioned the protectors' lands far to the south. He hoped that Keith was still all right. He should have taken the child with him. They would be at home now in *The Village*, the whole family and all their friends. *How could he have been so stupid?*

To be continued…

The above sketches were written to InkSplinters' prompts. I have tried to piece the stories together to build a picture of connection, disconnection and reconnection, of loss and uncertainty, of how the choices and decisions we make in life can lead us in directions we could never imagine and how life can become filled with regrets and isolation for some while others somehow manage to maintain and renew connections throughout life. What made Charley leave his son? What happened to Mary in New York and why did her friend Phil take his own life just when he was becoming a successful writer? How did Lorna hide the pain she must have felt for her lost son Keith?

These are just some of the unanswered questions raised by the sketches. I have really enjoyed pulling these pieces together for the InkSplinters first Anthology. I hope to return to this project in the future and try to complete the picture. I too would like to know what happened.

NEVER SPARE A TEAR

Alda Gomez

I will never spare you a tear, my child,
for tears bring depth and are needed
for growth.

I will never spare you a tear, my dear,
for tears will teach you about strength
and a truth that for you I cannot hold.

I will never spare you a tear, my love,
but I will hold your hand while you cry,
silently meeting your heart.

I will not spare you a tear, my soul,
for you need tears to smile and
laugh out loud in your life.

SUNNY SIDE UP

Brian Carroll

Sonny Nolan was a wedding singer fallen on hard times. Since the demand for his particular style of crooning dried up in the late 80's Sonny had sought to re-invent himself as a funeral singer. He dyed his one good suit black and revamped his repertoire to include songs more appropriate to the sombre sobriety of the church. Gone were the rabble-rousing songs of the boozy wedding reception days. In were the sad religious dirges which strained Sonny's limited vocal range. But he was nothing if not persistent and after a few early mishaps Sonny found his niche. In the inner city of Dublin where many an old dear of the blue rinse brigade would recommend Sonny to their friends who's nearest and dearest had departed.

Sonny had a mischievous streak that shone through however and he nearly ruined his reputation when he launched into an unrequested and lusty rendition of the Tom Jones classic 'Delilah' at the funeral of the late Delilah O'Doherty of Lower Gardiner Street. Sonny had taken a nip too many of brandy from his hip-flask that morning and thought his impromptu performance would bring the house down. Needless to say the parish priest didn't appreciate the secular songs and he had to take Sonny aside and have a quiet word in his ear after the grieving Mr O'Doherty had to be restrained and consoled.

Sonny was on his best behaviour for a good while after the 'Delilah' incident but he was fighting a losing battle with the booze and had to cancel several performances when he turned up at the church pink-eyed and unsteady on his feet. Sonny's final performance came at the funeral of

Gertrude O'Shaughnessy when he had a brainstorm and launched into his old wedding favourite, 'I Want To Break Free' by Queen. His swansong came during the guitar solo when he was miming along with some air guitar and he lost his balance. He plunged over the rail of the balcony and into the pews below. He cracked his soused noggin on the brass memorial plaque for the late Freddie Merrick, an irony that would has appealed to his off-kilter sense of humour.

Sonny's funeral mass was a great tribute to the man and his craft. Many of his fellow wedding-singers from the old days were in attendance and they brought the house down with their rendition of the classic, 'Keep Your Sunny Side Up.'

CLASSROOM WINDOWS

Bláithín Ní Liatháin

Grey and grim, and sovietesque the windows block
The light. Double glazed and insulated the windows
Hold in the heat and hold out the cold of winter.

Trees, the heralds of the seasons, through opaque glass
Become invisible. Faraway hills are not green, are not
purple
Are not snow covered, are not at all.

But in their desks the students sit in rows and face the
board.
They do not hear the birds sing, they do not see the poplars
Shake and shook by winds, nor beauty in winter clad
mountains.

In every class of every day roll is called. No mitching now.
Ye god homework is noted, dated, corrected and
commented on.

Lost to imaginations, clouds change shape and colour,
Darkening and lightening the sky. No daydreaming now.
Inside these windows is written what will be learned.

CREATIVE WRITING WORKSHOP

Frank George C. Moore

The ding, ding, of the electric tram made me relax as it always does since I first heard it ring it some fifteen years ago in Dublin city. It is as if the ghost of something fine that was here before, has returned from circa 1911.

> "Well Hello Louis
> yer lookin swell Louis
> It's so nice to see you back where
> you belong
> I feel da room swayin'
> and da bands playin'"

That song always plays Sachmo piano in my head, on our reconditioned Luas.

I got off at St. Stephen's Green, a nip of late October tipped my nose. Across the railings of the park I saw lord Ardilaun gazing across at the college of Surgeons. He had a bronze calm expression, he sitting on a granite dais, looking at his good works from heaven.

"To yourself Mr Guinness" I said in my mind eye "and isn't it a grand tram that we have again?"

Down Grafton Street in a half canter I walked as if in a walking race, I was Irish man late again. The evening light coming from the shop windows almost brought all the shop window people and the rest of us back into sunny July. The song by Tony Hatch played somewhere in my head.

Below beyond Trinity College outside the Royal Liver Insurance Company I waited for a bus and just as I arrived, a sixteen showed up, as if pre-arranged. Aboard we cut down by Trinity circus onto the bridge at O'Connell Street, to the north side of the river and into the beyond. A term we south siders have for all the world beyond the bridge and civilisation.

I'm wondering if you feel any different according to the buses you catch, to get somewhere specific.

For instance on a 16, I always feel a little younger. Maybe even a little sweeter. On a number 11, I feel a little more awkward, like a goose gob on a hot date with yer brother and his hot new amamorae, who every one fancies. Or a spare marrow at a wedding without a partner. Once I got a 77 and my back pain re appeared.

Old age by bus 'inus syndrome do you think? We won't mention the 69.

The reason I tell you this is I'm headed to a creative writing class tonight, so a bit of blarney is forgivable. Once, in a creative writing class I wrote a completely fictitious spy story. The facilitator said to me after they had a few pints, that story of yours, its freaked me out, do you know something about that stuff?

I smiled to myself thinking "it's a creative writing class, for god's sake. All blarney!"

Sure I've always known something about everything. It would be worse if I knew everything about everything, then I'd be a disnofascist or maybe God, or higher still Fintan the Tool.

I'm a great liar. Is that not the point of the exercise of creative classes?

Anyway I didn't feel quite sixteen getting off the bus or any sweeter. But I realised I was black late. I always seem to be late. So as I looked across at the rows of guest Hotels and B&B's on the west side of Parnell square.

Thought maybe I'll book in to one stay for a week so I'm not late next week? Would probably be late any way. 'Derirenach' is the Irish for late know this because last year I did a course in Irish, the lecturer used say.

"Aha an buachaill Derirenach" when I arrived. She never flogged me on my Derry air, if she had I would be going back to study Gaelic again. Don't tell anyone? I like that type of thing occasionally as Gaeilge of course and a Cailin muinteor deas dubh in charge of course. I also learned the Irish national anthem last year, because of the Irish class, bought an Arran ganzi and a pipe. If I'm late next week wonder if there's any chance of a severe flogging? No you say miss? Well it was worth an ask —

STORY FROM THE CITY, DARK

Anniekate Gillroon

We gather for our meal together, the three of us. She says her writing is too much work for her these days. She talks about her great grand-father again and tells us he once said, 'The city at night can be a haunting place. Dream about it but leave it to its haunting.' 'He hated nights sometimes because they reminded him of the black evenings of metal and shredded skin. And he would tell his dark war city story to his son, again and again' she says. I begin to prepare our meal. The tomatoes shine out, a silky red, as I put them on the board. Slices fall down gently against each other on the white plate. The bread, too fresh, soaks the honey. I put it on a tray and pour some more honey across the crusts. He and she sit there close to the fire, watching me prepare the food. 'He always said that there was healing in honey. Told his granddaughter once that he would have longed for it over there, where wounds opened, like the soft weeping mouths of children. Told her that he never heard young men cry so silently, ever in his life again,' she looks across at me, telling us this. 'How is it that something always reminds you of him? no matter what we talk about', he asks her. I stop cutting the blueberries in halves, almost cut my finger. 'You know well that it is because she is writing about him', I say, frowning at him. He laughs. The tray is heavy, the cups hit of each other as he takes it from me. The blueberries cling to the honey soaked bread. He asks her to tell us the war story again. We sit and eat and listen. She tells.

'Then the light crept upon us. We had stayed out under a cold lonely sky until five in the morning. The early morning light followed us into our tiredness. The city that night caught us in its ugliness and pain as we moved outwards from an early morning battle. He sat on the outskirts of the city alone. Nothing to comfort him at the empty walls and broken doors. Nothing until we came within sight of him. He turned and faced us. He had not yet left his childhood. It hung about him as a sadness in his deep eyes, his blond hair. His hand shaking with the weight of the gun he carried. We stopped, one of us called out but then became quiet. Him just standing there unable to move. His clothing covered in dust from hours, maybe days, his body on edge guarding this piece of ground for them. The gun drops from his hand. He looks down and later we say that we almost heard him cry. We walked towards him. He came forward, almost missing his steps on the fallen building. One of us put a hand out to him and he stood near us. None of us able to make him suffer as we were told to do, as we were trained to do. None of us.

> The sad city hung around us, uneasy,
> As we sat on the ground, a huddled group,
> Caught in this wrangled horror,
> Not of our creation,
> Morning, and he lay sleeping,
> A peaceful silence came from our tiredness,

In this silence we knew that he was going to stay living. His silence told us, that he edged towards peace in our presence. The city that night shared the full horrors of early morning. Beyond our huddled group, some as young as him lay face down, faces sideways. Eyes open, eyes pleading, caught in a wrangle of wreckage from their masters. Caught for trying to run away, as children do. One of ours, put a hand across and shaded his blue eyes from all the young blood that wept its way across and down to the next village'.

She finishes telling his story.

I pour tea for us and his hand shakes, as he lifts the knife to slice more tomatoes.

THE SAPONIFICATION OF
HENRI DE FRANOUX

Brian Carroll

Henri de Franoux was a stubborn man in life. He proved equally obstinate in death as his corpse steadfastly refused to decompose after four hundred years buried in the French Huguenot cemetery on Merrion Row in Dublin. His remarkable state of preservation remained concealed until his remains were accidentally disinterred. Builders disturbed his ancient slumber while digging the foundations for the new building next door.

Experts in forensic archaeology from Trinity College were called in to examine this most unusual case. The corpse was perfectly preserved in a thick coat of wax. At first it was thought to be a previously unknown preservation technique but closer examination revealed the source of the wax to be the corpse itself. Diligent students from Trinity managed to take a near perfect cast of the impression created by the wax exuded from the body. This was perhaps the most shocking revelation of all. The cast of the wax impression revealed a man not at peace but with a huge macabre grin spread across his face. The effect was rather disconcerting as the impression given was not one of jollity or mirth but of ghastly malevolence.

Such was the disquieting effect of the impression that it was deemed necessary to secretly store the remains in a locked room in the Department of Forensic Archaeology in Trinity College to which only the Professor of the Department held the key. Professor Andrew de Courcey jealously guarded his latest acquisition and would never allow it to be put on display or studied by other interested forensic scientists. In the six short months since the corpse's discovery, the Professor became obsessed with the remains of the long-dead Frenchman and devoted all his waking hours to the study of the man's life and indeed death. The Professor's absorption was such that he neglected all his other duties as well as his own health and mental well-being.

Eventually the Provost of the University had to have security guards break into the Professor's laboratory after he had locked himself in and failed to emerge after a Halloween Bank Holiday weekend. What they found shocked them so badly that they refuse to speak of it to this day. Rumours flew about and all sorts of bizarre and twisted tales of the Professors proclivities circulated around. All that is known for sure however, is that the Professor's body was found coated entirely in a waxy white substance and that his face was contorted into the same malevolent grin that adorned the deceased Huguenot's visage.

Nobody noticed until years later that the expression on the face of the late Henri de Franoux had gradually changed. A graduate student who studied the remains in some detail noticed that he now looked sad and despondent. The grin on his face had become a sad frown. Today, if you care to look closely at the remains, you could be persuaded that a tear escapes from his left eye.

ROSE GARDEN

John O'Farrell

"These are the rose bushes Uncle planted when he came here first, when he was young"

Bella looked at me without particular expression on her teenage face: this, she presented the bushes, is a fact, you can see they are here, I shall tell you how they came to be here. I didn't understand what she meant by "came here first" so I asked her.

"He used to be the gardener here long ago, that's how he knew about the place. He's always loved it."

She walked a little in front of me because she knew the way, suddenly she stumbled and I reached to catch her. She took a moment to steady herself then looked me in the eye and saw the concern there. She continued walking but her body seemed to relax. The tool shed was at the far end of the garden, hidden in a corner. This practice used to annoy my father, he believed tools should be stored somewhere convenient for the work. I asked him once - I was angry and wanted to hurt him - was he not ashamed of working in other people's gardens. He laughed so hard he couldn't answer, his laughter was hearty and sincere and not directed at me. "Other people's gardens...!" he managed to blurt out, he couldn't finish but only point at his chest and say "My gardens! My... gardens!"

Bella and I went into the shed even though there was no reason to. She lifted a pair of secateurs from the bench by one handle in a desultory way as if handling a dead bird. "Do you think you'll have everything you'll need?" I had already looked around; the tools were old, original, made to last until work wore them away. They had not been cared for but as each was required I would clean and sharpen them. In response to her question I picked up a stubby pruning knife and said: "I could do everything with this". I heard myself say it, I heard the pride in my voice. I tried to recover by showing my appreciation for the tools: "They'll need to be cleaned and sharpened but they're good tools. Look, here's an old clay spade, you don't see them around much anymore". Again I heard myself and winced. I felt I was pushing us away from talking about each other or just talking. I wanted to talk about her.

"I liked the story you read in English class," I said.

"Thanks".

I had liked it. I had liked being able to look at her without fear and listen to her voice without having to pay attention. It had been a story about a girl and a dog that had broken its leg. The dog was going to be put down but the girl promised to look after it and did so for most of her summer holidays. She began it with a scene of the girl having to stay behind as her family went to the circus. I said:

"I liked the way you sort of started in the middle."

"Yes," she said, "when you do that it's called in media res, I learned that at Billy Barry's." She stopped and looked at her feet.

There was no reason to stay any longer, I had not been expected to do any work that afternoon. We returned together following the paths. At one point I stopped and looked back; I tried to understand what my father had meant, "my garden". We came to the avenue, soon we were going to say goodbye. All this just so I could be near her. I wanted to kiss her cheek but I would be coming back tomorrow to begin mowing the lawns. She just stood there with her hands by her sides looking at me. I extended my hand, she took it falteringly, her palm was clammy.

"Goodbye," I said and shook her hand once. I cursed myself again and again on the walk home.

When I arrived at the door I was greeted by my sister. My name is Thomas but she still called me Domdom even though she was six. She had clung to my leg from the moment she could walk. It never bothered me. I was only eight years older than her but I knew somehow I was her father, we never played together.

My mother was in the sitting room watching television. It was half past five in the afternoon and they were still showing children's programmes. She used to tell her friends that children's programmes were great for relaxing as if this was a trick she had learned.

"I'm home Mam!" I called in to her. Mam, Mum, Mammy, Mother, sometimes Ma after I visited the home of a friend who used it, but never Cathy. I was always shocked when I heard someone call a parent by their Christian name. My sister was named for her but I always call her Catherine. A couple of years ago my mother said to me I could call her Cathy if I liked but I said that that would be confusing. I felt sorry for her when I realised that she must hardly ever hear her name spoken.

"Where were you?" my sister asked. "I almost had to start dinner!" She would have taken dinners out of the freezer and put them in the oven.

"I got a job."

"Mammy, Domdom got a job!"

My mother came out of the sitting room with a concerned look on her face.

"Thomas, what is this about?"

"I'll be gardening for Mr Silvers Mam, it's just for pocket money."

"I don't know Thomas, what about school?"

"I'm only going to do it for an hour after school and on Saturdays." She stroked the back of my head.

"Alright then Tom."

Mother wouldn't notice the extra money because I would use it to buy the things she forgot and pay more off the grocer's bill than she gave me. I could get the odd treat for Catherine as well.

The following day at school it was as if nothing had happened. At least Bella had not made me a source of fun, didn't look over at me before huddling closer to her friends and laughing. In fact she didn't look at me all day, except once when we met alone in the stairwell.

"Are you coming today?" she asked, smiling but without stopping, as though passing me for the first time that day.

"Yes, of course," I replied because that was in fact the arrangement I had made with her uncle.

"Ok then," she said looking over her shoulder as she continued her descent.

Later, when classes were over for the day, she stayed back talking to the geography teacher telling her friends to go on without her. I walked outside with a slow pace in the hope she would finish and we would find ourselves together but she didn't. I couldn't just wait for her outside the school door in full view of the teachers' room and any pupils on detention so I walked across the playing fields to the gate in the southern wall of the school grounds which was the one she used. I stopped under the horse chestnut tree near the gate.

I looked back at the school and saw her standing at the door looking in my direction. She turned and walked to the flower pots and bent down to smell the pansies there. Suddenly I couldn't breathe. She had stayed back talking to the geography teacher in order to avoid me. She had asked if I was coming that evening so that she could not be there. I immediately saw myself as a fool, my own fool, not her fool. She had no thought for me at all, she knew my father had been a gardener and she had asked me to come along and meet her uncle. Bella Silvers! Fool! I raised my eyes to look at her again, as if to apologise before going home, because home I would certainly go, only to find her half way across the playing field, looking straight at me, smiling.

"Mr Stevens was looking at me," she said as she came up to me, "do you think he's nosey? He asks about my uncle all the time."

"I don't know. Maybe."

"Who do you think is the nosiest teacher?"

"Mrs. Drake," I said, "she's all nose."

Bella laughed. After that we talked easily and quickly about school and people we both knew though we didn't really have any friends in common. She told me about her uncle and I told her about my father. I told her about the day he left for the last time. She squeezed my hand then with a look of concern on her face which made me feel mature and sent a shiver down my neck. She let my hand go again. It was too early for that I thought. When we got to her gate she stopped me and said she would go ahead, I was to follow in five minutes. I could have thought she was ashamed of me but I thought the opposite. I felt more important to her because I was a secret. I would keep her a secret too. In fact I would tell her to say, if anyone asked, that she would be ashamed to go out with me. I could say that I wouldn't go out with her because she was a snob. I watched her climb the steep driveway to the house.

When I realised I had been daydreaming I panicked and almost ran up the avenue. She answered the door and gave me a haughty look. She left the door open and simply turned and walked back into the house, calling out "Uncle! The gardener's here" as she did so. Before disappearing from sight she turned her head back over her shoulder and gave me a mischievous smile. That was the moment I fell in love with her.

Her uncle came out of a room to the left as though looking for his niece, seeing me he said: "Oh hello Tom. Do you know where the mower is?"

"No."

"It's in the coal shed."

I imagined this was one of the outhouses to the side of the house so I said:

"I'll find it, is there any petrol?"

"Yes, in the jerrycan, I filled it from the car."

Despite his being Uncle Silvers, he was practical man. I was beginning to like him.

"Ok then, I will start at the back."

"No, start at the front."

"Ok then," I said, and left.

I wheeled the mower down the paths to the front lawn, by far the largest. It was a fairly new machine, a Honda and a good size too. When I was working with my father we always asked to see the customer's mower, we had our own of course but sometimes the customer's was bigger if not better.

I mowed the front lawn and had mown the small lawn beside the tennis court when Bella arrived with a tray and two glasses of Coke. I was wary of this, I was working.

"Uncle said I was to bring you something to drink."

I relaxed when I heard this. The Coke was cold and delicious. I had never drunk it from a glass before. I tried not to gulp it down but when I saw her looking at me I did. It wasn't too fizzy, it must have been from a large bottle. They probably always had Coke.

Then Mr Silvers came and said to me: "Put the mower away and I'll drop you home."

"But I'm not finished," I said.

"There's time enough tomorrow, grass doesn't grow that fast!" he said.

"I don't need a lift, I can walk, thank you." I glanced at Bella but she was looking down at the tray.

"Well now, you've school tomorrow, I'd better get you home to your mother. I'll see you at the front door."

He went away before I could object. I shrugged my shoulders at Bella and did as I was asked.

I arrived at the front door determined to refuse the lift home but to my horror he had driven out his large Mercedes and was sitting behind the wheel, but it was not him I was looking at, Bella was sitting in the front passenger seat. I swallowed what felt like a conker. What was she doing there? Why was she doing this to me? Our eyes met as I walked towards the car and she looked away out the window. I sat into the back of the car and pulled the heavy door shut. The inside of the car was like a room. Mr Silvers looked at me in the rear-view mirror.

"I have to bring Bella to her lesson anyway, so it's no trouble, Belleview isn't it?"

"No Mr Silvers, Belmont," I said, stressing the second syllable, "number fifteen". I immediately regretted giving him the number.

No one talked during the journey and it was not long before I could say:

"Here is fine for me!" but Mr Silvers was already leaning forward over the wheel peering out the windscreen at the house numbers. "Now, now," he said, "I always get my man home".

It was a fine summer's evening and people on the estate were out chatting to one and other over the low hedges or walking their dogs. The children were on the green and of course my estate friends were out playing football. Many people stopped what they were doing when they saw the car, wondering what house it would stop at. I prayed my mother would not be at the door, it would not have been like her to be there but still I prayed. I wasn't worried that Catherine would come out; she never did anything to embarrass me.

"Is that your work?" Mr Silvers asked pulling up at my house and nodding to the front garden where you could see the small bed through the railings.

"Yes," I said.

It was my work. Not long after my father left my mother said it would be nice to have flowers at the front. I prepared a small bed and planted begonias and jezebels, all

288

of different hues, I knew she just wanted lots of colour. It was easy to keep. For a moment, all three of us looked through the car windows at the small flower bed. I slid across the rear bench seat and said thank you as I exited the car. I didn't look at Bella so I don't know if she looked at me. As I walked the seven paces to the door I heard the Mercedes pull away. I smiled at Catherine who was watching everything from the behind the net curtains.

The next day I went to school as usual, walking with Catherine, who still had questions about what she called the mansion. I left her at the door of her school and doubled back to my own. I slowed my pace down so as to arrive just as the bell for classes rang. Bella and I both had English first, Bella's place was the top of the class and mine was at the back. I passed down the aisle furthest from her. She was talking to someone and didn't see me. When the teacher came in she looked around and our eyes met briefly. When class was over she delayed a little gathering her books. As I was passing her by I slipped a note onto her desk. Her hand covered it immediately. The note read: "I can't come today." I knew she would understand. From then on I stopped looking at her.

BON CHANCE

Frank George C. Moore

I found myself in the gallery that morning. George
Bernard Shaw's art gallery in Merrion Square Dublin.
Early I was. I'm never early for anything. I'm am an Irish
man. She had said in French, you are not going to be late
after all the strings I pulled. You lazy dirty Irish potato
sucking sod. So get out of my sight. And   don't be late. I
picked up the word "sod" in French, she definitely said
sod, sounded very sophisticated in continental. *Bon
chance*, I replied looking at her sweet Gallic ass, it being
Saturday.

Hearing and seeing this, she swung the waffle
maker which was at hand as she had been making
breakfast. She had picked up my import faster than I had
anticipated. Her English was improving I thought. The
utensil caught me on the side of the face, made a mark like
a Hollywood injury. A perfect swelling arose I could feel
it. Of all the accoutrements she has for making breakfast
at hand it had to be that heavy one. A lovely crease arose
at the side of my face I could feel it. Very artistic shaped
injury, I thought. As I looked at myself in the mirror of
the bathroom by the front door, just on leaving the
apartment. She was always saying I was full of waffle I
thought. One of those sayings she had picked up from my
mother, who says she loves me too. Isn't the love of some
women a dangerous thing?

So I was at least forty minutes early for the
appointment, injured of course, pride too. If there's one
thing I resent losing more than money it's my sense of
calm. Equilibrium, balance it's what gives a man his

dignity. No breakfast I'd had, wearing the imprint of the first meal of the day I suppose you might say.

Bon appetite, I had heard her say as I left the apartment.

Yes, I wanted to regain my calm; ordinarily I'm a calm man. "It's as if you're constantly on holiday", that's how Morel puts it. You go on as if you're at a cocktail party all the time, out of work for five months you irresponsible sod. So pass the canapés waiter. I could hear my mother's tutelage here. "You're a married man now", of late always seemed to finish our conversations.

So here I was like a bridegroom at an arranged marriage, trying to find that picture again, the one that had fascinated me at a previous visit. A book launch is where I had first encountered it. Now in an attempt to commune with something peaceful I sought it out once again, that picture. I was alone, just before an arranged interview for a job at the National Gallery of Ireland. A Saturday morning in April it was, a lovely "April love day". I thought touching the swelling around my eye.

"What sort of an interview is conducted on a Saturday morning I hear you ask? I too had temporally forgot, I was back in Ireland. Everything to do with money, a job mortgage is always arranged here through acquaintance... Especially if it's mildly connected with the arts. Jobbery inverts grace and favour Ireland. How the emerald operates. I must tell you these things, if you don't know such. The thought irritated me. The cold marble floors of the gallery too, making me nervous, slippery floors I considered, bit like my life at that moment.

Mooching around by a huge naked marble sculpture depicting Mars. I found myself skittering sideways, trying to avoid looking up at its huge appendage. Not good for a man's ego that, before an interview I thought.

Suddenly a starched uniformed attendant stood motionless in front of me two piercing eyes above an uncle pop moustache. I moved over to a row of French paintings out of his line of vision. And there the picture was in front of me. Its subject set in a Parisian street, a young twenty something buxom girl selling flowers at a stall, a great plain tree filtering the light above her. The Seine glistening in full flow behind her. An old stone pedestrian bridge was set into the structure of the work, built before the French revolution in their year one. Or 1794.

It was the depiction of the light that was so striking. Its capture fascinated me and the uncanny resemblance of the subject to someone in my past. I had even considered if it might be her in the flesh, in the moment almost. After all it was painted in Paris. It wasn't very old, twenty five years perhaps. I examined the signature, couldn't make it out, but I then clearly read - *Paris "75.*

I had approached the painting too closely, hoping the uncle pop attendant was out of line of vision. I stared at the signature nervously.

At that moment someone tapped me on the shoulder. I turned around to look into the eyes of Patrice. "Bonjeur Môn ami Patrick", Morell told me you were to be interviewed today. It should go well", he said. A superior French grin on his Gallic face.

Now between you me and the Seine, can I make one thing clear, I don't like Frenchmen. There too slick with women and too fond of everyone else's money. This specimen in particular calling me Patrick My name is Glennpatrick. I told him this story a couple of times. My old man named me after his favourite Scotch. I thought he would have remembered that. - Glennpatrick a quality Scotch.

"You can always put G.P. after your sir name", my dad had said to me once. Confuse the buggers" My old man was laid back like myself, my dad; Its where I got my character which appears to irritate some women and most pompous men... He left me a packet of money; don't know where he got that from either. There were hints he might have been a successful upper class art criminal.

"I've had a word", Patrice said. It, the positions in the bag as you Paddies say. Just relax. The interview should go smoothly.

Patrice I must tell you was on secondment I remembered from the Louvre to the National Gallery of Ireland. I remembered Morel say. An old family friend from la belle.

Are you familiar with zis painting?" Patrice lifted his Gallic eyebrows.

You have views on it? "

Threes something strange about it, apart from its quality, I said. I even feel I could have met this girl. Can't recognise the location in the city can you Patrice?

Its *la route du Ray Lussac*, expensive street. But artists were tolerated there up to dee eighties. Been how it, gentrified is. It's a self portrait of an artist when she was a student, in fact this artist is in Dublin soon. I should know, it is I who "ave brought zis work here, Part of an exchange exhibition. She's now a professor of fine art in the *Sorbonne.* She is coming soon to Dublin You must meet her. French women seem to take a curious interest in allegedly rich Irishmen.

He had a bemused expression on his face.

He noticed I was examining my waffle mark as I touched my face, the crinkle imprint of the waffle maker reminding me of my inability, not to annoy Meroll these days. I remembered my old mum say to her. "The men in his father's family are very sedentary, you have to almost kick them into life. Lazy bastards in fact.

My mind at that moment drifted into considering "what if's". Was my tying the knot with Meroll a mistake? And could it be herself, the name came to me in that moment Zeta, be that French girl from the past, a strange coincidence relayed by a painting. It was turning out to be quite an interior morning I considered.

Patrice was grinning down at me said.

"Away with zea Connemara fairies Patrick?" he said.

His expression annoyed me. He was only three months in Dublin was beginning to speak English like a drunken educated Irish man. He added.

"Must vamoose Paddy, don't want to be zeen talking to a candidate for too long" He turned on his heel and vanished by a concealed service door. A door I hadn't noticed, left a scent of Gauloise and some expensive man perfume about. Nausea attacked. My calm had not returned. That slimy smooch ball was going to be on the interview panel.

I looked at the painting imagining Patrice's expert hands, fondle her. I believe he had screwed his way around the parlours of south Dublin since he arrived. I remembered a seven inch necked solicitor, a brother of a police commissioner as it happened. A clan no man messed with. Say to me at a party through a vat of brandy breath.

"G. P That French onion, he'll be done if he doesn't stop screwing certain gumbos wives and others. If yer a friend of his, tell him how things work in a civilised country. This lot I wouldn't mess with" I remembered thinking. "Serious men" I was quietly chuffed with the confidence from such a luminary. He had finished by saying, "G.P. only have sons" His eyes were glazed and a little moist. As he looked at Patrice who had been talking to Meroll at the time. I said to that mad solicitor Mick. "Join the queue Michael sir"

Sod, I muttered to myself. If that sleazy lizard has any input into me getting this job I'll tell them to derriere it. Despite Meroll, my mother and all the loving women in the world and their waffle makers. I looked at my watch.

295

Fifteen minutes to the bum ceremony interview. I straightened my tie took one more glance at the picture turned towards the administration office.

Later that day and pre six o'clock Saturday I found myself, as I do on most Saturdays when I am in my native city, dropping into a shop or two replenish my wardrobe. A habit my father gave me. He used say, "Always spend at least five per cent of your income on new clothes son. That way no matter how tight or in the pink finances are, nobody will guess" The other habit I have on Saturday is to treat myself to a new book or two. I have a few favourite shops, second hand books I prefer. You wouldn't believe the treasures I've found in the pages of recycled books.. Airline tickets to Johannesburg linked to an air ticket from Dublin to London and a train ticket from Clonmel to Dublin. A journey taken fifty years before the book was last closed...Left for me to open. So as usual, I adjourned then to Keoghs it's the pub, with my swag.

As it happened I had acquired a copy of Moby Dick. Hadn't read it since my father gave me a copy many years since. I was on the fifth page when my mobile phone rang. I had forgotten to turn the bugger to message minder.

I picked it up noticed Meroll's number on the screen.

Wveere are uouu?", she said in that panicky tone she takes when she is excited.

"My lovely", I said. Hoping for at least another hour's peace.

"Where are you Môn cher?" This surprised me.

"I'm in Keogh's"

Never mind", she said "News, I've news"

"The job" I said you couldn't know already. I didn't get it?

"Ohh that, it's yours" she said "shure I've told you. It's…no not that. Did you see the newspaper?"

"I've got it here" I said touching a copy of the Guardian.

"No" she said "Honestly sometimes you've got your head up your port.. No za Dublin "Eharald, did you see the headlines. Patrice hee ass, been found dead. Zay say, foul play zhaa police"

Just as she spoke, a figure came into the bar dripping wet, a bundle of papers under his arm. He stopped two bar standing customers in front of me" fixed me with a stare "Paper" he said. I pushed some loose change across the small round bar table, "Jinkria", a wet Polack voice said. Dropping a tablet paper onto the, table hustled on.

I could hear Morell's voice, Geee Peee are you there. I opened the folded paper. Headlines read;

-Eminent French art expert found, by landlady, dead in Dublin mews, - Foul play suspected.

I read on astonished. Patrice Maereau, Art Expert was found dead in his apartment on Haddington road today.

Morell's voice brought me back to the moment. "Hello gee pee did you see it"

"But, but" I said, "I only spoke to him this morning He was himself, full of vim beans his usual insufferable self" I said "Morell I could have been one of the last people to speak to him"

Maybe, or perhaps not" she said "He called your mother just after your interview and told her; Well he's got the job a shoo in. She phoned me. Added imagine what a way to go. Poor Patrice must have been a burglar. Where are you?"

I told her again. "I'll be there in half an hour" She rung off.

It was at that moment the bar door opened. I saw the figure of hand ball head Covney. A man I had attended school with even shared a desk with for a time. The quiff hadn't changed in thirty years.

Gibnet Barry Covney's path I had crossed in the intervening years. Always nodded we had exchanged pleasantries. Never had a longer conversation. I always thought of him as a Cork man. Although I knew he was born in Dublin, his father he once told me and back to Adam were from down there. "Ok a Cork man" I had said. When he joined the police force when we finished secondary school. Frankly it had surprised no one when he became not just a police man but an up and coming

298

detective. He kept to himself then we had all noticed. Always polite with everyone but apart. The job I suppose. He nodded towards me. I nodded back said "Barry"

I returned to reading Moby Dick. Then noticed a shadow come over the page. When I looked up he was standing looking down at me.

"G.P" he said, "still practising medicine? So you're back from France. I met your new wife at a reception, congratulations. Quite a looker" I looked up at him. "Still in Pearse Street Sergeant Barry" I said.

"No its Chief Detective Inspector now" he said "I"m up in HQ in the Park"

Congratulations your way" I said "always knew you had it in you"

"Can I join you?" He said "long time since I talked to some one I shared class room with"

Of course, please sit, Hand ball" He smiled that tooth gap grin he has.

He sat down opposite me. "Yep hand ball never lost it. Do you still play?" I said. "A little" he said. "It's mainly squash now"

"More sophisticated" I said.

"Aren't we all these days. Still collecting ancient books?" He picking up my copy of Moby Dick.

"Grand tale" he said. "Morality story. Never hold contempt or transfer your ire to another even if it"s taken yer leg, or your woman or your money. The Leviathan Poor dumb animal. A swimming mammal" He said.

The words, your woman, hung in the air.

The sun slanted in through the bar window as it has a habit to do in good Dublin pubs. The silhouette of the word bonder lit the table and both of us.

He looked into my eyes said. "Been in the wars G.P.? Quite a shiner"

"Accident in the kitchen a passionate French woman" I said He let it drop.

"Ahh passionate women," he said.

He asked, "What you planning to do now your back Liffey side?"

Strange how your vanity or whatever it is when you are dealing with someone you were educated with asks how your life is turning out. What you up to now?

"Just lined up a job in the gallery matter a fact" I said.

To my astonishment he said, "So I've heard. Glenn pat a mhich"

He looked at me with those cold beady eyes. I remembered then despite the years and our polite glancing association we had shared over the intervening years. We still didn't like one another even as mellowing men.

The years began to fall away. We were eighteen again. Handball narrowed his eyes said

"G.P. Tell me. What happened - I've just come from Patrice Maereau's apartment, droch olla GP. Droch olla. He's dead, mort as the French say. Do you know G.P...? Can't but remember old Sac, our French teacher, lovely old gent. Gave him an awful time. Never listened to him GP. Do you remember some shit sent in that request to radio Caroline, asking that diddy man disc jockey to play? "My nineteenth nervous breakdown. When we heard he was taking time off, to recover from our collective endeavours to drive a good teacher down. We were bastards G.P... Ahh human nature me and all." If I had listened to him. Ye know he was a brilliant French teacher. When he died .I discovered he had fought in the French resistance agent those barbarous Nazis. And us G.P what we did to him? I could have even a beautiful French wife, travelled the world like you?" I looked at him a new respect for him and the law.

Just at that moment the bar door opened Meroll appeared. She stopped, looked at us, made her way slowly to our table

"Ahh Handball" l said "Meroll will tell you about my eye and no waffle hand ball" I said.

He stood as Meroll joined us. "What "ill it be, he said? My twist."

301

"Twist?" She said "Ahh to drink you Irishmen. Crème de Menthe on ice" she said.

The bar man wasn't behind the bar I noticed. To my surprise Handball left us to go through the door out to the dingy lounge.

It occurred to me he was giving us an opportunity to speak to one another. It was the first time I saw Meroll without her cool chic French composure. She kissed me on the neck, breathed out that special way she does. "Gleen Patrice" she whispered into my ear "I love you so deeply Môn Cheri. Things will be said. My dalliance with Patrice ended months ago. It is you I love my Irish potato. With zis man we must be careful"

The hand ball reappeared at the door He looked at both of us. Did I see contempt perhaps a look of jealousy in his eyes? No I realised somehow, it was, I detected, concern, even empathy for both of us. Somehow we were back in those class rooms thirty years back. Or in that dance hall down by Parnell square when as I remember I lifted a girl from him. Her saying to me there's sort of bad and good about that one.

"To the happy couple" he said. Placing the drinks on the table. He opened the Evening Herald glanced down at it. Said almost apologetically. "GP you probably realise by now, this is why I'm here. Would you know anything about this? I'm sure you can tell me where you have been since you left the art gallery at twelve fifteen. Explain the mark on your face. And how can I put it delicately Mrs. Gilbert what can you tell us about your relationship with Patrice Maereau? I am sure you both can be of assistance and we'll have this matter cleared up in jig time. But when you finish your drinks I am sure you won't mind calling down to Pearse Street station. We have an incident room set aside. Talk to this man"

He took a card from his pocket placed it on the table.

"I took this task on myself GP knew you would be cooperative" He stood up looked at Morell turned and left the bar.

She looked at me said "We will get through this GP" I took a long pull from my black pint, nodded towards the bar man indicating, same again. Began to read the report in the evening paper of a violent assault on the French lover Patrice. Morell began to sob. As I touched the swollen imprint around my eye. Thinking of my young wife's passionate nature. A cold insight touched my heart.

"Wee'zd better make our way down there GP, to za police bureau" she said. She sounded very wifely and vulnerable through her sobs.

"No I said. Don't worry about that, let's finish these drinks. It's Ireland they are Irishman. Tradition to be late" I took a sip from the newly arrive pint of black Guinness. Said "Hand ball 'ill understand"

"But he "asnt been murdered" she said. "Can you think of why anyone would want to murder a Frenchman?" I smiled looking at my beautiful intelligent passionate new young French wife. Alarm eased its icy hand on the back of my neck.

It would be easy to recount my movements of that day. Dublin is such a small and intimate inner living town. But as I looked at Meroll I counted her passionate nature and charming gift of flashing into physical expression of feelings. A cold realisation entered my mind. She began to shake. "Can you imagine being murdered" she asked. The word, Murdered hung in the air. "It will be all right Morell" I said putting my arm around her. She seemed so frail, as if life itself had left her. I said "It'll be grand my love" and in a gentle whisper she replied "Bon chance, Môn Cheri"

Kenneth Nolan is a Writer and Poet originally from Tallaght, currently living in Lucan.

He has been published in Tallaght Soundings, Optic Magazine, Van Gogh's Ear Anthology, Headspace Magazine, In-Tallaght Magazine plus The Echo and Tallaght Express newspapers.

In 2012 he won the CDVEC Sports & Cultural Council Award for Poetry and in 2013 he was short listed for the Jonathon Swift Award.

He's dedicated to his writing, when he's not writing he's thinking about writing. He's easy going and very straightforward. *"If it barks it's a dog"*

Blog// kennethnolan6.wordpress.com

Alda Gomez is a SpIrish woman who's been writing in her native Spanish for as long as she can remember. A couple of years ago a bolt of lightning struck her on the forehead and she got a marvellous wonderful idea! She could start writing in English.

Ever since then poems in English have been pouring onto blank pages, into notebooks and upon dusty keyboards.

Brian Carroll likes genre fiction, fountain pens and fluffy bunnies. He is a computer nerd who rides his silver bicycle everywhere. He writes because the alternative is not pretty and is rather fond of dark chocolate.

Brian Browne officially joined 'the old farts club' earlier in January 2014 so he is now entitled to call himself a grumpy old man. He is still discovering, to his amazement, that sometimes others are kind enough to listen to his ramblings.

Cathy Power is a Dublin woman with an identity crisis and a passion for Kilkenny hurling. She is an occasional contributor to RTE's *Sunday Miscellany* and is just about starting her first novel. She lives in Dublin 9 with her daughter and two old dogs.

Dublin born Bláithín Ní Liatháin is a teacher of Irish and English.
Having taught all she wants to teach it's time to start learning.

For forty years as a public administrator Pat Nolan's job was to write:
Reports, policy papers, and replies to parliamentary questions. So, on retirement, he decided he would like to ... write. But this time for himself, and ideally for you, dear reader.

Camillus John was bored and braised in Dublin. He has been writing fiction since Lenny, the dog that can lick your mind out, licked his mind out, when he was six. He's been shortlisted in RTE's *New Planet Cabaret*, *The RTE Guide/Penguin Ireland Short Story Competition* and published in *Boyne Berries*. His *Pervert's Guide to Modern Fiction* is due to appear shortly in *The Stinging Fly* and *The Rise and Fall of Cinderella's Left Testicle,* his novel, is now nearing completion. The attached is a photo of *The Flying Superhero Clothes Horse* himself, Howie B, as unfortunately, Camillus accidently burst himself invisible at a Pats match in late 2013, when they won the league.

Susan Cooney's poetry deals in large part with the passing of Time. She qualified as a language teacher in Dublin, where she is teaching languages and she has lived in Madrid and the U.S.A. She has been writing poetry since she was eighteen.

Harry Browne is an old guy who started the writing thing late in life. He has written and published a time travel novel called 'Time and Time Again' and is currently working on the sequel. He is patiently waiting for his literary genius to be discovered and his book to be taken up by a mainline publisher and a major movie house.

Geralyn Rownan lives on the east coast of Ireland and works in Dublin. She's smart, gorgeous and great fun. That's according to her therapist and the members of her creative writing group, Inksplinters, who are, of course, totally unbiased. She likes writing stories with happy endings

Katie Dwyer believes in travel—in writing stories while looking out the windows of trains or in seeking out stories in new and distant lands. She comes to Ireland by way of Colorado and Oregon, first to study Human Rights Law in Belfast and Galway, and now is living and writing in Dublin. She likes castle ruins, stone walls, quiet seasides, steep cliffs, and the feeling of arriving in a place she's never been before.

E.M. Ollivander is an occasional scribbler who like to exercise the mind with words and pictures and the body with walks in nature.

Breda McAteer joined the Ink Splinters creative writing group in 2012. She studied English at Liberties College Dublin, and St Patrick's College (DCU). Her father encouraged her to write at a young age through his own appreciation of literature and his interest in writing poetry. She contributes her poems based on nature, to her experience of living in Ireland and North Wales. The inspiration behind her poem Peters Painting is from a member of the Ink splinters group who is also a talented artist. This is Breda's first published work, and she is currently in the process of writing a short story.

John O'Farrell has only recently started writing regularly despite harbouring the ambition to do so for many years. He comes from the Waterford area but emigrated to Dublin as a young man. Notoriously he is a civil servant.

After having failed in her attempt to write a romance novel, there was nothing for it but to attempt literary fiction. So, Kay Dunne left Australia for Ireland and completed a master's degree in creative writing, joined Ink Splinters and found she liked writing poetry. She's still working on the poetry, and, in the meantime, has had a couple of short stories published in commercial magazines in Australia, a humorous piece in the Sydney Morning Herald, and has been placed in competitions in short story, memoir and synopsis writing.

Mimi Goodman

All those ideas & thoughts, the discipline needed to put pen to paper. The nightmare of trying to type. Keep going.

Photo by Wendy Ip

Volker Gebhart much enjoyed being part of the InkSplinters group when he lived in Dublin. He originally comes from Bremen in Germany and has a background in journalism. He is currently working on a novel; he also writes short stories and contributed to the screenplay for Mark Nielson's 'Land of Sky Blue Water' (US, 2011) as story consultant. He works in online media.

Anniekate Gillroon lives in Dublin. Writes. Her writing never was short listed for any prize, never won a prize, never was published. She will always write. Her biographical picture is the flowering shrub in their garden. It never won any prizes but it flowers every year. Its beauty will always bloom and flower within its natural lifespan.

Martina Carroll wrote a poem in the summer of 2012. Then she discovered the InkSlingers workshops and the offshoot group InkSplinters. In order to be a member she had to go to the sessions and write more poems. One thing led to another and with the influence of the group she started writing prose. She has dabbled in art for years and previously worked with conceptual texts associated with paintings. Much of her poetry is inspired by art. Now creative writing is a part of her life and she has many new writer friends and acquaintances in the city. She has discovered a great writers' scene Dublin.

Pronsias O Mordha. (Frank George C. Moore)
Published social journalist. Poetry writer of the Dublin's Pale.
Sometimes short story writer.
Of Thomas and George.

42 Imaginary Things I Think People Might Be Saying About *Inksplinters Anthology 2014* In The Near Future. Possibly.
Camillus John.

"Like most people, I hate creative-writing anthologies. But this one is ok." *Inda Kinny.*

"This anthology is dynamite, it blew my brains out and smeared them all over my living room walls." *Paddy Tarantino.*

"It's better than sex." *Pope Francis.*

"This book is superglue, I couldn't put it down." *Sticky Fingers McGurk.*

"Very absorbing. The best toilet-book I've read all year. It was right up my alley. In fact, it kept me going for weeks." *Elias Crapper.*

"Others have carped that *Inksplinters Anthology 2014* contains too much sex, drugs and rock 'n' roll. But I disagree. In my opinion, you can never have enough of that sort of thing in a book. I bought ten copies." *Desperate Dan.*

"Finnegan's awake? Finnegan's asleep more like. Hold on, he's awake again with a well-thumbed copy of *Inksplinters Anthology 2014* popping his eyeballs and steaming his ears!" *Jimmy Joyce*

"This book has so much depth, you'll drown." *Russell Brand.*

"Reading *Inksplinters Anthology 2014* was about the only thing that kept me sane when I was off cockling for a gang-master earlier this year. Buy at least two copies forthwith." *Spike Milligan.*

"The writing is so sharp in this book, you could shave both your legs with it." *Panti Bliss.*

"Inksplinters Anthology 2014 was so riveting, it made me eat all the rasher sandwiches in my Hambag* in one go." *Janey Macken Street. *(Hambag© By Pravda).*

"What could have emerged as a monumental act of hubris is rescued by Editor, Harry Browne's humility, wit and intelligence in dealing with such a ragtag, moth-eaten bunch of egotistical "writers", who couldn't hand something in on time to save their lives." *Harry Browne.*

"I read *Inksplinters Anthology 2014* and found it so seductively charming, that I wanted to marry it and have it babies." *Roy Keane.*

"At the start this book certainly rings all the right bells, but in the end it just gave me the hump to be honest." *Quasimodo.*

"*Inksplinters Anthology 2014* reminded me of T.S. Eliot's *The Waste Land.* I couldn't finish that either." *T.S. Eliot.*

"This excellent book allows the reader a fascinating glimpse into how much heart and soul a modern writer puts into making people nauseous. Can't wait for the sequel though." *The spirit of Ernest Hemingway.*

"Today everybody Googles. No one Yahoo's any more. Buy *Inksplinters Anthology 2014* – because everybody else is – even the Yahoos." *Google sales and marketing department.*

"Does this work live up to the hype? No." *Nine out of ten discriminating readers.*

"This anthology has the power to mesmerize. All human life is contained in these pages and Harry Browne, Editor, deserves a medal for getting all contributors to keep taking the tablets during its making." *Harry Browne.*

"*Inksplinters Anthology 2014* lingers in the unconscious and is full of other books. If there's an author they haven't ripped off, please let them know and they're sure to rectify it in the sequel." *Nine out of ten established authors.*

"This book is toffee, it'll give you something to chew on for weeks. As the bishop said to the altar boy." *Bernard Cleeves.*

"*Inksplinters Anthology 2014* held me rapt from beginning to end and sent me back at break-neck speed to all the other things I should have been doing instead." *Deeply disturbed, Dublin 4.*

"Deep seriousness, wild humour, disarming tenderness – and more exploding monkeys per chapter than you can shake a stick at." *Mr C Lion C/O Dublin Zoo.*

"Like Joyce's, *Ulysses*, the action of which takes place over the course of a single day, 16th June

1904, *Inksplinters Anthology 2014* takes place over the course of the last two years." *Buck Mulligan.*

"This anthology is like a splinter, once it gets in, it'll travel all the way to your heart and kill you stone dead – but in a good way mind." *Jack Frost.*

"I used to think that writers in Ireland were just a sad bunch of melancholy naturalists with the arse out of their trousers. Until, of course, *Inksplinters Anthology 2014*, sprouted legs, put on a pair of cherry-red Doctor Marten boots and "persuaded" me otherwise. I don't think like that anymore. It's actually deadly. *(Is that all right? Will you let me go now Mister?)*" *Nine out of ten disgruntled non established authors.*

"Why did the chicken cross the road? To buy ten copies of *Inksplinters Anthology 2014*. Duh." *Chicken Little. Oh shit, the sky is falling*

"Jim Joyce, Sammy Beckett and Oscar Wilde went in to a pub and said to the bartender – *"We'll have three copies of Inksplinters Anthology 2014* please kind sir –with three whiskey chasers on the side."* I'd advise everyone to do the same." *Brendan Behan.*

"The only thing better than having *Inksplinters Anthology 2014* handy to read on the train is not having *Inksplinters Anthology 2014* handy to read on the train." *Oscar Wilde.*

"Have you ever fallen asleep on a bus and then suddenly woken up with drool dribbling from both sides of your mouth simultaneously and then, as a result, you end up with a massive pain in the neck for the rest of the week?

No? Well buy *Inksplinters Anthology 2014* and experience this for yourself." *The driver of the Number ten bus.*

"So good, I threw my husband out the window." *Madonna.*

"Genius. I read it on the train home the day I received it and spent the whole evening crying." *Miranda Hackensack.*

"The writing in this anthology is a perfect alchemy of lightly worn erudition and priests with red trousers." *Uriah Heep*

"I've seen the best minds of my generation destroyed by Inksplinters, starving hysterical naked, dragging themselves through the Dublin streets at dawn looking for an angry fix. Angelheaded hipsters." *Allen Ginsberg.*

"It's a groove and a gas man. Bord Gosh man. Bord Golly Gosh man. Bord Thundering Jaysus man. People should send them all their money, all their cigars, and all their daughters and sons too! Peace, love and you know what man." *Pete Seeger.*

"Reading *Inkplinters Anthology 2014* gives you an unrivalled picture of the rumours, suspicions and treacheries inherent in all writing groups the world over, without having to lower yourself in any way by joining a group yourself. Five stars." *El Zorro.*

"Written with verve, purpose and fancy French pencils of assorted colours." *The one-eyed, one-horned, flyin' purple people eater.*

"Jack Kerouac's *On the Road* sold a trillion Levi's and a million espresso machines, whereas, the writers within *Inksplinters Anthology 2014* hope to sell their soul to the first publisher who comes knocking with any small pile of cash. Or even a Garth Brooks ticket would do at this stage, I suppose." *All of the Inksplinters, without exception*

"You will want to read its most provoking parts over and over and chances are twenty months from now you won't be able to remember a fecking word. Which is very nice and decent of them I think. Bravo." *The seventh dwarf.*

"Strafes each page with a cacophonous range of voices, sad, kooky, funny, poignant – and trouserless too for the most part of this anthology, for some strange reason." *Omar Bradley.*

"This anthology kicks experimentation in the groin, pokes convention in the eyes and drops ice-cubes down the neck of all common-sense. Or was that my mother? Hold on, I think it was. What were you talking about again?" *Your Mother.*

"If you ever watched a sponge cake sink in the middle of the oven, then you'll probably have a fair idea of the contents of this fine book." *Mrs. Beeton.*

"Prometheus stole fire from the Gods, whereas the Inksplinters will be happy to steal a tenner per book from any hodgepodge of confused individuals that happen to wander past unawares." *Jack The Ripper*

"Between heaven and hell. Between the devil and the deep blue sea. Between the canals. Between your arse and your elbow. *Inksplinters Anthology 2014.* Not available in the shops." *Horatio Hornblower.*

"*Inksplinters Anthology 2014* is a big, fat, happy, smiley book with a tinselled cherry on top. It's the perfect Christmas present for bouncing people like flying pinballs into the happy-go-lucky bag of a new year." *The Grinch.*